After Michael

Betty O'Rourke

Other titles published by transita

Elissa's Castle by Juliet Greenwood
Emotional Geology by Linda Gilliard
Forgotten Dreams by Doris Leadbetter
Pond Lane and Paris by Susie Vereker
Scuba Dancing by Nicola Slade
Stage by Stage by Jan Jones
The Waiting Time by Sara Banerji
Turning Point by Bowering Sivers
Uphill All the Way by Sue Moorcroft

transita

Transita books reflect the lives of mature women. Contemporary women with rich and interesting stories to tell, stories that explore the truths and desires that colour their lives.

To find out more about transita, our books and our authors visit **www.transita.co.uk**

After Michael

Betty O'Rourke

transita

Published by Transita
3 Newtec Place, Magdalen Road,
Oxford OX4 1RE. United Kingdom.
Tel: (01865) 204393. Fax: (01865) 248780.
email: info@transita.co.uk
http://www.transita.co.uk

British Library Cataloguing in Publication Data
A catalogue record for this book is available from the British Library

Cover design by Baseline Arts Ltd, Oxford
Produced for Transita by Deer Park Productions, Tavistock
Typeset by PDQ Typesetting, Newcastle-under-Lyme
Printed and bound by Bookmarque, Croydon

ABOUT THE AUTHOR

As a child, **Betty O'Rourke** wanted to live in a caravan and write books, or alternatively, be a lighthouse keeper, because she had the idea that all she needed to do would be to turn the light on at dusk and off again at dawn, giving her plenty of time and solitude to write.

At the age of 20 Betty went to work in Foyles Bookshop in Charing Cross Road. Later she became a Library Assistant, and studied to become a Chartered Librarian. She met her future husband at Library School. They spent the first two years of married life in the United States where she worked as a children's librarian at Brooklyn Public Libraries.

On return from the States they started a family. As soon as their four children were sufficiently independent to give Betty some time to herself, she began writing seriously.

Betty joined the Romantic Novelists' Association and through their New Writers' Scheme became published by Robert Hale. She has had subsequent successes with Hale, D.C. Thomson, Ulverscroft Large Print and now Transita.

Having written mainly romance with a thread of mystery in the past, Betty wanted to reverse the focus and write a mystery with a thread of romance – *After Michael* is the result.

Betty now lives in Reading with her husband.

For more information about Betty and her work visit www.transita.co.uk

CHAPTER 1

'**M**AN THAT IS BORN OF WOMAN hath but a short time to live – he cometh up and is cut down like a flower – in the midst of life we are in death.'

Fiona heard the vicar's voice drone on tonelessly at the head of the grave, without the words registering in her brain. She felt numb. She had felt numb ever since they'd told her of Michael's death. Even now, seeing his coffin lying there in front of her, she couldn't believe it, couldn't take in that he was dead. She felt as if she were a character in a play, not real, watching herself act out a part, something outside herself.

They'd called her brave, a stoic because she hadn't been able to cry. She wished she could cry, then they might leave her alone, stop fussing and worrying over her.

She looked across towards Eleanor, her best friend, standing beside Colin on the far side of the gaping hole. Really, Colin should be here, beside her, supporting his mother, comforting her, but Eleanor had been the one to break down at the service, sobbing heart-breakingly in the church. Fiona had pushed Colin away when he came up to take her arm to lead her towards the graveside. 'Look after Eleanor. She's very distressed,' she'd said, almost implying that she wasn't.

Colin had his arm round Eleanor's shoulders now, awkwardly, as if he felt uncomfortable in the situation, as well he might. Her eyes turned to the other people in this small, select group, then paused. Who was that young woman standing behind and slightly to Colin's right? Fiona knew everyone else gathered here; mainly neighbours, local people, but she was quite sure she had never seen this young woman before. She was in her twenties, with light brown hair blowing loosely round a pretty, oval face; a dark suit, neat white blouse. She was probably a secretary from Michael's office, Fiona decided. They'd have sent a representative, she supposed. Nice of this girl to come. Perhaps she'd been Michael's secretary once, or he'd helped her in some way. She must speak to her, ask her name and thank her for coming, once this ordeal was over and the wretched vicar had ceased droning on about death and dust and ashes.

When the coffin was finally lowered and the group began to disperse, Fiona was caught up in conversation with neighbours, people she hadn't seen for some time, who all wanted to press her arm, kiss her cheek, express the trite sentiments that people fall back on who don't know what to say in these circumstances. She forgot about the girl until she was in the car with Colin, driving back to Little Paddocks.

'Colin, there was someone at the graveside I hadn't seen before. She was standing just behind you and Eleanor. Did you know who she was?'

'If she was standing behind me I wouldn't have seen her.' Colin was in his logical mode.

'I thought you might have noticed her earlier. You'd have remembered her if you'd seen her, she was rather attractive and about your age.'

Colin sighed. Fiona recognised the unspoken 'match-making mother – even at a funeral!'

'There's no reason why we should know all the people who came today – Dad must have known a great many people through his work.'

'But only local people and a few close friends came to the graveside.'

'Maybe she didn't realise that. Or maybe she had a reason to be grateful to Dad for something.'

'All the same, I'd liked to have asked her name, spoken to her before we left. So many people mobbed me as soon as the vicar stopped, and when I looked round, she'd gone.'

'Curious local. You get them; people who cluster round the church gates for a wedding. There must be those who do the same at a funeral.' Colin's tone was dismissive. Fiona wondered if the funeral had been more of a strain for him than he would admit; he had never been particularly close to Michael but the young took things to heart sometimes.

Mrs Burdett was waiting in the hall by the open front door when their car drew up outside.

'Food's laid out in the dining room, Mrs Latimer.' She thrust a glass of sherry into Fiona's hands. 'I've put drinks in the drawing room. About two dozen coming back, you thought? There's plenty more of everything in the kitchen if need be.'

'Thank you, Mrs Burdett, you're a treasure.' Fiona said, with genuine gratitude. Mrs Burdett came up from the village three times a week as cleaner, but as a widow with children long left home she was available and willing to be called on to come and help out in an emergency. Michael's funeral, following his sudden and unexpected death, had been just such an emergency.

'Take your hat and coat off before they start arriving, Madam. I'll take them upstairs for you.'

Mrs Burdett's motherly helpfulness was comforting. Fiona obediently took off her coat and handed it, with her hat and handbag, to Mrs Burdett. She paused a moment in front of the mirror, fluffing out her hair and checking her make up. No sign of tears, but there wouldn't be; she hadn't cried. Her hair was immaculate in its elegant chignon, no grey hairs yet among the honey blonde colour, and her skin was smooth and unlined. Not too bad for a fifty-year-old, she thought, turning away and taking a sip of sherry. As she did so, the first of the cars swept up the drive with its cargo of mourners.

There were at least two dozen of them, more, Fiona thought, than she had estimated to have been at the graveside. People can never resist a free drink and some food! She passed among the guests with a plate of Mrs Burdett's dainty canapés in each hand, accepting sympathy, condolences and trite phrases in equal measure. Thank goodness the vicar had declined the invitation to come!

When she wasn't nearby, she had the distinct impression people were treating the event more in the nature of a cocktail party; no one actually mentioned Michael by name, it was merely that her presence seemed to remind some of them that they needed to lower their voices as though

4

conversing near the bed of someone terminally ill. Fiona found it at first amusing, then irritating.

She went out into the hall, then into the kitchen in the hope of being able to help Mrs Burdett. Perhaps serving coffee might remind some of them that they had stayed long enough. She wanted her home to herself again.

'You've provided too much delicious food,' she told Mrs Burdett. 'They're staying too long. They won't go until it's all finished.'

'I'll start collecting up a few plates. Always works at the village institute dos,' Mrs Burdett smiled. 'You stay here and watch the kettle. Need a bit of peace and quiet at a time like this.'

Fiona heard the sound of the front door opening and wondered if her hopes had been answered and they were beginning to leave. She went out to the hall and saw someone already on the steps outside. It was the stranger from the graveside.

'Oh! I say! Just a moment!' She hurried forward but the door opened wider again and a man came in, blocking her way. He clasped both her hands in his own, smiling down at her.

'Fiona my dear! Can you forgive me? Only just arrived – lost my way and missed the church service altogether.'

She stared up into a face that she hadn't seen for more years than she wanted to admit.

'Simon?'

He drew her towards him, kissing her on each cheek. 'My dear, I had to come. It's been so long – I should have come to see you earlier, but I didn't know if that would have been what you wanted – '

'I'd always be glad to see you, Simon.'

The words sounded conventional but she meant them. As she stood there, her hands still clasped ridiculously in his, as if they were about to begin some movement in a country dance, the years were rolling back. Simon Neville, an old sweetheart from the years before she'd met Michael! Simon Neville, her mind said before she could suppress the thought, the man she should have married instead of Michael.

Fiona looked up at him, his still-handsome face strong featured and healthily tanned. His thick hair was lightly sprinkled with grey but his body had not increased in girth since she'd last seen him. Yes, Simon had worn well.

Over his shoulder she saw the stranger walking down the drive and realised that her last chance of finding out who the girl was, was about to be lost forever.

'A moment, Simon, please.' She withdrew her hands and quickly stepped into the drawing room. To her relief, Colin was standing near the door.

'Colin! That girl – she was here! She's just this moment gone. Run after her and find out who she is, please. We have another guest just arrived – I can't go myself.'

Colin put down his plate, wiped a handkerchief across his lips and strode towards the front door. He barely noticed the tall, middle-aged man who was standing beside his mother with a look of tender affection on his face.

The girl was already some way down the drive and as Colin hurried after her she paused beside a dark green, open-topped sports car, parked facing the gates.

'Er – excuse me!' For once, his mother had been right. She was a most attractive girl, a real stunner. He felt a little shy, asking her who she was, almost as if challenging her right to have come.

She glanced back at the sound of his voice, but then opened the car door and slipped into the driver's seat. Colin rested his hands on the top of the door to prevent her driving off.

'My mother wanted to thank you for coming,' he said. 'It was much appreciated.'

'That's all right.' She fitted the key into the ignition and Colin realised he was going to have to be quick if he was to discover her name before she drove off.

'I'm sorry – ' he blurted out. 'I – we – I don't know your name. This is embarrassing – '

'It's Anthea.' She smiled at him, a quick, amused glance which might have been sympathy towards his embarrassment or amusement at his awkwardness. Then the key was turned in the ignition, the car spurted into life and she shot forward down the drive. Colin had time only to take his hands off the door and step back quickly and she was gone.

He walked slowly back towards the house but did not go back inside. Little Paddocks was a large house, set in its own grounds of some ten acres or so, an elegant gentleman's house that Michael had bought for them some five years ago. Colin didn't care for it much, beautiful as it was. He'd been at university when his parents had moved in, not one of the older foundations that Michael had wanted, but one of the newer, less well-thought-of but more practical establishments. He'd have disliked Oxford or Cambridge, Colin decided, just as he disliked the upper class aura that went with living at Little Paddocks. He wondered if his mother felt the same way.

It had all been Michael's idea to live as though they were upper class county people. Michael had been a snob. Colin had always known that and it had always riled him. They weren't county people, not upper class, not even, probably, truly upper middle class. He knew his mother had come from a quite humble background and suspected that his father had, too, though Michael's background had always been a bit of a mystery. There were no living relatives on that side, and none ever mentioned. Colin had always assumed that his grandparents had died years ago and Michael had been an only child, but now he reflected that he didn't actually know anything about Michael's early life. Certainly, there hadn't been any of Michael's side of the family at the funeral today, but perhaps this Anthea was some sort of cousin they'd never heard of? His spirits rose a little. She certainly had been a stunner. He wouldn't mind seeing her again.

Back in the hall Fiona was getting her breath back after the shock of seeing Simon again after so many years.

'I should have telephoned you first – it was stupid of me to think I could come barging in like this, without warning,' Simon was saying apologetically.

She was suddenly afraid that he might decide he shouldn't have come, and go away at once.

'I saw the death notice in the *Times*,' he continued. 'And I thought – that's Fiona's chap. Then I thought I'd go to the church and afterwards slip away. I didn't know whether you'd want to see me, I mean, so soon. But these damned country lanes – '

'Of course I would have wanted to see you. I'd have been terribly disappointed if you'd gone to the church and not come on here. It's wonderful to see you again after all this time,' Fiona said warmly. 'Won't you come into the drawing room and have a drink, and something to eat?' As she spoke, she was aware that she didn't want to bring him in amongst all those people, having to introduce him, having to explain him. How did one say at one's husband's funeral 'and this is Simon Neville, my first love, the man I really should have married?'

When Simon hesitated, she seized her opportunity, touching him lightly on the arm. 'Come into the kitchen. There's plenty of extra food and drink there and we can talk undisturbed. I think the party will be breaking up soon, anyway.'

'Party?' Simon raised his eyebrows. He followed Fiona into the kitchen. 'Who came to the funeral, then?'

'Mostly neighbours and local people that I hardly know. One or two friends of mine from the village but mainly, I suspect, they came out of curiosity. We never entertained the locals much and there must be a good many people who would love to see inside the house.'

The long kitchen table was half covered with plates of sandwiches and canapés. Beyond, in the scullery, Fiona could hear Mrs Burdett washing up.

'Sit down.' She pulled out one of the wooden kitchen chairs at the bare end of the table, for Simon, and sat down opposite him. She reached for one of the half-empty wine bottles next to her but he shook his head.

'I'd prefer coffee, if it's not too much trouble. But these sandwiches – they look delicious. Did you – ?'

'Mrs Burdett, my daily, did all this. She's a treasure. She's just made coffee for everyone so I'll fetch you a cup.' Fiona went into the scullery, where two large percolators were bubbling on the stove.

'I'll take them in coffee ready poured. Easier and quicker.' Mrs Burdett wiped her hands on a roller towel hanging against the door. 'Have you had anything to eat yourself, Mrs Latimer? Now, don't you go neglecting yourself. You need to keep your strength up.'

'I'm going to eat something in a moment. How could I resist any of your delicious sandwiches? I've an old friend, come unexpectedly, so I'm entertaining him in the kitchen. I'll take two cups of coffee and we'll have some of the spare food laid out there.'

Mrs Burdett pursed her lips at the idea of Fiona entertaining one of her guests in the kitchen but she was of the old school who knew her place, so made no comment, except to acknowledge Simon's presence with a deferential 'afternoon, Sir' when she brought the tray of coffee cups through the kitchen on her way to the drawing room. She was surprised and touched when he leapt to his feet to open the door into the hall for her, and even glanced ahead to make sure the drawing room door was open as well.

'Wonderful spread, Mrs Burdett,' he murmured as she passed, giving her a glow of pride as she swept into the drawing room. None of the other guests had commented on her catering, even though she could see they'd made considerable inroads into it.

'I can see you've done well for yourself, these last twenty-five years.' Simon spoke sincerely, looking round at the high-ceilinged kitchen, out of the window at the garden, stretching away to woods in the distance. 'This is a beautiful house.'

'Yes. Michael saw that we never lacked for any material comforts.' Fiona's voice was flat and Simon wondered if there had been a slight emphasis on the word 'material'.

'How long have you lived here?'

'Five years. We had a flat in London so this was quite a change. Michael kept a small pied-à-terre there for when he stayed overnight on business. I think he thought the country would be better for Colin than London, not that Colin's been here all that much. Colin's my son. He was hurrying out of the door when you arrived.'

'I did wonder if he was yours. A good-looking chap, same fair colouring as you.'

Fiona felt a flush of pleasure at the thought that Colin resembled her, rather than Michael. She should have wanted him to look like her dead husband, a constant reminder of the man she'd loved and married, but part of her had always been relieved that Colin didn't look at all like Michael or have any of his personality traits.

'Was Michael, er, ill, before – ?' Simon asked delicately, helping himself to several of the sandwiches beside him.

'No. It was all very sudden. That's the odd thing, really. He was always very fit; kept himself in good shape. He built a gym in one of the stables and he used to work out regularly. And he was relatively young, not yet fifty-five. His death was totally unexpected. It seems he had a heart attack in the night and apparently – just went, just like that.' She snapped her fingers.

'My poor dear. It must have been awful, a terrible shock for you.' Simon's outstretched hand covered Fiona's, resting on the table. 'Were you there when – ? Forgive me, you don't want to talk about it.' Simon picked up his coffee cup.

'No, I don't mind talking about it. In fact, it's rather a relief. There hasn't been anyone I could talk to; only Colin, and I couldn't burden him by going on about it. Michael was at his London flat, so I was spared the messiness of finding him dead. I believe someone – a hall porter or concierge, someone like that, broke in and found him, after one of his clients became concerned when he hadn't turned up for a meeting. It was all handled very discreetly. Michael's flat is in an area where they don't like the thought of anyone lying dead in one of the apartments. They organised an undertaker and took him away before they even telephoned to tell me he'd died. There was a post-mortem, of course, but the result was clear. Doctor seemed to think he might have been pushing himself too far, too fast. Michael always was something of a workaholic, though I'd always thought he could cope.'

Simon smiled fondly across the table at her. 'He wanted you to have the best. And you have. This is far more than I could ever have aspired to; more than I could ever have offered you.'

'If he worked himself to death to provide this, then I ought to feel guilty, but I can't,' Fiona said. 'I didn't want all this, lovely as the house is. Michael's first and only love was money, and what he could buy with it.' She dropped her eyes and said quietly 'I don't think he ever forgave me for the fact that he couldn't buy me.' She looked directly at Simon and added 'though, judging by what I seem to have ended up with, anyone might be forgiven for thinking it had been just that.'

'No! Not you!' Simon took her hands in his. 'You could never have been persuaded against your nature.'

'I was, though.'

'Look, my dear. I ought not to keep you from your guests any longer. I ought to be getting back now, anyway. But don't let's leave it so long next time.' Simon stood up. 'I may see you again, mayn't I? In a week or so, when you've had time – when all this has settled a bit.'

'Yes! I'd like that very much.' He bent to kiss her cheek, a quick, almost boyishly shy kiss. Fiona was touched.

'Simon keep in touch, please,' she begged as she saw him to the door. 'I don't want to lose you again.'

'No fear of that my dear. Not now.' He uttered the last words under his breath, but Fiona heard them.

She watched him walk down the drive, noting his upright figure and long, easy strides. Simon had always been an attractive man and now, in late middle age, he still was, to her at least. She wondered why she had let Michael sweep her off her feet all those years ago, rejecting Simon for him. To be fair, and Fiona wanted to be fair, her marriage had been happy enough, at least in the early years, and Michael had provided for her generously. He had given her Colin, a son she adored, and, even if there had never been the daughter she would have longed to have, Colin was enough. Some people couldn't have children at all, or, if they did, the children turned out a disappointment. She must never forget that, in spite of everything, she had been blessed with a great deal more than most. Fiona sighed and turned back into the hall, shutting the front door. She had no right to wish for more. No one had everything. But sometimes it had seemed that she had too much of the wrong things.

The funeral guests were on the point of leaving. Fiona apologised for neglecting them, but her words were brushed aside. They understood, or thought they understood. Some may have thought she had been overcome, needing time to herself alone; some thought the distinguished looking man who arrived later but had not been at the service, must have been the family solicitor, requiring her attention. She let them think what they wanted. She thanked them all for coming, thanked them for their flowers, their good wishes, their support. In the end she was thanking them for going.

As the door closed behind the last of them, she turned to Colin. 'Thank God that's over. I thought they'd never go. You fed them too well, Mrs Burdett.'

Out of the shadows Eleanor stepped into the hall. 'I'm going too,' she said. 'Ring me when and if you need me. Right now, all you want is to put your feet up and have a large G and T.'

Fiona blushed. 'Nell – I wasn't including you among them. You know I – '

'Yes, you were. And if I'd done my stuff as a good friend I'd have steered them towards the door a lot sooner. Funerals are always stressful, almost as bad as weddings, always having to make small talk to people you never wanted around in the first place.'

Fiona giggled. 'I like the idea of comparing a funeral to a wedding. Some weddings you must have been to.'

'Well, they are similar. The main character, or characters in the case of a wedding, gets to escape early on, and the hostess is left having to cope with the guests, who invariably stay far too long. Goodbye, Fee dear, call me soon.' She clasped Fiona's shoulders and kissed her briefly, smiled at Colin and squeezed his arm. 'Look after her, Colin. She's all yours now.'

Eleanor opened the front door and slipped through it. They heard her high heels clattering down the steps to the gravel drive.

Almost on cue, Mrs Burdett appeared from the kitchen.

'Pot of fresh tea for you, Mrs Latimer? Or would you prefer something stronger? Don't worry about anything, I'll soon have the place to rights again. Go and put your feet up in the study and I'll bring a tray along straight away.'

'Thank you, Mrs Burdett. Tea would be lovely. Come along, Colin, we'll have a cup of tea and half an hour with our feet up before we even think of doing anything else.'

The study had a comfortable window seat where it was possible to stretch out full length if need be; and an adjustable reclining chair which Michael had bought years ago but rarely used. The room had been described as the study originally and did in fact contain a desk where Fiona wrote letters, and a bookcase full of leather-bound classics, but for years she'd used it as a retreat, a small room where she could escape by herself. The larger rooms sometimes seemed overpowering, especially when she was alone in the house, and in winter they were invariably cold.

Mrs Burdett brought in tea and a plate of buttered scones. She was wise enough not to proffer the remains of the funeral feast, delicious though they'd been. Mrs Latimer had said she would spend half an hour having tea with Master Colin, and by the end of that time all trace of the guests would have been wiped from the drawing room and dining room.

Mrs Burdett, fiercely loyal to her employer, understood Fiona better than anyone realised. She wanted, as far as it was possible, to forget this day ever happened. Not, Mrs Burdett knew, because the funeral had been a sad and poignant reminder of a happy life gone now forever, but because Mrs Latimer was the kind of person who disliked deceit in any form, and would not have cared to spend the best part of the day pretending to a sorrow she did not feel. Mrs Burdett did not count herself as a confidante of Mrs Latimer; it would not have been proper, given their different social positions, but she could read between the lines, pick up signals, understand what was in the air. Mrs Latimer was not distressed by her husband's death; shocked by the unexpectedness, perhaps, but, in the main, little moved.

In the study, Fiona reached for her second cup of tea that Colin poured for her. 'It went off all right, didn't it? Though the vicar was a bit over-enthusiastic, I suppose.'

'I think he'd have preferred it if you'd thrown a mild fit of the vapours and had to be taken to the vestry,' Colin said. 'Stoicism isn't what he's used to. Clearly, he didn't know how to handle it.'

'I couldn't cry,' Fiona said. 'Perhaps I may, eventually, but not yet. Oh, that girl! Did you find out who she was? She looked vaguely familiar, but I couldn't place her.'

'Not really. All she said was "I'm Anthea" as though she expected me to know her. Didn't like to admit I hadn't the foggiest who she was.'

'Anthea.' Fiona rolled the name thoughtfully round her tongue. 'No, doesn't mean a thing to me either. Oh, well, I

17

don't suppose it matters.' She dismissed the girl from her mind, but Colin did not.

CHAPTER 2

SOME THREE DAYS LATER FIONA broached the subject which had been on her mind ever since the funeral. 'Colin, I suppose I should make a start clearing out all Michael's things, his clothes and everything. What on earth am I going to do with them?'

'Oxfam shop in the village?' Colin suggested.

'Not in the village, darling! I couldn't bear to think of some of the locals going round wearing Michael's cast-offs! But a charity shop is probably the answer. One in Winchester or Salisbury, perhaps. That's far enough away to be anonymous.'

'I'll give you a hand if you like. When do you want to start?' Colin looked up from that morning's paper. They were in the study; they sat there often in preference to the larger, more formal room on the other side of the house.

'Why not now?' Fiona rose from her chair. 'That's if you're not too busy.'

Colin tossed the paper aside and got to his feet. 'No time like the present,' he said.

In spite of her gratitude for his help, Fiona couldn't help wincing at the cliché. Colin, at twenty-four, was growing into middle age. He was beginning to act and speak like a man nearly twice his age and she had started to fear that no suitable girlfriends would be seriously interested in him for long. She must do something to help him, but she wasn't sure what she could do. There were girls in the village, of course, and he was friendly with them all, but none of the friendships had ever looked likely to develop further. Now he was down from university, with no employment prospects as yet, she could hardly expect him to be thinking of any serious relationship with a girl. Once the dust had settled over Michael, she would have to think about encouraging him in some career. He could take his time, though. Fortunately, money wouldn't be a problem and he could choose something that would interest him without having to concern himself about earning a decent salary. It was a good thing that Colin wasn't as money obsessed as Michael had been.

They went upstairs to Michael's room. He and Fiona had slept separately for several years now. She couldn't remember exactly why the decision had been made, but it had seemed reasonable at the time. Something to do with Michael wanting to go on working late in the evening and not disturb her, she thought, though later on Michael had been away from home a good deal and it would have been nice to have been together on the occasions when he was there, Fiona thought wistfully.

When they stepped into Michael's room, neat, tidy, with an unlived-in feeling almost as impersonal as an hotel room, Fiona felt embarrassed, almost with a need to explain to Colin why they had had separate bedrooms.

'Your father was a considerate man,' she said. 'He never liked to disturb me when he came up to bed late.'

Colin nodded, accepting the remark without interest. Fiona wondered what he thought about the arrangement.

Heaven forbid that he'd grown up thinking this kind of lifestyle was normal!

'I'll sort his personal things.' She said quickly. 'You sort his clothes. Better make two piles, one the reasonable stuff that can go to a charity shop, the rest we can throw out or Mrs Burdett can take to a jumble sale.'

Colin did not answer but strode across to the mirror-fronted cupboards which ran the length of one wall. He slid back the doors and surveyed the rows of suits and jackets in front of him.

'Did he really need all these clothes? Or was he the kind of chap who never threw anything away?'

'I don't suppose his business suits got a lot of wear,' Fiona said. 'So many of them, and all much the same.'

Colin began taking them from their hangers and piling them on the bed. 'All these might as well go to the charity shop. What can we put them in? Do you think Mrs Burdett has some bin bags in the kitchen, or is there an old suitcase we can use?'

'You'll need to check pockets for the odd handkerchief and loose change,' Fiona said over her shoulder. She had the top drawer of the tallboy open and was piling the contents on top. She looked at each item as she took it from the drawer. Colin could see it was going to be a long job.

As instructed, he went through trouser and jacket pockets, rescuing a crumpled handkerchief and some theatre ticket stubs which he tossed into the waste paper basket with barely a glance.

The pile of suits grew. Now he was on to sports jackets and casual trousers. He pulled one jacket from the rack, an oatmeal coloured tweed, almost new.

'I don't ever remember him wearing this,' he remarked. He hadn't remembered his father wearing most of the clothes here, but then, he supposed he had never really seen much of Michael for several years now.

Fiona glanced in his direction. 'Mmm, I don't, either. It must be either very new or very old. Don't throw it out, try it on yourself.'

Colin slipped his arms into the sleeves and regarded himself in the mirror. He didn't think the jacket was his father's usual style; it looked more suitable for someone younger, nearer his own age. He would quite have liked it himself but the sleeves were a little too long and it had been made for a fuller figure. His father had been half a head taller and a couple of stones heavier.

Reluctantly, he took it off, tossing it on the pile for the charity shop. 'Doesn't fit,' he muttered, for Fiona's benefit. He reached for the next garment, then remembered he hadn't checked the pockets. Unlikely there would be anything in any of them; it looked barely worn, but he might as well be thorough. He slid his hands into the side pockets and then the breast pocket. His fingers felt something square and flat, but not in the pocket itself. He turned the jacket out, seeing an inner breast pocket. Piece of paper. Probably the receipt for it. Curious, he felt inside.

It wasn't a receipt. In his hands he held a snapshot. He didn't need to turn it over to see if there was a name on the back; he had recognised Anthea at once.

He glanced over his shoulder at his mother. She was unrolling pairs of socks, checking for holes or darns, then folding them together again, absorbed in the task. Surreptitiously, he stuffed the snapshot into his pocket and went on with sorting the clothes, but his mind was no longer on it. Who was this Anthea? Clearly not merely someone from the office who had once worked with Michael, not even an ambitious young executive who thought of him as an admired mentor. Instinctively, Colin knew there was more to this than just a business friendship. For one thing, why the photo kept in a jacket never worn for work, never, as far as he knew, worn here at home? When had his father worn that jacket? What had he been doing when he'd worn it?

It came as no surprise to Colin to think his father might have had a mistress. He knew that his parents' marriage had always been rather cool and undemonstrative. Though they rarely rowed, and seemed to get along together tolerably well, for years Michael and Fiona had led very separate lives. Even the separate bedrooms told their own tale. Colin wondered if his mother had ever suspected that there might be someone else. If so, she certainly couldn't have thought it might be Anthea. The girl and the name had meant nothing to her. He wouldn't say anything at this stage, certainly not show her the photo, but he'd do a little detective work on his own and find out some more about this mysterious Anthea.

Finally, they finished sorting out everything in Michael's room. Colin took the black bin bags of clothing downstairs, some to the kitchen for Mrs Burdett's Women's Institute village hall jumble sales, the rest to await being taken into Winchester to one of the charity shops.

Fiona looked at the piles of papers, diaries, letters, and photographs that made up the remaining contents of the drawers in the room. 'I don't want to go through all of this,' she said wearily, gesturing at the pile. 'Can I put the lot on a bonfire, do you think? If there are any unpaid bills they can send them in again, but, really, Colin, I can't face any more.'

'I'll deal with them for you, if you like.' Colin put his arm around Fiona's shoulders. She looked tired and drawn. Michael's death was beginning to get through to her.

He led her downstairs and called to Mrs Burdett to make a pot of tea and bring it into the study. When she came in with the laden tray, Mrs Burdett clucked in her motherly way and began fussing over Fiona.

'Trying to do too much too soon, Mrs Latimer,' she chided. 'There's no call to clear away everything all at once. Take time over it, and let Master Colin do what he can to help. He'll be glad to, I know.'

Colin was glad to help. He took the piles of paper, diaries and notebooks, stacked into grocery cartons, out to the garden and began to build a small bonfire in a corner far away from the house. While the twigs and dry leaves took hold, he sat down to go through each carton systematically, looking for a reference to Anthea. He supposed he should feel that he was invading Michael's privacy and that he had no right to be reading through everything, yet he felt no guilt about it. He and his father had never been close. If Michael had been cheating on Fiona, Colin felt he had a right to know. What use he made of any evidence he might uncover, he hadn't yet decided.

There were photographs, but not another of Anthea. Mostly they were holiday snaps dating from years ago, with himself building sandcastles and a youthful Fiona in a modest swimsuit lying in a deckchair. There were a few professional photos taken at business dinners, showing Michael and Fiona grouped at a table with other guests; some of them showed Michael by himself. Colin scrutinised all these very carefully, noting particularly people in the background, sitting at other tables and not intended to be included, but there was no one in any of them who looked even remotely like Anthea. After a moment's hesitation, he tossed them on to the bonfire.

There was a batch of diaries going back some eight or ten years and he latched on to these eagerly, but they proved to be disappointing. Entries such as 'dentist 10.30' and 'car service due' filled most of the pages. There were a few entries he did not understand, initials and a time on some pages, about once a month in the later diaries, but the initials did not include an A. Whatever they referred to, he had no means of learning now. One by one, he tossed the diaries aside, but something held him back from consigning them to the fire alongside the photos.

There were letters, but they were no more revealing; a few receipts; some formal letters, a couple of letters dated eight years previously, from an elderly aunt, Michael's only known relative, who was now dead, little else. There seemed very little here to show for a man's life. Colin wondered if Michael kept his personal papers in the office, or at his London flat. Reluctantly, he tipped them on to the fire. There were two boxes still left untouched. He wanted more time to look through them before he destroyed them completely so he left them where they were, kicked the small fire apart and came back to the house.

Back in the hall, Fiona took a phone call. 'Mrs Latimer? Nigel Williams here, from Chumley and Williams. I really must apologise. I should have contacted you sooner but things have been – ah! – a little chaotic here.'

'You are my husband's solicitor?'

'Yes. I rang to ask when it would be convenient to come and see you regarding the – er – will and the estate.' Nigel sounded a little embarrassed. Fiona supposed he thought she was still a distraught widow, something she could not imagine herself ever being. She spoke briskly, to put him at his ease.

'Come any time you like, Mr Williams. How about tomorrow? Would eleven o'clock suit? I shall be here all day but I don't imagine it will take long.' She knew Michael had made a will, years ago, soon after they had married, leaving everything to her. It could only be a matter of changing everything into her name, perhaps updating her own will to leave everything now to Colin.

Mr Williams arrived promptly the following day. He was in late middle age, a sleek, dapper man, every inch the solicitor. Mrs Burdett showed him into the study and hurried off to make coffee.

After the conventional pleasantries and condolences were over, Nigel Williams sat down at the little table by the window and opened his briefcase, reluctantly, it seemed to Fiona. She was beginning to think he was a pompous man, making a formal occasion out of the simple act of reading her husband's will.

'Mrs Latimer,' he began at last. 'I find myself in somewhat of a quandary.'

'Oh?' Had they lost the wretched will, perhaps? She could have told them what it said, but they probably wouldn't accept her word.

'Normally, I would have arranged to come and see you before the funeral, but when I came to examine your late husband's papers, I found certain anomalies – '

'What do you mean, anomalies? Michael's will is perfectly straightforward. I was with him when it was drawn up, twenty-five years ago. He left everything to me.'

'Yes, I am aware of that will.' Nigel squirmed awkwardly in his chair.

'Are you saying he made another will, later?' Surely not; Michael would have told her if he had been thinking of anything like that. They might not have been close, in these last years, but Michael wouldn't have changed anything without discussing it with her first. And why would he have wanted to change anything?

'No, no. There's only the original will, as far as we are aware, made out in 1979, when, I believe, you were first married.'

'That's right.' Fiona remembered that day, the visit to the solicitor's office, a rather giggly and happy lunch afterwards in a very expensive restaurant. Michael had said 'I'm leaving you all my worldly goods. They don't add up to much right now, but by the time you inherit them, they'll be worth a packet, I can assure you.'

'Your husband, Michael Latimer, left you everything of which he died possessed.'

'Yes, I am aware of that. This house, mainly, but he also had some stocks and shares I believe, and the London flat. And there will be his company pension, of course. As you know, he worked for Brightmans and Wellings, in the City.'

Mr Williams squirmed some more. 'Mr Latimer *did* work for Brightmans and Wellings, to be sure, but my understanding is that he left that company nearly a year ago, and that at the time, his pension rights were converted into a cash sum.'

'But that's impossible! He was nowhere near retirement age! And he was working in the City right up until his death. He died in London, at his flat.'

'I'm sorry if this has come as a shock to you, Mrs Latimer. It was something of a surprise to us, too, when we made enquiries. I have been in touch with Brightmans and they told me Mr Latimer left the company several months ago, and at the time special arrangements were made for him to redeem his entire pension rights. It's very unusual, I know, but it seems there were unusual circumstances – '

'So are you telling me there is no pension to come from his work?' Fiona stared at Nigel. 'I would have thought, Mr Williams, that as his solicitor, you would have pointed out to him the great disadvantage of cashing in his pension early, explained to him that it was not in his best interests – his and mine – '

'I certainly would have done, had I been consulted about the matter,' Nigel said tetchily. 'I can assure you, Mrs Latimer, that I knew nothing about this arrangement until I contacted Brightmans and Wellings.'

'But can they do that? Legally, I mean?'

Nigel Williams looked even more uncomfortable. 'It is a very unusual arrangement. Normally, of course, it wouldn't be possible. But I understand there were special circumstances.'

'What special circumstances? Look, you'd better tell me exactly what it is you know and are having difficulty in telling me.' Fiona was about to lose her temper with the man.

Reluctantly, Nigel said 'I'm sorry, Mrs Latimer, but I know very little about the situation. Brightmans were very reluctant to discuss anything with me but it would seem that his entire pension rights were converted into a lump sum when he left and he signed an agreement renouncing any future financial claim on the company. I realise now that you knew nothing of this – '

'Of course I knew nothing about this! Are you telling me my husband made some arrangement to be given his pension early, and took the entire amount, including whatever he might have had in the future, in cash? What on earth would he have done that for? It must have involved an enormous amount.'

'It was. Some two million, I would estimate.'

'What! But what on earth could have happened to it? Michael certainly couldn't have spent that much in the last year. Neither I nor my son has seen any benefit from money of that amount.'

'That is what we have been wondering too, Mrs Latimer. Would you know if your husband had any foreign bank accounts, Cayman Islands, Switzerland, for example?'

'Certainly not! Michael never had anything like that, I'm sure. We've always lived comfortably but hardly ostentatiously. I can't believe that Michael could have asked for and received that amount of money. There must be some mistake.'

Nigel shook his head but said nothing. After a moment, Fiona said 'so I am to expect no income from Michael's company pension? But at least there's still this house. I suppose I might have to consider selling up and finding somewhere smaller, but this house would probably raise sufficient capital – '

'There again, Mrs Latimer, I'm afraid I have bad news for you. This property is subject to a mortgage.'

'I know that. But its value must have practically doubled in the years since we bought it,' Fiona snapped.

'You were not aware, then, that a second mortgage was taken out on this property, some six months ago? I am very much afraid that, were you to sell, and I think you may very well be forced to do so, the money you might expect to receive for the house would be very little, practically nil, once the debt on the two mortgages have been cleared.'

'You mean to tell me that I don't even own my house now?' Fiona said. This was something she could barely take in. Her mind was telling her all this wasn't happening. It was some kind of terrible nightmare and soon she would wake up and find that it hadn't really happened, that Mr Williams was due to come and visit and tell her that she would have a comfortable income from Michael's pension and the house was hers outright. Hadn't there been some sort of insurance Michael had mentioned, about the mortgage being paid off in the event of his death? She hadn't, admittedly, paid much attention when he'd told her, assuming that it was all something far in the future which probably would never concern her. She wished now that she was more clued up about money. Michael had always taken care of everything and she'd never given much thought about day to day living. There had always been plenty and she'd assumed that state of affairs would continue indefinitely.

Nigel looked at her apologetically, as if he felt that he, himself, was responsible for her situation. He had been taken aback when he had investigated Michael Latimer's financial situation, and discovered that it was anything but straight-forward. There seemed to be a vast amount of cash unaccounted for, and Michael's company, Brightmans, was being extremely unhelpful. They had seemed so cagey and unforthcoming about the extraordinary pension arrangements he might almost have thought they were being deliberately obstructive.

That second mortgage, too. What had the man wanted with even more money when he had persuaded his company to advance him, almost certainly illegally, two million in future pension rights? And where had it all gone? Clearly, Latimer hadn't spent it on his wife or home, or on a wild consumer spending spree. When he had arrived at Little Paddocks, he had assumed that the man's widow had at least known something of the situation, though possibly not in any detail, or exactly how much was involved. He had thought that perhaps Latimer had planned to set up his own business but his method of financing it appeared both risky and highly inadvisable. Now he was faced with the situation that the widow knew nothing whatever of the situation, and had been calmly expecting the comforting news that she would be financially secure for the rest of her life. He would have to advise her on managing her straitened circumstances, and he had no idea how to do so.

'What am I going to do?' Fiona stared at Nigel, her face ashen. 'I have nothing. I left all the money side of things to Michael. I always believed – he gave me to understand – we were and always would be, comfortably off, well provided for, whatever happened. Michael never gave me any indication that he was in financial trouble, but he must have been, mustn't he? All this money – where has it all gone? Certainly we haven't seen any of it.'

'Certainly I agree it's hard to see why he might have needed to raise as much capital as he apparently has done. You are sure he never mentioned anything about plans for setting up a business on his own?'

'Certainly not! He seemed to be settled at Brightmans, happy there, with no ambitions to leave. I assumed he would stay on until retirement, which might have been another ten years away. And why did he need to remortgage this house, without telling me what he was going to do?'

'I think you are going to have to put this house on the market,' Nigel said gently. 'I would suggest you do so as a matter of urgency. And look for somewhere else, somewhere smaller. There is just you and your son Colin living here now, isn't there?'

Fiona nodded. 'Yes. I suppose this is far too big for the two of us. Always was too big, I used to think. But it's a beautiful house. I shall miss living here. I don't want to end up in a poky little flat somewhere horrid.'

Nigel glanced round the room. The furnishings were expensive and he'd noticed a couple of fine pictures hanging in the hall on his way in. They might fetch enough to tide her over for the immediate future. So far, Mrs Latimer hadn't asked about the money in the bank, the stocks and shares she knew her husband had held. She'd think of it eventually, and then, almost as if the thought had passed from his mind into hers, Fiona spoke.

'There must be some money. Michael always kept a sizeable amount in our joint bank account. And I know he had stocks and shares. Surely, they can be sold to cover at least part of the mortgage, or the income from them would keep us for the foreseeable future. It isn't all doom and gloom, after all.'

'Mrs Latimer, there are no stocks and shares.' Nigel's voice was gentle, yet clear. 'Your husband sold them all about six months ago. And I think you will find there is just a little over five hundred pounds in your joint account. A large withdrawal was made some six weeks ago.'

'Six weeks! But he would hardly have had time to spend any of it before he died! It must still be among his things!'

Nigel put a sheaf of papers back in his briefcase. 'I am truly sorry, Mrs Latimer, to have had to have been the bearer of such shocking news. What more can I say? I was as astounded as you when I learnt what the situation was. If I can be of any further help, please don't hesitate to get in touch with me at the London office. Any time.' He stood up, holding out his hand to shake Fiona's. When completely at a loss with a client, resort to safe clichés, his father, who had founded the business, had advised him. At the front door, he became aware that mere platitudes were not enough to leave this nice woman, who was clearly shaken to her very depths, and in no way to blame for her husband's insane actions.

'As time goes on, you may find things are not so black as they appear right now,' he said, taking her hand and holding it a little longer than convention decreed. 'There may be developments – some of the money may yet be recovered. I can't think that Mr Latimer could have disposed of so much in such a short time. We shall see. Rest assured I will be investigating into everything to do with his estate; I shall go through everything I have and everything I can find. I ask you to do the same, Mrs Latimer. If you come across anything that might shed light on the matter, please let me know at once. Look, here is my personal card.' On an impulse he handed her a card from his inner pocket. 'My home number is on that. Call me at any time, day or night, if you discover anything. Meanwhile, I'll work on a financial plan for your immediate future, and I'll be in touch again very soon.'

Fiona murmured her thanks. She was almost sorry for him, having to break such devastating news to her. As soon as his car had driven through the gates at the end of the drive, she was running upstairs to find Colin.

Part of her mind said she ought not to burden him with her financial problems, but this concerned Colin just as much as herself. She was on the edge of panic and needed to share Nigel Williams' devastating news with someone. Colin was the obvious person.

'He cashed in everything he could lay his hands on?' Colin stared at her in disbelief when she told him. 'What on earth did he want so much money for? It must have run into hundreds of thousands.'

'More. This house was worth over half a million when he bought it,' Fiona said. 'And he's taken all the pension rights. We have practically nothing at all. What's been going on, Colin? I feel as if I've been married to a stranger all these years. Why did he never say anything about what he was doing? What *was* he doing, to need so much money and then let it disappear?'

'Williams said it all happened not much more than a few months ago?' Colin frowned. 'The money, or a good proportion of it, must still be around somewhere. He couldn't have spent it. He wasn't away much, not more than the odd night or so, and that was on Brightmans' business. He didn't spend all that much on the house, either; some more furniture when we moved in, redecorating, that sort of thing.'

'Those nights away. They weren't on Brightmans' business. They couldn't have been. He had left the company by then. Mr Williams said he hadn't been working there for more than six months.'

'Then where was he working? Didn't he leave the house every morning and catch the London train?'

'I don't know. He did act as if he was going to work as usual, but where he went I don't know.' Fiona shook her head wearily. 'Colin, what are we going to do? Mr Williams says sell this house as soon as possible. We can't afford to live here any longer.'

'I'll get a job,' Colin said at once. 'Really, I've been thinking about that, ever since I came down from Uni. I was waiting to see what sort of decent offers came up, but now it's urgent. I'll take anything I can find. We'll manage.'

Fiona rested her hand on his arm, regarding him fondly. He seemed to have grown up, suddenly, and become prepared to take care of her as the man of the house. But what kind of job could he possibly do, with a rather obscure degree in classics and no experience of anything practical?

'Dear Colin. You're all I have, now,' she murmured. 'But don't think this means I'm going to turn into a possessive mother, all clingy and dependent. I can work too. Heavens, I'm barely fifty. There must be a job I can do that will earn us enough to live reasonably well.'

'Not round here, there won't. Not for either of us,' Colin said. 'What work is there in a village like this? Serving in the local shop, or taking over some of Mrs Burdett's clients? I suppose I might find something as a jobbing gardener, or help on one of the farms. It's laughable, Ma, and what can we do but laugh? I simply refuse to believe that the situation is quite as extreme as old Williams says. Solicitors always paint the worst scenario. Dad *couldn't* have made away with such a vast amount of money in such a short time. Whatever he did it for, he didn't reckon on having a heart attack just a few months later. He must still have the money somewhere, and I'm determined that I'll find it.'

'Thank you, dear. Now, after all that, I think we deserve a rather good lunch. I'll ask Mrs Burdett to see if she can find us something special. I won't, of course, mention a word about our situation. Time enough to face that if we have to dispense with her, as I suppose we will have to, if we're to move into somewhere much smaller. Oh, I shall miss her more than anything!'

'I suppose we should keep all this to ourselves for the time being.'

'Colin, I'm not about to inform the whole village that my husband has deprived me of a pension! The vicar would be round, asking if we wanted to be given parish relief, or whatever it is that they do for the poor these days.'

'I was thinking of Eleanor,' Colin said.

'Eleanor? You know, although she's a good friend, my very best and oldest, I don't want to talk to her about Michael yet. I don't want to tell anyone. I don't even want to think about it.' Fiona turned back, on her way out of the room, to say 'We're going to have a splendid lunch, even if it's the last good meal we eat in this house.'

Left to himself, Colin sat down on his bed to absorb the solicitor's news. He found it hard to believe that it could really be true, but he wasn't about to accept it all without asking questions, a lot of questions. His mind went to Anthea, the mystery girl at the funeral. He was sure she had some connection with Brightmans, and therefore must surely know something about the circumstances surrounding Michael's resignation. He needed to contact her urgently, talk to her and find out exactly who she was and why she had come to the funeral. Not just a secretary or assistant, he was sure. Michael had kept her photo in his pocket, the pocket of a jacket he had never worn at home. That, in itself, spoke of something which would be worth a closer investigation.

CHAPTER 3

COLIN WANDERED OUT INTO THE GARDEN, walking down to the place where he had made the bonfire. He was kicking himself that he had burnt so many of his father's diaries and papers already, but he remembered that he had not completed the job. There was still a pile of diaries and notebooks lying in two cartons beside the dead remains of his fire. He tipped them up, turning over the notebooks as they spilt on to the ground. It was imperative that he searched through everything again to see if there was any clue that would lead him to finding Anthea's whereabouts.

Painstakingly, he thumbed through each diary, page by page, year by year. Though there were regular entries, with initials and a time, there was no mention of Anthea by name, or any initials which contained an A.

At the back of some of the diaries were a few pages for addresses, telephone numbers and other notes. Colin went through these particularly carefully and at last he thought he might have struck oil. At the back of one diary three years old, he found a pencilled note, an A against a London telephone number.

As he raced back up the path to the house, he wondered what he was going to say to her. His pace slowed while he gave it some thought. The telephone operator would not give out an address for a number, he knew. He remembered how Anthea had driven off speedily before he could ask her any questions. If the number was hers and she put the receiver down on him, he'd have achieved nothing.

Fiona was in the kitchen with Mrs Burdett. Colin went into the study to use the extension there and closed the door. He keyed in the number from the diary and after a few moments a woman's voice answered. He thought it was Anthea, but he could not be sure.

The idea came to him, in a flash. 'Good morning, Madam.' He made his voice sound deeper, and slightly rough, like a workman. 'Telephone engineer here. I'm sorry to trouble you, but we've been having problems with crossed lines. Could you please confirm your name and address for me?'

'There hasn't been any problem with my telephone.' The voice sounded puzzled, but not, Colin thought, suspicious.

'No, Madam. It's another line, but I have to eliminate all connections.' He hoped that sounded technical enough to convince her, and yet be vague. 'If you could just confirm your name and the address you are speaking from, then I probably won't need to trouble you again.'

'Very well. I'm Anthea Ransom. The address is number three, Chomley Mews, Chelsea. Do you need the post code?'

Colin, a pen in his hand poised over the diary page, nearly shouted 'yes!!' in triumph, but restrained himself enough to reply in the same tones 'No, that won't be necessary. Thank you very much for your help, Madam. We won't need to trouble you further.' He replaced the receiver and punched the air in delight. He hadn't thought it could be so easy.

A sobering thought occurred to him, moments later. He had forgotten to withhold his number, so if she did have any suspicions about the call, Anthea had only to dial 1471 and she would know where the call had come from. She would certainly recognise it as Michael's number. That was, if he had ever called her from here.

There was no puzzled or indignant return call in the next few minutes. Colin looked in the desk and found a London train timetable, from which he saw there was a service to Paddington in less than an hour's time. He'd call on Anthea now, straight away, while his enthusiasm was at its height. His anger, too. Michael had cheated his mother out of her financial rights, and somewhere a fortune had gone missing. He was going to find out what had happened to it, starting right now with the only clue he had.

He went into the kitchen, where Fiona and Mrs Burdett were setting out lunch on the kitchen table.

'Just in time to eat, dear. Mrs Burdett has made us a quiche, with some salad,' Fiona greeted him.

'Sorry, Mother. Can't stop for lunch. I'm going up to London by the next train.'

'But, dear, you must have something before you go! And why are you off in such a hurry? It's rather sudden, isn't it?'

The last thing he wanted to do was to tell her about Anthea just yet. While he hesitated, thinking of an excuse that would sound reasonable, Mrs Burdett came in from the scullery with a pot of tea, which she put on the table.

'You ought to have something, Master Colin. Must keep your strength up,' she chided.

The quiche did look tasty. He reached out and cut himself a slice. 'I'll eat it on the way,' he said. 'I'll be back this evening, Ma.'

Fiona frowned. She disliked being called Ma. So common, she thought. And he was intending to eat his lunch in the street, like some urchin. 'Why do you have to rush off now?' she asked plaintively. 'What's so important that it cannot wait until you've eaten properly?'

'I have to hurry to catch the train.' There was plenty of time before it left the local station, but Fiona wouldn't know that. If he stayed, he might be persuaded into saying where he was going, and he wasn't sure that Fiona would entirely approve. 'I'll tell you all about it when I get back,' he said, heading for the door. Perhaps he would tell her, perhaps not. It all depended on what Anthea had to say.

Fiona followed him into the hall, intending to continue the discussion, but was distracted by the telephone ringing. While she paused to answer it, Colin scurried out of the front door.

The call was from Simon Neville, ringing to ask her how she was bearing up, and inviting himself to visit that afternoon. He suggested taking her out to dinner later, and was prepared for Fiona to make up her mind if she wanted to or not, when he arrived. In her pleasure at the unexpected visit, Fiona forgot all about Colin.

By the time Simon arrived, Fiona had decided that she would tell him about Nigel Williams' visit, and the revelations about Michael's money situation. It would be impossible, she knew, to spend a whole afternoon and evening in his company and not blurt out the news. She needed to tell somebody, too. It was all very well, just talking to Colin about it. After all, it affected him almost as much, but he was young and had his own problems. She didn't want him to feel he had to be responsible for her, just when he needed to think about his own future.

Before Simon arrived Fiona had another telephone call, this time from Eleanor. 'How are you, Fee? Feeling back to your old self a bit, now?'

Why did people talk as if she was recovering from some long-term illness? She had thought better of Eleanor. 'I'm angry,' she said. It was plain truth; anger was the predominant emotion she had felt ever since Nigel Williams' visit.

'I bet you're angry! I mean, why on earth should he have dropped dead like that at his age, with no warning, no health problems.' Eleanor spoke briskly. 'What I really meant was, have people stopped pussy footing around you as though they're afraid you are going to have a fit of weeping hysterics?'

'I'd have hoped people would know me better. I'm not the type, whatever happened,' Fiona replied. 'I'll admit, Michael's death came as a shock. I had no idea he had any health problems, though I suppose he must have had some kind of heart trouble. Probably he didn't even realise it himself. He always seemed very fit, and he was still only in his early fifties. He shouldn't have gone like that, so suddenly.'

'Men do, though. He smoked and drank, didn't he? And he must have had pressures at work – '

'Ah, that!' She wasn't going to be able to keep it from Eleanor, her closest friend, for long, and if she didn't come out with it straight away, she would have to dissemble now. 'What kind of pressures he was under, I have no idea. Even what kind of work he was doing, I don't know. Did you know he had left Brightmans nearly a year ago? He never told me anything about that and he was still leaving here each morning to take the train up to London. Well, at least I suppose that's where he went. He kept to the same hours as he'd always done.'

'What!' Eleanor gasped. 'And he never told you? What was he playing at, for goodness sake?'

'I wish I knew,' Fiona said wearily. 'But whatever it was, it involved money. Lots of it. He made some deal with Brightmans to take his pension rights early. He had everything he would have been entitled to at sixty-five, everything, in fact, that I would have been entitled to as his widow. He's left me nothing, Nell.'

'Taken his pension rights early! He can't do that! It's illegal!'

'Legal or not, that's what he did. And he remortgaged the house, too. Whatever he did with it all, there's no money now. The family solicitor has just given me the news but I'm finding it hard to take in.'

'You want to go up to Brightmans and insist on seeing their Managing Director and find out what it's all about. It sounds crazy. You don't want to take the word of that doddery old solicitor of yours.'

'Nigel Williams has been our solicitor for years. He's a family friend and I'm sure he knows what he's talking about,' Fiona protested.

'But he's a bit long in the tooth, isn't he? Are you sure he hasn't got confused somehow? It probably isn't nearly as bad as you think. You really ought to go to Brightmans and find out exactly what the situation is.'

'I don't think I could face the humiliation of going there and admitting my total ignorance of what Michael was doing. Nigel said he would see what could be salvaged and he's working out a financial plan for my future. It looks as if I may have to sell Little Paddocks, though.'

'Sell up! Oh, Fee, no!'

'I was never all that keen on the place. It was Michael's choice, not mine. It's far too big for Colin and me, and Colin will be off soon, I'm sure. He won't want to spend his youth looking after his mother. No, a little cottage somewhere in the village will be far more suitable for me.'

'You could come and live with me!' Eleanor sounded eager. 'Or, better still, we could join forces and buy one of those very nice little houses they are building along the main road. Fee, it would be splendid! We could do all sorts of things together! Just think!'

'I don't think so. Nell, much as I love you, I can't see us sharing a home. We both appreciate our independence and there would be too many problems.'

'Well, think about it. Promise me you'll do that, at least. You know we always said we'd have a little cottage together, roses round the door, in some little country village some day.'

'But that was when we were still at school!' Fiona laughed. 'Even then, we could never agree about the decorations, or even where we'd have this little cottage. But listen to this, Nell! One good thing came out of it all, though. Simon Neville made contact again. You do remember him, don't you? He and I went out together long before I met Michael. He telephoned at lunch time, and he's coming to take me out to dinner tonight.'

'That's nice.' Eleanor's voice lacked enthusiasm. 'Fee – you will be careful, won't you?'

'Careful? Whatever do you mean?' Fiona detected a change in Eleanor's tones. 'Careful of what?'

'You're in a rather vulnerable state right now. You've had a shock and you haven't had enough time to take in all the implications.' Eleanor sounded embarrassed.

'Nell! It's Simon Neville, for heaven's sake! Not some fortune-hunting Romeo planning to prey on a helpless widow! And it's just for dinner. He's not having designs on me.'

'How do you know?'

'I haven't seen or heard anything of him for more than twenty-five years, that's why. And Simon isn't like that. He's a very kind, considerate man and I'm looking forward to talking over old times with him, thinking for once about the days before I even knew Michael.'

'Why's he turned up now, if you haven't heard from him in twenty-five years?'

'He read the notice about Michael's death in the *Times*, and recognised the name. Poor man, he got lost round all the little lanes, and missed the service completely. Turned up when we were having the wake, or whatever one calls the funeral do.'

'So that's why I didn't see him at the church. Well, all I can say is, he picked his moment to turn up again.'

Fiona was beginning to lose patience. 'I really don't know what you are implying, Nell, but I'd like to point out that I am perfectly capable of looking after myself and I shall see whoever I wish to see, whenever I wish. Nobody tells me what I can or cannot do.'

'I'm sorry.' Eleanor sounded contrite. 'It's just that I worry about you, Fee.'

'You've no need to. I can take care of myself perfectly well. Goodness knows, I've had to manage alone enough in the last few years.'

'And you still have Colin. He'd be ready and capable of seeing off any unwanted suitors if need be.'

'Only if I needed him to. Goodbye, Nell. I'm going to be rather busy now.' Fiona put down the receiver before Eleanor could say more. Nell seemed in a funny mood, unlike her usual self. Would she be like this, irritatingly protective, if they did set up a home together? No, it wouldn't work, Fiona told herself. Close friends they might be, but she could never imagine herself sharing a home with Nell. For one thing, she seemed to have some objection to Simon but Fiona couldn't

47

imagine what possible reason she could have. They had all been friends and had gone round in a group together in the days when they had all been young and heart free.

Simon was the most upright and straightforward man she had ever known, in many ways the complete opposite of Michael. Perhaps that was why she had been swept off her feet, all those years ago? Simon had represented safety and Michael excitement, the glamour of the London City world. And money. Reluctantly, Fiona admitted it to herself. Michael had had money, or appeared to. He'd been generous, and had led her into a lifestyle she knew she could never have achieved with Simon.

He arrived promptly at half past three, bearing an enormous bunch of tawny orange roses.

'These always used to be your favourites,' he said. 'I remembered you used to say you didn't like red ones.'

'They're still my favourites. How clever of you to remember.' Fiona buried her nose in the bunch and inhaled their strong perfume with pleasure.

'I suppose flowers are really a bit much,' Simon said. 'You've probably still got loads of them around the house.'

'No, actually. A few people sent wreaths, which are still on the grave, I suppose. Only Nell sent flowers for myself – carnations. You remember Nell, don't you – Eleanor Pagett?'

'Nell Pagett? She still around? Of course I remember her! What is she doing with herself these days?' Simon followed Fiona into the sitting room and Mrs Burdett, hovering by the kitchen door, took charge of the roses.

'Nell lives in the village. She moved into a cottage in the High Street about a year after we came here. She's much the same as she always was. She never married, you know.'

'Always thought that odd,' Simon remarked. 'You and Nell – the two prettiest girls around. Well, so most of us chaps thought. For me, there was only ever the one. No one ever came up to your standard, in my book.'

'Simon!'

'Suppose I shouldn't be saying things like that, so soon after your husband's funeral. It's just that – seeing you again has made the years roll back. Looking at you makes me feel young again.'

'I know. It makes me feel the last twenty-five years never happened. In some ways, I wish they never had, but then, I'd never have had Colin. He's been such a comfort, and so helpful, these last weeks.'

'You've every reason to be proud of him,' Simon said. 'He sounds a splendid chap and I hope I'm going to be able to meet him soon.'

'He's gone to London today,' said Fiona. 'Rushed off at lunch time without a word of explanation, clutching a piece of quiche to eat on the way to the station. I hope he might be back this evening so you can meet him, but he didn't say. I suppose he might be rushing off to a job interview. Earning some money is becoming rather urgent now.'

'But Michael left you well provided for, didn't he? I can imagine Colin wants to be independent now he's finished as a student, but he'll want to look for something interesting, won't he? Or has he heard of the perfect job already?'

'I don't know what he wants to do. But he's anxious to find a job. He was talking about being a jobbing gardener in the village, or working on one of the farms.'

'Temporary, of course? Well, there's nothing like a bit of experience of how the other half live, to start him off. Stand him in good stead when he comes to the serious work.'

Before Fiona could say more, Mrs Burdett wheeled in the tea trolley. 'My goodness, what a splendid spread!' Simon exclaimed. 'I see you are looking after Mrs Latimer very well, Mrs Burdett, helping to keep her strength and spirits up.'

Mrs Burdett looked pleased. 'I do my best, Sir. And Madam is always very appreciative of my efforts.' She glanced at Fiona. 'Ring if you want any more hot water, won't you, Mrs Latimer?'

After she had gone, Simon said, 'We can dispense with all the formal small talk, now. Tell me truly, how has it really been? For you, I mean?'

'The funeral? Bit of a strain. I suppose all funerals are. It's the ritual which gets you through, I suppose.' Fiona leant forward to pour tea.

'I didn't mean the funeral. You know that. I meant, how has it been these last years? Have you been happy?'

'Happy?' Fiona considered the question. She had to be completely truthful with Simon. 'I suppose content might be a better word. I *was* happy with Michael at first – he was generous and we had a comfortable lifestyle. He was fun to be with. I suppose I could say I found him exciting.'

'Exciting enough to sweep you off your feet? That's how it seemed to all of us who watched him snap you up and whisk you away from us. We were all a bit taken aback when you married Michael, I think.'

'It all happened too quickly, you thought? Yes, I suppose it did. And you are right, he did sweep me off my feet. He was so different from anyone I'd ever met – oh, dear, that does sound very tactless and unkind – there were several very sweet men in the group we used to go round with and you were quite the nicest of them all – '

'But not rich and exciting? No, I know I was never that. None of us were, in those days.' Simon sounded rueful.

'It makes me sound as if I married Michael for his money,' Fiona said. 'I admit, I liked the lifestyle his money and business contacts brought. Perhaps that does make me sound very shallow, but it wasn't only that. I did love him, and I hated being poor. Dad worked on the railways, you know. We were never going to do more than merely get by. I trained as a typist. The best I could have hoped for was to end up as somebody's secretary. And if I'd married – '

'If you'd married me, you'd still have had a good many years of merely getting by. I made it in the end. I have several consultancies and I'm pretty well off now but it took a long time and even now, I don't suppose I'm anywhere near being in Michael's league.'

'Michael's league? I wonder now, what that was,' Fiona said thoughtfully.

'You have a beautiful home and you're clearly comfortably provided for. I could never have given you all this, in the early days. Not even now, perhaps. Look, my dear, I want to be honest and up front about all this. I want to see you again, but I do realise that I have to be discreet. The last thing I'd want would be for the locals in a small village like this to start gossiping, saying that I was after you for your money.'

Fiona's laugh had a slightly hysterical edge to it. 'That's the last thing they'd be saying!'

'My dear, you don't know what these small communities can be like. They may not be country yokels any more, in fact, I would think a good many of the people living here are city commuters or retired, but that doesn't mean they don't love to gossip. There's not much going on here, so anything that looks as if it could have a whiff of scandal, is meat and drink to them.'

'They'll certainly have plenty to gossip about soon, then,' Fiona said, with a touch of bitterness. 'But it won't have anything to do with your coming here. I dare say that, whatever I do, it won't be long before everyone knows that the rich widow living in Little Paddocks is a complete sham.'

'What do you mean?' Simon was looking at her intently. Fiona couldn't fathom his expression.

'I mean that, though Michael appeared to have money, it all seems to have disappeared. This house, which I had always assumed would come to me debt-free, has a second mortgage on it which I haven't a hope of meeting. And the pension from his company doesn't exist. I never knew, but he had left Brightmans nearly a year ago, and somehow managed to cash in his pension rights. He accumulated hundreds of thousands of pounds in the last year, but there's no sign of any of it left. No one seems to know what he did with it, but there's no money, Simon. No money at all.'

Simon looked at her, shocked. 'Oh, my dear!' he whispered. 'I am so very, very sorry. I had no idea. But surely – he couldn't cash in his pension – that's unheard of.'

'It seems he did. I don't know what he was doing this last year or so. As far as I know, he still went up to London and I thought he was still working at Brightmans, but my solicitor told me he'd left there over six months ago. And it would seem that he amassed a huge amount of cash in the last year. What he's done with it, God alone knows. I was asked if he had an offshore account in the Caymans, or Switzerland, or somewhere. I laughed at the idea but now I'm beginning to wonder. There is so much coming out that I didn't know about, it's as though I have been married to a stranger all these years.'

'And you never had any inkling – any feelings that something was not quite as it should be?'

'Never. He behaved just as usual. Sometimes he stayed up in London in the week; he had a small flat which he rented when we moved down here. I understood there were evening meetings, conferences which went on late, occasional trips abroad which he had to make on Brightmans' behalf. I never questioned that; there were dinners, social functions that we both went to in the past, so I knew such occasions genuinely happened. And, to be frank, I was never all that keen on them, so when we moved down here I stopped going with him. He said he had to attend as there were clients to entertain and they'd be talking business, which made me even less keen. I never imagined for a moment that everything wasn't going on just as it always had. He was alone in the flat when he had his heart attack and he was dead when the night porter found him. I felt so sorry that he'd died alone, but I was told that it must have been quite sudden, and he probably didn't suffer anything.'

There was a catch in Fiona's voice as she added 'I never saw him again, not even in his coffin. A London undertaker dealt with all the necessary formalities. It all seemed so unreal.'

Simon reached out and took both her hands in his. 'What can I say? There must be something I can do to help. Have you spoken to Brightmans about his pension? There must be some mistake.'

'Nigel Williams, our family solicitor, went into it all for me. He didn't manage to get much out of Brightmans; he said they sounded a bit cagey and wouldn't explain why they'd let him take his pension – our pension – early. I suppose it wasn't strictly legal and they were worried that he'd make a fuss and report them to the tax inspectors, or whoever. Nigel advised me to put this house on the market as soon as possible and look for somewhere smaller. He thinks there may be a little money left over from the sale, and there are quite a lot of good pieces of furniture I'll have to get rid of anyway if I'm to move to a cottage somewhere. There are some pictures which might bring in something; they would be out of place anywhere else.'

'Fiona, I can only say that I think you are being incredibly brave.' Simon still held her hands and she began to feel rather foolish.

'You know, I rather like the idea of a little cottage somewhere in the village. It'll take me back to my roots. I was born in a railwayman's cottage.'

'But this Nigel Williams is not going to let things rest as they are, I hope? He'll go on investigating. Find out what Michael's done with all that money. What he wanted it for. If he died so soon after he got it, there must surely be a sizeable amount of it still left, somewhere.'

'One would think so. I still can't take it all in. I won't mind leaving this house; it wasn't my choice and I always thought it was too big for just the three of us. It's silly, I know, but the only thing I'm going to miss will be Mrs Burdett. She's been such a treasure, a real bulwark. She's much more than just a daily woman.'

'Women like that don't disappear,' Simon comforted. 'You may not be able to employ her any more, but you'll still have her as a friend. You can be sure of that. But will you be able to bear to go on living in the village once you've sold up? Won't it be too hard, too embarrassing?'

'I know most of the people here. They have always been friendly; friendly to me, not particularly Michael. And there's Eleanor. She goes right back to our schooldays. We'll be company for each other, two women growing old disgracefully, keeping the village in gossip. She suggested we shared a home together and I must say, for a moment I was tempted, but I know, deep down, that it wouldn't work. We both need our own space, the freedom to live our own lives. Nell's a dear, but she'd drive me mad if I lived with her.'

'I can imagine it, if my memory of Nell Pagett is correct,' Simon said dryly. 'You're a strong woman, Fiona, and you'll overcome all this. I'd like to help, but I don't want you to feel that I'd be taking over. Let me just say that I'm here if you need me. Whatever I can do, you have only to ask. And there will be no strings attached, I promise you. It will be for old friendship's sake.'

'Thanks, Simon. You are kind. I value your friendship more than I can say.'

' Now, even after that splendid tea, I'm going to take you out for dinner. A drive in the country first, then we'll end up in a little, hidden away country manor where the food is out of this world. And for the next few hours we can both pretend we are twenty years old again.'

'Simon, I think you are exactly what I need, right now.' Fiona leaned forward and kissed his cheek and he thought, with a sense of excitement stirring within him, that perhaps it might not be too late for him, after all.

CHAPTER 4

COLIN ARRIVED AT CHOMLEY MEWS late that afternoon. Standing outside the rather pretty mews terrace, he had sudden misgivings. What could he say to her? How could he ask the kind of questions that were burning in his mind, without giving offence? He wanted to say – who are you? Are you in some way linked to my father's strange and probably criminal behaviour? Are you his girlfriend, or mistress? He'd have the door slammed in his face if he started off asking questions like that. Yet how could he explain why he had come to see her? How could he explain, without embarrassment, how he had found out where Anthea lived? Even now, the memory of his pretending to be a Telecom engineer made him squirm.

Before he could change his mind and leave, he made himself walk forward and press the doorbell. Perhaps she'd be out. More than likely she'd be out, in the middle of the afternoon. In which case, he'd do what he should have done first, go to a café somewhere and plan what he was going to say, then return when he'd worked it out fully. He'd thought about it on the journey up to London, but still he hadn't made any proper plan.

The door opened while he was still deciding whether to leave. Anthea stood in the doorway.

'Er – hallo,' Colin stuttered. 'It's Anthea, isn't it? Anthea Ransom?'

'Yes, that's right.' She still stood there, making no move to invite him in. Colin realised she looked even more attractive than he had remembered from their brief encounter after the funeral; auburn hair, softly curling round her shoulders, deep cornflower-blue eyes and a slender figure that he had a sudden urge to hold.

'I'm Colin. Colin Latimer.'

'Yes, I know who you are.' She still stood there, not making it easy for him, but at least she hadn't shut the door on him yet.

'I came to – to thank you for coming to my father's funeral,' he said. 'It was kind of you. And – and appreciated.'

She had a faintly amused look on her face, as if she knew her presence at the funeral had merely been puzzling, no more.

'My mother wondered – she wanted me to ask you – I mean – ' How he wished he had worked out exactly what he was going to say! Now, coming out with that crass line "my mother wanted me to ask you" made him sound like a schoolboy still acting under parental orders. And, frankly, faced by the cool, amused expression of this sophisticated girl, he did indeed feel no more than a gauche schoolboy.

Anthea relented. 'You'd better come in,' she said, stepping back.

The mews house, one in a terrace tucked away behind larger houses, had a country cottage look to it. Originally it had been part of stables, then garages, and the lane running past was narrow and cobblestoned. Inside the rooms were small, the front door opening directly on to the sitting room.

This was furnished with good quality pieces, and added to the cottagey feel with chintz-covered armchairs and curtains. It looked the home of a single person, someone not wealthy but comfortably off.

'Do sit down. Can I offer you anything? Tea, perhaps, unless you could do with something stronger?'

Colin felt he could well do with a stiff drink, and her way of offering one suggested she knew he was nervous. Her manner wasn't helping, either. But it was too early for alcohol and he wanted to ensure he kept a clear head. 'A cup of tea would be lovely,' he said. At least that would give him the excuse to stay a while longer.

There was a tiny kitchen off the sitting room, through an archway. Anthea filled a kettle and put mugs on a tray. She turned back and stared at him.

'Why have you come to see me?'

'I – well, I – '

'You were curious about who I was.' She laughed softly and came into the room to sit on the arm of the other chair, facing him. 'Neither you nor your mother had the faintest idea who I was, had you?'

'We thought you must be someone sent from his office, from Brightmans. One of his assistants, perhaps, or a secretary.'

Anthea nodded. 'Yes, I suppose you would be likely to think that.' She gave no indication as to whether Colin's assumption had been correct.

'We thought – my mother thought that perhaps my father had helped you in some particular way, or that you'd worked together on some project. No one else came from Brightmans, you see.'

Anthea gave a gentle, rather attractive chuckle. 'And I bet your mother wondered a few other things about me and my connection with your father,' she said. 'Things that she must have been curious about, or maybe would rather not want to know.'

'Weren't you representing Brightmans?' Colin asked bluntly. He was getting rather tired of the way she seemed to be playing games with him.

Anthea shook her head. 'I've never worked for Brightmans,' she said. 'I knew your father slightly and I rather liked him. That's why I came to his funeral.'

'Oh, I see.'

'No, you don't see at all. You don't know who I am and you want to know my connection with your father, but you are too polite or too shy, or too worried about what the answer might be, to ask me outright.'

'That's about the size of it.' There was something about the frank way Anthea spoke that made Colin feel relieved.

'You could have asked me at the funeral, though I suppose I left too soon, before you or your mother got round to speaking to me. That was deliberate; I hadn't meant to go back to the house. I didn't want to speak to anyone. It didn't occur to me that you'd be curious enough to track me down.'

'Naturally, we wondered who you were. You could have been a long-lost relation of Dad's that we knew nothing about.'

'Now that *would* have been intriguing!' Anthea laughed again. 'You came out to my car to ask me, didn't you? But I drove off without explaining myself so you had to play detective to find me. How did you do that, by the way?'

'Your telephone number was in one of Dad's diaries. I found it when we were clearing out his things. Well, I thought it could possibly be you, just an A beside the number.'

'So you played at being a Telecom engineer to get my full name and address?'

Colin flushed scarlet. 'I didn't know how else – '

'It was a good wheeze, except that nowadays the telephone has a good system for tracing calls. Telephone engineers don't need to ask one's name and address, so I called up 1471 and discovered the engineer had used the Little Paddocks telephone. I've been expecting a development of some kind since then.'

'I think you should accept that we had reason to be curious about you, since you seemed rather cagey about introducing yourself,' Colin said. 'And even more so, after we discovered some very odd things about Dad's life, during the last year before he died.'

'You discovered things about him? Do you mean there were things in his diaries?' Anthea asked sharply.

'No, not from his diaries. At least, not the diaries that were among his things at home. There was nothing in them except notes about dentist appointments, car servicing, that kind of thing, apart from a few addresses and telephone numbers which meant nothing. Our family solicitor broke the news to my mother that Dad hadn't worked at Bright-mans for nearly a year. We'd had no idea that he'd left. He still went up to London each day and now we have no idea what he *did* do for that last year.'

'That must have been rather a shock for your mother, for both of you.'

'You *knew*?' He was guessing, but some instinct told Colin that Anthea knew a great deal more than she was willing to say. He was determined that he wasn't going to leave until he had found out as much as he could.

'I knew Michael hadn't been working at Brightmans for several months. I didn't know where he *was* working.'

'How come you know that, if you didn't work there, have never worked there?' Colin demanded.

'My mother works at Brightmans.'

'Oh, I see.' Colin didn't.

'I'll get that tea.' Anthea stood up. At the entrance to the kitchen she turned her head to say 'I suppose you think you know the worst about Michael now. Your mother may find she's not as well off as she believed she would be. It's better not to be too curious about Michael, though. He was a secretive man. Probably there's no one who knows every-thing there was to know about him. You'll have to accept there are things it's better not to pry into too deeply.' She turned her back and began pouring hot water into a teapot.

'But you know things, more than you are telling me,' Colin said, exasperated.

'I know very little. As I said, I only met him a few times.' She brought the tray into the sitting room and put it down on a small table. 'Milk and sugar?' she asked, conversationally.

Colin ignored her. 'You met him through your mother, did you, since she worked at Brightmans?'

Anthea nodded. 'Yes, that's right.'

'I'd like to meet your mother. Could you arrange it, please?'

Anthea burst out laughing. 'Well! I've never heard of anyone *asking* to meet my mother! It's a bit sudden, isn't it? And I'm not sure if she'd be willing to meet you. She wouldn't want to talk about Brightmans and your father, anyway. That's confidential.'

'They wouldn't talk to our family solicitor about what happened, why he left or why they allowed him to take his pension in advance. But surely they could tell his son, his widow? We're the ones most closely affected by what they allowed him to do. I think we have a right to know, particularly as Michael isn't here to explain his actions to us.'

'I don't know.' Anthea looked down at the floor, trailing patterns on the rug with her foot. 'I must say, it does seem hard on both of you. But it was all done in strictest confidence. Brightmans would never give any details of the arrangement to anyone. I'm sure of that.'

'But you know what happened, don't you?'

'Not really. My mother never said very much about it to me. Believe me, Colin, I don't know anything. I couldn't help you, even though I have some sympathy for you.'

'I'm not at all sure that the pension arrangement is legal. If we were to challenge it in the courts, Brightmans would have to come clean and explain why they had done it. I think, if we don't get any satisfactory answers, to that and several other questions, too, then we *will* go to court and bring the whole situation out into the open.'

'No, don't do that.' Anthea looked up at him, her face anxious. 'You don't know what kind of can of worms you would be opening if you make Michael's arrangement with Brightmans public.'

'Then at least they should let his family know the full facts.' Anthea's fear of courts and publicity had convinced Colin that there must be something decidedly fishy about the whole situation, and he was determined to find out what it was.

'My mother wouldn't see you, anyway. It would be more than her job was worth to discuss Brightmans' business with anyone,' Anthea said.

Colin had finished his tea, and there didn't seem to be any further excuse to stay longer. So far, the meeting with Anthea hadn't yielded any light on Michael's behaviour, although it had confirmed his suspicions that there was something very odd going on.

He stood up. 'I'd like to see you again,' he said. 'Not to try to pump you about things that you clearly know no more about than I do, but because I'd like to get to know you better. May I take you out to dinner one day soon?'

Anthea smiled. 'What a quaint, old-fashioned invitation! How could I resist? Thank you, Colin. I'd like that.'

'How about Wednesday? And where would you like to eat?'

'Wednesday would be fine. Call for me here at half past seven. I don't mind where we eat, except that I don't go much for burgers and chips.'

He grinned, relaxing for the first time since his arrival. 'Neither do I. Thank you for seeing me, Anthea.'

At the door she said, 'Don't go ferreting about in Michael's affairs. It wouldn't be a good idea.'

He was tempted to say 'But I have to. We haven't any income to live on, now he's taken all our future funds and disposed of them somehow,' but he couldn't bring himself to risk sounding whingeing and poverty stricken. 'I hope I won't have to, but the situation has hit my mother pretty hard,' he muttered, and turned away before either of them could say more. He strode down the cobblestones to join the main road at the end. The visit hadn't been a complete waste, he was going to see her again and even if he never found out anything more, that at least was a big something.

Colin was half way down the escalator at the tube station when it occurred to him that while he was in London it might be a good idea to visit the flat where Michael had been staying when he died. He wasn't sure what he hoped to gain from such a visit, but the opportunity was too good to miss. He had thought of going to call in to the London headquarters of Brightmans, but it was too late in the day now to expect anyone to be there with the time to see him, even if they were willing to. And such a visit would be far better left until he had planned exactly what he was going to say and what questions he would ask.

Michael's flat was in an old apartment block in a back street near Paddington station. It looked run down and dingy from the outside, but, once past the overly ornate entrance, it was clean and surprisingly well appointed.

Colin had no key to the flat. As far as he knew, only Michael had ever held one and there had never been a spare left at home. He wondered what had happened to Michael's keys, to all the personal items which would have been on him when he died. Fiona had not seen him after his death, everything had been dealt with by a local undertaker, which in itself sounded very unusual. Presumably, the contents of his pockets and other personal effects had been passed to her at some point, though now he came to think of it, Colin had no recollection of there ever having been a parcel delivered to Little Paddocks.

There was a glass-fronted office in a corner of the main hall, no more than a large broom cupboard, but he could see through the frosted window in the door that there was someone inside, hopefully a hall porter or someone with the authority to help him. Colin went over to it and knocked.

The man, in a uniform with epaulettes and brass buttons, opened the door.

'Can I help you, Sir?' He sounded well-spoken and helpful.

Colin abandoned his first idea that he should pretend he was looking for a flat to rent, and decided to come clean about who he was. If this man, or one of his colleagues, had found Michael, he might be willing to talk frankly about it, unless there was something to hide.

'I'm Michael Latimer's son,' he said. 'My father died here in one of the flats, a week or so ago. I wonder – could you tell me what has happened to the flat since? Is it still empty or has it been re-let?' It didn't seem likely that it would have been relet so soon, but he knew that accommodation was snapped up quickly in London.

'I remember it all very well,' the man said. 'I was the one to find him. Brought up his milk and paper as I always do, and couldn't get any answer when I knocked. I knew he was staying there; seen him come in the previous evening, so I was a bit surprised at not making him hear. Got the pass key in the end, and there he was, lying on the floor in the living room. Must have been there some time, I reckon, too.'

'What has happened to the flat? Is it still empty?'

'Yes. Still left as it was. Rent was paid up until the end of the quarter, you see, so we can't do anything with it until after then.'

'Can I go up and see it?'

The man looked doubtful. 'How do I know you're Mr Latimer's son?' he asked. 'You might be a reporter from some newspaper, looking for a story?'

'No, I really am Michael Latimer's son. Look, here's my driving licence, with my photo and address. Will that do?' Colin opened his wallet and held out his licence.

'Well, in that case, I suppose you can. It's still rented out to him, or to his heirs, I guess. You might want to take any bits and pieces that were his, but most of the stuff, furniture and things, came with the place, so they'll be cleaned and re-let after the end of next month. There is still some of his personal stuff there, clothes and things, though not much. Used the place when he was working late, he told me. Cheaper and more convenient than a hotel room, but he didn't live here, not what I'd call live, all the time, like.'

'I haven't got a key. And I don't know which number,' Colin felt foolish. 'We never came here, you see.'

'I'll take you and open up.' The man leant back into his cubby hole and took down a bunch of keys from a hook on the wall. 'Nice man, Mr Latimer,' he remarked, leading the way up the stairs. 'No trouble at all. Good, quiet tenant and kept himself to himself, though he was friendly enough when we met in the hall.'

On the first floor the porter opened a door a short way down a corridor. Colin noticed the place didn't appear to have a lift.

'Here we are!' The porter pushed open the door and stepped back for Colin to go inside. 'Just shut the door when you've finished, will you?'

Colin didn't want to be left alone in the flat. 'You said you found him lying on the floor in the living room?' he asked. 'Show me.'

The porter pushed open a door to the left of the small entrance hall. 'In here,' he said. 'He was lying beside the sofa, just as if he'd slipped off it. I went to call an ambulance from his phone, but he said he had already done that.'

'He *what?*' Colin gasped.

'He said "I've called them. No need for you to do so. They'll be here soon." Those were the last words he spoke. I bent down to put a cushion under his head but he'd drifted off. I reckon that was when he died.'

'You mean he *wasn't* dead when you found him?'

'Alive enough to speak to me. And, sure enough, two men with a stretcher came along within a few minutes. They checked him over, but I heard one of them mutter to the other that he was a goner.'

'They didn't try to resuscitate him?'

'No point. Try that too long after the heart stops and you end up with brain damage. At least, that's if you succeed, and he'd gone by then. I could tell. He was a funny colour, blue round the lips and yellowy white skin. Well, you'll excuse me if I don't hang around here, won't you, Sir? Gives me a funny feeling, seeing where it all happened. Never had a death like that here before.'

'Of course. Sorry I made you relive it all. Thanks for your help. All right if I collect any of his clothes and personal things, is it?'

'Certainly. Flat's his, or yours now, I suppose. Till the end of the month, anyway. There aren't many things of his still around, though.'

'I'd like to see where he used to live. Get some feel for the place,' Colin said. 'Oh, by the way, I'm a bit puzzled – we thought it was the undertakers who collected him from here, not the ambulance.'

'Ambulance men probably took him straight to the undertakers.' The porter shrugged.

They wouldn't do that, Colin thought at once. They'd take him to the hospital, or to the morgue. There'd be a post-mortem, if they didn't know how he'd died. And yet Fiona hadn't had a call from any hospital; the first she'd known about Michael's death was from a firm of undertakers somewhere in the East End of London, telling her that they had, on instructions, collected Michael's body and were preparing it for burial. What were her funeral wishes regarding the ceremony and could they help liaise with any officials? Fiona had been in such a state of shock that she hadn't thought to ask on whose instructions they had collected Michael's body, and from where?

Colin sat for a long time on the sofa, deep in thought. The whole situation was getting stranger and stranger, and more and more unlikely. Fiona hadn't said much about the call from the undertakers. She hadn't even picked up their name properly. He assumed it had been such a shock she hadn't been able to take it all in, but then, why hadn't she asked him to take over and manage things? He wasn't a child, or someone so close to his father that news of his death would have been a devastating blow. Colin thought he would have been better able to cope with handling the details of the death than his mother. He wished now that she had turned to him. But would he, then, have thought to ask all the questions that he wanted to ask now? Probably not, any more than Fiona had done.

After a while, he stood up and began to explore the rest of the flat. There wasn't much of it; a small kitchen, clearly tidied up by the porter or someone since Michael's death; a bathroom, and bedroom.

He went into the bedroom and looked round. He pulled out drawers in a tallboy and opened the wardrobe. There were a few clothes hanging inside, a raincoat and a dark suit, the one Michael used for formal meetings or dining out, and a couple of sets of underwear and several shirts in the tallboy. But where were any papers, files or anything connected with work, whatever Michael's work had been, in these last months? There ought, at least, to have been a briefcase of some sort. There was nothing.

Colin searched the whole flat, opening drawers and cupboards in all the rooms, but there was nothing else of a personal nature anywhere. The refrigerator was empty, but probably the porter had removed any food likely to decay. He would have a word with the man again before he left. There was no point in staying longer; the place was empty, far too empty to be normal. The few clothes Colin could understand; Michael had only stayed here overnight occasionally, but he would never be without his briefcase, or papers relating to work. There would have had to be something here, and yet there wasn't a single thing. Someone must have been here after Michael's body had been taken away and removed everything that might have given a clue as to what he had been doing in the last weeks. Colin closed the door and walked downstairs to the porter's room.

'Did anyone come to the flat, after my father was taken away?' he asked.

'Not as far as I know, Sir. I didn't see anyone.' The porter shrugged. 'I went up shortly afterwards and tidied up a bit, took away the milk and some perishables from the fridge. If they're left inside, they make the fridge stink and it's a job cleaning it up. I shut the place up and that's how it was left.'

'Where was his briefcase? He must have had it there with him, must have had some papers and files at least, but there's nothing like that there, nothing at all.'

'I didn't see a briefcase or papers of any sort when I was there,' the man said. 'Perhaps the ambulance people took it with them when they took him.'

'Hardly likely.'

'Might have done in case there was medication inside.'

Colin forbore from asking what a dead man would want with medication. He turned away, but the porter added 'Course, I suppose someone might have gone in while I wasn't here. I'm not on twenty-four seven. There is another chap does weekends, but he would have said if anyone had asked for the key. We're supposed to log it if anyone but the tenant wants to be let in.'

'And when is he on duty again?'

'Next Friday. Does eight am till ten pm over the weekend.'

'What happens if someone wants the porter after ten?' Colin asked.

'They don't get one. Can't get at the keys 'cause this place is locked up. Tenants all know that; if they've forgotten their keys they'll have to come back before ten or sleep in the corridor.'

'So if anyone did come to collect things from the flat, you'd know, unless they had a key themselves?' Colin asked.

'That's right. It's all logged here. And there wasn't anyone asking to be let into Mr Latimer's flat until you came.'

'Thanks for your help.' The man hadn't been much help, but Colin supposed he had told as much as he knew. The next thing to do was to investigate the ambulance service, and he might as well do that by telephone from home.

Fiona was out when he arrived back at Little Paddocks, for which Colin was relieved. There was a note for him on the kitchen table, telling him that she had gone out to dinner with a friend, and wouldn't be back until late.

He gave a wry smile at the 'friend.' It wouldn't be Eleanor, otherwise Fiona would have said. Almost certainly it was the chap who had turned up late at the funeral, what was his name, now? Simon. Simon Neville, who had apparently been an old flame of hers way back before Fiona had met Michael.

What was the man up to? Colin had no objection to his mother having a male admirer if she chose, but it was odd that he turned up so promptly as soon as Michael had gone. Well, if he was a fortune hunter, impressed by the look of Little Paddocks and their supposed lifestyle and hoping to cash in on a fortune, he was in for a disappointment, a shock, even. Colin hoped that wasn't Simon's intention; the last thing Fiona wanted now was to be disillusioned by yet another man in her life.

He helped himself to the remains of Mrs Burdett's quiche and some salad, then went into the study to consult the London telephone books and look up the Ambulance service, but he was distracted and found himself looking up the addresses of restaurants around the Chelsea area. Where would Anthea like to go to eat? Would she want to dine locally or prefer somewhere new, where she would be less likely to know people, less chance of having to explain who Colin was if she met a friend? Everything was becoming more complicated, the more he thought about it.

CHAPTER 5

SIMON'S CAR WAS COMFORTABLE, expensive but not opulent, and he drove competently. Fiona found herself relaxing against the leather seats and idly watching the countryside flash past. The area was new to her; she had no idea where he was taking her, and, at that moment, she didn't care. Simon could drive her half way round the world and she would be happy just to sit beside him, listen to the soft, unobtrusive music on the car radio and make desultory conversation about nothing in particular, watching his well-groomed hands on the steering wheel, taking the occasional glance at his strong profile.

Why, she wondered, had she ever thought of him as dull, and Michael as the exciting man in her life? She had made a mistake, all those years ago, when she had made the wrong choice of life partner. A frisson of excitement shuddered through her as Simon glanced at her briefly and smiled, before returning his gaze to the road.

'Not far now,' he said. 'I hope you're feeling hungry, Anton will expect us to do full justice to his culinary expertise.'

It felt as though she were back to her carefree teenage days, reliving the excitement of a first date. This is ridiculous, Fiona told herself. I'm fifty, for heaven's sake, not a silly teenager. And Simon is – well, he's older than I am, but he has certainly worn well, over the years. But we're not youngsters again, we can't go back and relive our youth, however much we may want to. Too much has happened in the intervening years, too much which has shaped and changed our characters and personalities. I'm not the girl I was when I first knew Simon, and he isn't – cannot be – the same person I knew then.

Simon broke into her thoughts. 'We're here,' he said, turning into a drive between high iron gates. Trees on either side screened any sight of a building and so it was a complete surprise and shock when they turned a corner and she saw a perfect Elizabethan manor house in front of them.

'*Here?*' Fiona asked. 'But this looks like someone's home. You're not going to tell me – '

Simon laughed. 'No, not mine. How I wish it were! It was someone's home once, though. Now it's a very exclusive country club and restaurant. So exclusive that we have to park out of sight, behind those trees to the left. It's all part of giving the illusion that one is the personal guest of the owner and no one else has that privilege. Not entirely successful, of course. They can't hide away all the other diners, but one does have the feeling that one is rather special. And why shouldn't we cosset ourselves, once in a while?'

'You've been here before?' Fiona regretted the remark as soon as she'd uttered it. Obviously Simon had been here before but it must have been a rather special occasion. One didn't come to a place like this often. It occurred to her that she knew nothing about Simon's life in the years since they had last known each other. He knew about Michael, she had told him a great deal, probably too much, but he had said very little about himself. She would have to remedy that tonight.

A suave *maître d'* greeted them at the door and ushered them into a comfortable small sitting room, with no other guests. A waiter brought drinks and a menu, which seemed to contain everything one could possibly think of wishing to eat. Knowledgeably he guided them through it, tactfully suggesting dishes, asking their tastes and preferences. Finally, he left them, saying that their table would be ready in twenty minutes.

'They cook all that in so short a time?'

'You'd be surprised. Anton is one of the top world chefs and he has a formidable team under him. I can't begin to imagine how they manage it, but they do. Yes, I have been here before; several times, but only once to dine,' Simon said. 'You see, Anton is a particular friend of mine, well, a kind of relation, in a way, so I count as a rather special guest.'

'I see.'

'No, you don't. You're just being polite, while you wonder if I can really afford to take you to a place like this.' Simon smiled at her, his eyes twinkling. 'Well, I think a first date is rather special, don't you? And this is a first date – the first for over twenty-five years, anyway. Don't expect to be wined and dined at this level in future – that is, if you want to see me again. I do realise I might be assuming too much.'

'Michael being hardly cold in his grave,' Fiona said, with a shrug. 'Please don't think his grieving widow ought not to be dining out with another man so soon. I told you, Michael and I led separate lives for the last few years, and, after the way he has treated Colin and me, I feel I owe him nothing, certainly not affection. I'm angry, and frustrated that I can't ask him just what he thought he was doing, leaving us with nothing. What *was* he doing, anyway? Every day leaving by train, and all the time he wasn't going to work at Brightmans at all. He must have been going somewhere. Oh, don't get me going on Michael! I don't want to spoil a glorious evening by talking about him. I don't even want to think about him.'

The waiter arrived to conduct them to their table. The dining room was large, but tables were set in alcoves screened from each other so there was a feeling of dining quite separately.

The food was, of course, utterly delicious. When the waiter had finally left them, Fiona said, 'Now you must fill me in with your own life. You know what happened to me, these last thirty years, but I know nothing about what happened to you. I don't even know – do you have children? A wife?'

Simon laughed. 'Not a wife now. I married Margaret twenty years ago and I was widowed five years ago. We didn't have children. She was something of an invalid, she had multiple sclerosis and was in a wheelchair for the last few years of her life. We managed to get about and travelled in Europe before it all got too much for her and I suppose we had a good life, in spite of the restrictions of her illness. We were happy, I think, in a gentle, undemanding way. We loved each other, but it was in many ways like a brother-sister relationship. We cared for each other, looked after each other. I always felt very protective of Margaret, though she claimed she didn't need protecting. I suppose it's the male thing, a need to be needed, a need to look after one's partner.'

'How did you meet her?'

'At a wedding, of all the conventional situations. My cousin was marrying her brother and she was a bridesmaid. Beautiful, I thought she looked. She far outshone the poor bride, who was overweight and spotty. Traditionally, the best man is supposed to look after the bridesmaids but Charlie's friend quickly became rather sozzled and I took over the job. Not of being best man, but of looking after Margaret. It all went on from there.'

'You've been a caring person all your life,' Fiona said gently. 'It's your nature. But who has there ever been to care about you?'

'Me? Oh, I get by. I'm doing quite well nowadays, well enough to have a housekeeper so it's not as if I'm doing my own housework and living off ready meals and take-aways,' Simon laughed. 'Actually, the housekeeper came when Margaret wasn't well enough to do things like dress herself, and she stayed after Margaret died. She's a bit like your Mrs Burdett, but not so efficient – or such an excellent cook. Mavis Eggerton is a rock, and I don't know what I would have done without her, during the last year of Margaret's life. But she has a husband and family of her own and I rather suspect she may be quietly training me for the day when she decides I can look after myself perfectly well, with the help of a cleaner, perhaps.'

'And what did you do once you'd finished university? You always wanted to be something in the medical profession, I seem to remember,' Fiona said.

'Alas, that turned out not to be for me. There wasn't the money for further training, but an uncle gave me a position in his company, and it was there I learnt a helpful amount about the business world. Eventually, I started my own business, in a small way to begin with. It was a struggle, and there were a couple of times when I thought we would go under, but eventually it steadied and now we're doing well, importing raw materials, trading with countries all over the world. I can afford to take things a little easier now. In fact, I consider myself semi-retired, though I still keep an eye on the business and keep the accounts, and so on. It suits me. Keeps my mind active but gives me time to enjoy life again – time to spend with old friends from my youth – if they'll put up with a tedious old bore like me.'

'You're not a bore! Anything but! I don't know when I've enjoyed myself more, tonight,' Fiona exclaimed.

'Yes, I've enjoyed myself, too. I've felt like I was twenty-three again, just being with you.' Simon took her hands in his, across the table. 'Shall we go now, and drive home by moonlight, like the days when we used to walk across Hyde Park and count the stars?'

'We couldn't do that now,' Fiona said sadly, rising from the table. 'Too much pollution to see many stars, and it wouldn't be safe to walk anywhere like that at night.'

'Perhaps not, but we still have our memories of having done that, in an earlier, more innocent age.' Simon took her arm and steered her out of the restaurant. An attendant was waiting with her coat and Simon's car had been brought round to the front door. Fiona felt cossetted as the doorman helped her into the passenger seat and closed the door after her.

Their way back lay through open fields where the grass was silvered by the moon, but after a while they entered a small beechwood where shadows played among the trees. A magical place, Fiona thought. Simon slowed the car and pulled over into a layby. 'I just want you to listen to the night sounds in this spot,' he said. 'I've always thought it a magical place.'

Almost like a echo of her own thoughts, Fiona thought. Unbidden, the words came into her mind, 'Michael would never have thought of stopping to listen to the night sounds in a wood.' She pushed the thought away, feeling disloyal. Michael hadn't ever been like that, he was always eminently practical, his interests centred solely on his priorities in life, money, making money, enjoying the things in life money could buy...

Simon wound down the window. 'Listen,' he said. 'There's an owl over there. Murder is about to be committed. Wait.'

A moment later there was a sudden whoosh overhead and a scream as some small animal was seized in its talons.

'Such beautiful creatures, owls,' Fiona sighed. 'But they have to eat, too.'

Simon leant towards her. His arm slid round her shoulders and his face was close to hers. Fiona looked up at him, knowing what he was about to do.

'Is this too soon?' he whispered.

'Too soon? Simon, we've known each other for more than thirty years!' She gave a little, nervous laugh.

'I meant – ' He hesitated, drew back a little.

'I know what you meant. I've only buried Michael less than a week ago. And no, I won't feel guilty or disloyal to him, or his memory. I'm beginning to think I wasn't married to him at all. I married a stranger, not at all the man I thought I was marrying.' Not the man I should have married, Fiona thought to herself.

Simon's kiss was gentle at first, caressing her mouth with his lips as he drew her closer. His free hand brushed across her breast and his touch, though fleeting, stirred her deeply. His kiss became more demanding, and then she was swept up into the glorious memory of being twenty again, of kissing Simon for the very first time, under the stars in an empty Hyde Park.

'I don't want to let you go again, Fiona,' Simon said, when finally he moved to draw breath. 'You will let me see you again, won't you?'

'Yes. Oh, yes, please!' She clung to him. His lovemaking was as she had remembered it, tender and gentle, yet there was more now than in the years of his youth. He was a man, not a young, unsure boy and the years in between had given him experience and understanding of a woman's needs.

She lay, basking in the supreme bliss of having found, at last, someone with whom she could be close, could trust to understand her very thoughts without expressing them.

It was some time later, when streaks of light in the sky signalled that dawn was not far off, that they drove into the village and through the wrought iron gates of Little Paddocks.

'In a small place like this I wouldn't put it past the lace curtains to be twitching, even at this hour,' Simon remarked.

'Let them!' Fiona rested her head on his shoulder. 'There'll be gossip enough once they get to hear about Michael's financial wrangles. And they will, somehow, you can bet on it.'

'And that won't worry you?'

'It won't worry me that everyone will know. I hope they don't start pitying me, that's all. But if they've seen us coming home tonight, or, rather, this morning, they'll be more likely to envy me, and I'll enjoy that.'

'That's the stuff!' Simon pulled up at the door. 'What's Colin going to think?'

'He'll have been asleep long ago and won't know what time we came back. Anyway, he'll be happy for me. He was never close to Michael, he won't feel I've been disloyal. Michael forfeited any loyalty from Colin once he heard about the pension scam. Look, will you come in and rest? You surely don't want to drive back at this hour. I've a spare room if you want.'

'Thanks. It's tempting, but I ought to go back. It's not too long, just an hour or so and the roads will be empty. And after tonight, I feel I could stay awake for ever.'

'Drive carefully, then.' Fiona leant across to kiss him goodbye.

'I'll telephone later. Thanks for tonight, Fee. You've made me feel like a young man again.'

Simon watched her put her key into the door, turn to wave and disappear inside. He turned the car, hoping he wasn't making too much noise on the gravel, and that Colin's room was in the back of the house, then he was off, through the village and as soon as he was out in the country again, singing an old student song that he hadn't sung for thirty years.

Fiona slept well and awoke late. When she came downstairs into the kitchen she found Colin, already breakfasted, making himself mid-morning coffee.

'Good evening?' he asked.

'Mmm, lovely, thanks.' She didn't want to elaborate, or even tell him that she had been out with Simon. Not yet. Fortunately, Colin was absorbed in his own thoughts and didn't notice the glow in her face.

'Did you sort something out, yesterday, in London?' she asked.

'What?' Colin looked up, startled.

'A job? Didn't you go looking for a job? Any luck?'

'A job?' He stared at her, then, remembering that Fiona must have assumed he was rushing off to an interview yesterday, and that he didn't want her to know where he had gone, said vaguely, 'Oh, no I didn't find anything suitable. But I promise I won't stay lazing around here doing nothing.'

'That's all right, darling. We're really not that poverty stricken that you need to grab the first opportunity of work that comes along. Nigel Williams will come up with something. He's promised to design a financial plan for us, and there must be some money coming to us from the house. At least, your father's pictures must be worth a bit.'

'You're really going ahead with selling Little Paddocks?'

'Darling, it's too big for the two of us. And I didn't think you cared for it all that much, anyway.'

'I don't.' Colin picked up his coffee cup and prepared to depart towards the study. 'It's just that – I don't like the idea of being *forced* to move into somewhere else.'

'I know. It feels like Michael is still manipulating our lives from beyond the grave.'

'Look, Mum.' Colin paused by the door. 'I will find myself a job, I promise, but I do think I ought to stay around here until all this is settled. I mean, until we know exactly why Dad did whatever he did with the money, and where it's all gone.'

Fiona gave a scornful laugh. 'That may take years. We may never know. Nigel doesn't think there's any way we can find out much, with Brightmans being so cagey and refusing to tell us anything.'

'All the same, I'd like to try to find out for myself as much as I can. I rather fancy myself as a sleuth, a private eye. Perhaps, if I do manage to find out what he's been up to, I can take it up as a profession. Are you going to mind your son going around in a dirty raincoat and a Homburg pushed over one eye?'

Fiona didn't smile. She looked at him anxiously. 'Colin, do be careful and don't do anything silly, will you? This is all best left to Nigel Williams and his firm. You don't know what you might be getting into if you go probing into financial matters.'

'My father, the Mafia boss!' Colin joked, then wished he hadn't when he saw the frightened expression on his mother's face. 'Yes, I'll be discreet,' he said. 'But Nigel Williams isn't doing anything, is he? He's letting Brightmans con him into thinking there's some confidential deal when anyone can see the whole thing's illegal.'

'Nigel is doing his best. After all, he hasn't had much time yet.'

'That's true.' Plenty of time, Colin thought sourly, but he wasn't going to let her see that he was determined to ignore Williams and make his own investigations. He moved off towards the study, calling over his shoulder 'I'll be out for the evening on Wednesday. Probably late. I won't want a meal and don't wait up.'

'I may even be out myself,' Fiona murmured, but he had already left and didn't hear her.

In the study Colin picked up the London telephone directory and settled himself beside the desk, close to the telephone. Yesterday, he had had no luck in tracing the ambulance crew who had attended the Paddington flats to collect his father's body. None of the places he called had any record of such a call-out. Now, he was going to make a systematic search.

'This is ridiculous!' he exclaimed. 'Ambulance services always keep records of every call-out. How is it that there is nothing logged about a visit to the flats that day?' He went on to check with the Accident and Emergency departments of all the London hospitals, beginning with those closest to Paddington, then working his way throughout the whole of central London. No one had any record of either a heart attack patient or a dead body being brought in from the Paddington flats.

They had no copy of the *Yellow Pages* for London, otherwise he might have worked his way through East End undertakers. Instead, he tossed the directory aside and stared out of the window, deep in thought. There was no reason to suppose that any of the hospitals' or ambulance stations' records were wrong, in which case either the hall porter was lying, or the people who had collected Michael's body were not official ambulancemen.

I suppose they *could* have come from a private company, Colin thought. But where would they have taken him? They must have taken him to a hospital morgue, unless they took him directly to the undertakers. But that would be illegal. A doctor would have had to certify death. Where is the death certificate? Where is the undertaker's bill? They must have sent us one.

A search through the desk drawers and pigeon holes revealed a death certificate, but nothing more. Colin spread it out on the desk. Michael's name and age were given clearly, and his address at death was given as the Paddington flat. Cause of death was noted as heart failure, but the signatures of a doctor or registrar were undecipherable. The address of the registry office was printed on the certificate, and that was the next call to make.

Colin was hardly surprised when the assistant at the other end, after some moments when she was clearly trying her best to trace the details, came back with the news that she couldn't find any record of such a certificate having been issued. Colin was too dispirited to argue that he had the actual form in his hand, and replaced the receiver with thanks for her time and trouble.

Fiona was reading in the drawing room when he came looking for her.

'Mum, have the undertakers sent in their bill yet?' he asked, as casually as he could.

'No, dear. It's really rather a relief, but they sent me a letter only yesterday, telling me that Michael had taken out a funeral plan with them, actually some time ago, it would seem. There was nothing further to pay; the plan covered all the costs and they said they would settle with the vicar for any outstanding payments. To the gravediggers, and the organist, and so on.'

'Who were the undertakers? Where is the letter?' Colin spoke more sharply than he had intended, and Fiona looked up in surprise.

'Really, dear, I don't remember. Does it matter? I threw the letter away. In fact, I threw away everything to do with the funeral when I heard about what Michael had been doing. At least, I suppose he must have had some twinge of conscience when he knew he was going to deprive us of most of our money.'

Colin tried to hide his annoyance and frustration at coming up against yet another blank wall. He could, he supposed, speak to the vicar next, as presumably he would have received some money in the form of a cheque, for the funeral service itself. At the moment, though, he was reluctant to involve anyone from the village in the deepening mystery of Michael's death. He was sure there was something illegal, probably criminal, in the whole affair and the more he probed, the more he became determined to find out the truth.

For now, though, there was little else he could do, so he returned to the study and spent a few enjoyable moments with a London guide, choosing a suitable restaurant to take Anthea to, on Wednesday night.

CHAPTER 6

COLIN GAVE A GREAT DEAL OF THOUGHT to the coming evening with Anthea. He was not going to be fobbed off, nor was he going to appear to her as a tongue-tied, callow youth. He was going to plan his questions carefully, and ensure that this time he found out the answers he wanted. At least, that he found out as much as Anthea herself knew, and not merely what she wished him to know.

He dressed smartly but casually, in clothes he felt were suitable for the place he was intending to take her, an Italian restaurant which had been recommended to him by one of his London-based student friends, whom in desperation he'd telephoned for advice. As a fall-back plan, he had the address of a Greek taverna, in case Anthea didn't care for Italian food. He had enough money to pay for a good meal for them both, though he knew he would have to start watching his spending on his credit card. There would be no more casual use of it as he had been in the habit of doing as a student, secure in the knowledge that the generous allowance he'd enjoyed then would cover his debts, and if it did not, Michael or his mother would take care of any shortfall.

Michael simply *couldn't* have disposed of hundreds of thousands of pounds in a matter of a few months, he told himself again, as he sat in the train to London. It must be somewhere, in a secret account. I wonder how one finds out about money in foreign bank accounts? The best person to ask, I suppose, would be Nigel Williams, who might possibly have contacts that other people didn't have, able to investigate such matters. Colin was hesitant about leaving things to the family solicitor, as he seemed too elderly and out of his depth in dealing with a situation like theirs. He hadn't managed to prise any information about the pension arrangements from Brightmans, whereas Colin was sure that the threat of a court case and bringing matters publically into the open would have frightened them into giving at least some sort of explanation. He decided that he must find out exactly what position Anthea's mother held with the company, and whether she would be able to tell him anything, or put him in touch with someone who would, even if it was strictly unofficial.

Anthea opened the door to him promptly and welcomed him inside. She was wearing a pretty, filmy dress that seemed to float round her and made Colin feel relieved that he had made the effort himself to dress smartly.

'Would you like a drink before we go?' she asked.

'That would be nice. Do you have any white wine?' Colin was a beer man himself, but that didn't seem appropriate and he knew he would show up his ignorance if he asked for a cocktail or spirits. Besides, he needed to keep a clear head if he wanted to pump Anthea for information and remember it afterwards.

'Do you like Italian food?' he asked, sipping a cold, crisp wine and covertly studying her as they sat opposite each other on the chintz armchairs.

'Love it. Is that where we're going?'

'I thought Luigi's in Bolton Street. Unless you'd prefer to eat Greek. I've provisionally booked a table at both.'

He saw her raise her eyebrows and felt pleased. 'Yes, I know Luigi's but I haven't been there for ages. Frankly, I don't often eat out so it's a special event for me.' Anthea smiled at him, a rather young, innocent smile which touched him.

'What do you do, Anthea?' he asked. 'You were at home in the afternoon that first time I called, so do you have a job?'

'I'm a design consultant,' Anthea replied casually. 'I work from home, advising people on their furnishings, curtains, upholstery and so on. I go out to their homes and tell them what I think they ought to do to make their expensive apartments look even more expensive. It was chance that you found me in, that day. I was surprised you came then; you obviously thought I was some kind of typist dogsbody at Brightmans with a crush on your father, or worse. Or, perhaps you didn't expect me to be in, and wanted to have a snoop round at where I lived. This mews cottage wasn't cheap; I bet you wondered how I could afford it. I can assure you, it was all honestly earned. My job pays very well, I only deal with the very well-heeled. If you're wondering, I can reassure you that there wasn't any of Michael's money that went towards paying for it.'

'You certainly believe in speaking frankly,' Colin said, a little taken aback by her. 'I didn't think for a moment that you were – that my father had given you money. But it is a nice house and it must have cost a good deal.'

'And I earn good money. As I said, my clients are well-off. But you have been wondering about me, haven't you? You thought I might have had an affair with your father, didn't you?'

'I did wonder how you came to know him, yes.' Colin felt embarrassed.

'I told you before. My mother knew him. She works at Brightmans and knew him there. I met him a few times, through her. I thought I would like to come to his funeral, as I'd liked him and I thought there wouldn't be too many who genuinely did. I didn't intend to come back to the house and I didn't even intend that anyone should notice me, but I gather your mother did, and wanted to know who I was.'

'She knew everyone else, and she was curious. And I am curious about your mother. If she works at Brightmans she must know about this extraordinary arrangement about my father's pension. It's left us virtually without any money, except what we can salvage from selling some of our furniture and some pictures Dad had. That won't keep us for long. I am certain the pension arrangement is illegal, and both our family solicitor and I are intending to challenge it in the courts. If Brightmans is guilty of acting illegally, it will cause a huge scandal to be brought out into the open, and I'm sure the company won't want that. For ourselves, Mother and I are past caring about scandal. My mother was relying on my father's pension – she's unlikely to find herself a job at her age and with her lack of skills. If your mother can understand what that must feel like, then at least, ask her to talk to us and explain why Michael was allowed to take his whole pension money, and what he wanted it for. If she's concerned that she'd be breaking company confidentiality, then won't she at least explain unofficially, and I'll see her name is kept out of things.'

'You're quite good at speaking bluntly, too, aren't you?' Anthea held out the wine bottle but Colin shook his head, his hand over his glass. 'What makes you think she knows anything about it? Brightmans is a big company and she doesn't work in Accounts.'

'No, but she does know what went on, doesn't she?' Colin persisted. 'I know she must. The way you spoke the first time I came here, I was sure that she must know about it, even if she hadn't told you. Please, Anthea, arrange for me to meet your mother and I promise I won't say another word about my father, or Brightmans all evening.' He stood up. 'We should be going. I booked the table for eight o'clock and it's nearly that now.'

'It won't do you any good. You can wine and dine me all you want – '

'I didn't ask you out just so I could pump you about Dad and Brightmans. I asked you out because I wanted to see you again. I would have wanted to see you even if you had nothing whatever to do with any of this.'

'Did you? That's sweet of you. I'll get my coat.' Anthea picked up her coat and handbag from the back of her chair. 'Shall we go, then? But I bet you won't be able to avoid talking about Michael or Brightmans or my mother for the rest of the evening.'

The meal was a success and Colin made a real effort to keep the conversation on general topics. Anthea was happy to talk about her work, her fascinating and sometimes frankly eccentric clients and their weird tastes in furnishings, which needed to be tactfully curbed if her reputation as a designer of taste was not to be compromised. Colin found her very good company. He talked about his own searches for a job, his lack of any practical skills and the difficulty of finding work of any sort in the village or neighbourhood.

'I was seriously thinking about looking for work as a jobbing gardener,' he said. 'That's about all there is that's available in the village.'

'And do you know anything about gardening?'

'Not a thing. When I think about it, I suppose I couldn't do even that. I wouldn't last long, once I'd pulled up someone's prize plants and carefully nurtured the weeds.'

Anthea laughed. 'But you must have *some* skills. What are you – twenty-five? Twenty-six? What have you been doing with yourself since you left school?'

'I'm twenty-four. I've been at university, studying classics. I got quite a good degree but a knowledge of the ancient Greeks and Romans isn't going to be of much use in the real world.'

'At least you must be bright.' Anthea finished eating the lasagne on her plate and wiped her mouth on the napkin. 'Didn't you want to work in the City, do the same kind of brokering that your father did?'

Colin shook his head. 'That's never appealed. I couldn't bear the idea of being stuck in an office all the time. Frankly, I wasn't even interested enough to find out what Dad was doing at Brightmans.'

'That's obvious!' Anthea picked up her wine glass and drained it. 'You're not a bit like Michael, are you? You don't even look much like him.'

'I suppose not. He and I were never very close. He was away a lot on business and I was away at a boarding school and then university, so our paths didn't cross very often.'

'He was away a lot on business? Did he say it was on Brightmans' business?'

'Well, we supposed it was. He didn't talk much about work. He said he had to entertain clients and my mother wasn't keen on company dinners. When he had to go away overnight it was work all the time, he said, so there wasn't much point in her going. He said he never went anywhere interesting, just business capitals if it was abroad.'

'I don't think Brightmans send their employees away to see clients very often. It's probably too late to check now, but I think you'd find it wasn't on Brightmans' business when Michael was away.'

'You mean – he was lying? Moonlighting?' Colin sat up, dropping his fork on his plate. 'What do you know about it, Anthea? Please tell me!'

'I don't know anything. Truly. But I do know enough about Brightmans from my mother to know that employees are rarely sent out of the office on business.'

'So he might have had some other business interests that he kept secret from mother,' Colin said thoughtfully. 'Perhaps that's where the hundreds of thousands he's amassed have gone. He left no clues at home. There was nothing personal in his room. It was bare of any papers except a few old diaries and letters which didn't tell us anything. It was almost unnaturally bare, now I come to think of it. I assumed that he had kept all his papers at his London flat, but there was nothing there, either. And I assume there wouldn't have been anything left at Brightmans.'

'Look at us! You promised you wouldn't talk about your father, or Brightmans, for the whole evening, and now, here we are, both of us discussing Michael as if he was the only interesting topic!' Anthea said, laughing. 'You're even getting me involved, and I vowed I wouldn't have anything to do with it. Come on, take me home. I have a heavy workload tomorrow; I'm seeing a woman with far more money than taste, and I shall have to be tactful about her choices or my reputation will be in shreds when her friends see what her house looks like.'

Colin found them a taxi although it was only a short distance from the restaurant to Anthea's home. On the doorstep he wondered if she would ask him in and, if she did, whether if would end up with him staying the night. As a student, he had had no difficulties with dating girls and having casual, friendly relationships with many of them, but Anthea was different. As well as exuding a confidence and independence that he had rarely found in his student friends, he didn't want to antagonise her and lose her, at least not before he had found out all she and her mother could tell him about Michael's arrangement with Brightmans.

On the doorstep he hesitated. Should he kiss her and say goodnight here, or ask to come in? The question was resolved when Anthea opened her door, then turned to him and said, 'I'll ask you in for coffee, but it really is only coffee. I've had a pleasant evening but I have to be up early tomorrow.'

'Thanks. Coffee would be nice.' Colin followed her over the threshold, wondering how he was going to reintroduce the subject of meeting her mother. He simply had to talk to her; he felt sure she held the key to the explanation of the pension arrangements, and probably much more, too.

Anthea went into the kitchen and put on the kettle. 'Only instant, I'm afraid,' she said. 'That was a nice meal. Thank you, Colin.'

'Are these your pattern swatches?' He saw a bulky folder lying on one of the chairs and picked it up. Anything to create a delay while he thought of some way of bringing up the subject of seeing her mother.

'Yes. Don't touch them, they're sorted into order. Here's your coffee.' Anthea brought a mug in from the kitchen and handed it to him. 'I'm not having any. Keeps me awake.'

He tried to make it last while he made small talk, but he had barely drunk half when she took back the mug. 'You'll have to go now. You'd miss your last train if you stay any longer, anyway.'

Colin stood up. 'Anthea, I'd like to see you again. I – '

'Can you come up on Sunday afternoon?' she asked abruptly.

Colin hesitated. Sundays were difficult. Fiona still liked to cook a traditional roast for lunch, even though there were just the two of them, and she wouldn't be pleased if he went out. He'd have to leave before lunch if he was to be in London in the afternoon; there weren't many trains on a Sunday.

'Sundays are a bit of a problem. My mother likes me to be home then.' It sounded wet, like a little boy, he felt.

Anthea shrugged. 'Suit yourself. My mother will be here around three o'clock and I thought you wanted to meet her. I can't guarantee she'll be willing to tell you anything, or even if she knows anything. But she knew your father and I suppose she might be able to tell you something about him, since you said you didn't feel you knew him all that well.'

'I'll be here. Thank you very much, Anthea.' Colin stood up and kissed her on her cheek. 'It's good of you to arrange for me to see her.'

At the door she said, 'She doesn't know you'll be here. And, as I said, she may not be willing to tell you anything. Her name's Moira, by the way. Moira Ransom.'

Colin had a spring in his step as he walked towards the tube station. Today was Wednesday, nearly Thursday morning, three days before he would meet Moira Ransom, three days in which he could plan what he would ask her, how he would persuade her to tell him everything he wanted to know. He debated whether he should tell Fiona, but decided against it. Time enough when he knew all the facts, and still, as Anthea had warned, her mother might refuse to tell him anything. Brightmans had refused to tell Nigel Williams, a solicitor, any details, so it might be that it would be more than Moira's job was worth to discuss anything, especially if it involved Brightmans in something illegal.

The following day Colin was alone in the house while Fiona went to Winchester. He hadn't told her yet that he would not be there for Sunday lunch and was wondering what excuse he could make which would be plausible enough, without having to explain about Anthea. He hadn't told her about meeting her again after the funeral.

The doorbell rang and when Colin went to open it, Simon Neville was on the step.

'Oh, hallo!' He wasn't sure what he should call this elderly friend of his mother's. Simon sounded a bit informal, so he decided to stick to formalities. 'Mr Neville, isn't it? I'm afraid my mother is out at present. She's gone to Winchester to see an estate agent.'

'That's all right. I knew she wouldn't be here. It's really you I came to see. May I come in? And, please call me Simon.'

Once inside, Simon seemed ill at ease. 'You're not doing anything in particular, are you? Look old chap, why don't we go down to a pub somewhere – not the one in the village, too many gossips – but somewhere a bit away from here, where we can talk, man to man?'

Colin was surprised, but didn't comment. 'There's a pub about three miles down the road. The Farrier's Arms. I don't think many of the locals go there. Farmers, mainly, no one who would know the family. Would that do?'

'Fine. Get in the car and you can give me directions. Sorry to behave rather cloak and dagger but I wanted to talk to you and I didn't want us to be interrupted.' Simon's car was outside and they were soon negotiating the country lanes outside the village.

'It's here,' Colin said, indicating a small, thatched building set back from the road. 'I've never been here myself, and I don't suppose Mother or Dad have either.'

'Looks ideal.' Simon pulled into the car park, which already held two muddy four-by-fours and a tractor. They went into the low-ceilinged bar and Simon said 'Beer for you? Take a seat in the corner and I'll bring them over.'

Once they had settled Simon said, 'You must be wondering what this is all about. You know who I am, of course. The man who missed your father's funeral because he got himself lost, and turned up just as everyone was about to leave.'

'I remember hurrying past you in the doorway on my way down the drive. Mum asked me to speak to one of the mourners. I didn't know who you were, but then I didn't know who most of the people there were. I don't know many of the locals, except some of the girls.'

'I knew your mother years ago, before she married your father,' Simon began. 'We used to go round in a group, a few chaps and girls, and your mother and Eleanor Pagett were among them. Eleanor lives in the village, Fiona said, so you must know her.'

'Yes, I know Eleanor. She's Mum's closest friend,' Colin said. 'I didn't know about you, though.'

'I was very fond of your mother in those days. In fact, I was in love with her. She was the sweetest, prettiest girl I had ever seen, but I knew I had very little hope of winning her, because in those days I hadn't any money or prospects. I wasn't in a position to ask her to marry me, though I would have liked to, and then your father came along and I lost my chance. I never forgot her, though. I did eventually marry, and happily, but I've been widowed now for several years. When I saw the death notice in the *Times* for your father, I realised at once it must be Fiona's chap, and I thought I should go to the funeral, even though I barely knew your father. Met him a couple of times, years ago, before he and Fiona married. And when I saw your mother again, well, she had barely changed in all those years. All my old feelings came back to me.

'Now, Colin, I can understand you might feel a bit uneasy about someone from the past turning up again, especially so soon after your father's death. I want to assure you that I have nothing but the greatest respect for your mother, and I would do nothing to hurt or upset her in any way. Nor do I wish to offend you. If you feel that I might be taking too much for granted, that it's all too soon after your father's death to begin seeing Fiona – '

'I don't think that at all,' Colin broke in. 'I'm glad Mum has someone who cares about her, that she feels she can trust. Dad's death was a shock, but it was the suddenness which was a shock, not the fact that he died. They had lived quite separate lives for some time. They were more like two acquaintances sharing a house than a married couple.'

'I don't want you to think I am a fortune hunter,' Simon continued. 'I'm well enough off myself not to think about money. And I know your mother's situation. She told me about that extraordinary arrangement with your father's pension rights – '

'If you had been a fortune hunter, you'd have run a mile by now,' Colin said bluntly. 'In spite of appearances, the expensive house and grounds, she hasn't got a bean. She's having to put Little Paddocks on the market, and as soon as possible. And look for somewhere much smaller to live.'

'Is she upset about leaving such a lovely house? She has put on a brave face but it must be a terrible wrench to lose all that.'

'No, I really think she isn't bothered. The house was Dad's choice, and I think she went along with it because that's what she always did, but she'd have been happier with somewhere smaller, less pretentious. I never cared for the place, but then, I wasn't here much, only in the vac, and then I was usually out with friends somewhere. Now I come to think of it, Mum must have spent a good deal of her time alone in that place. No wonder she doesn't really like it and will be quite happy to leave it.'

'And what about yourself, Colin? What plans have you for your future?'

'Honestly, I don't know. When I came down from uni I hadn't a clue what I wanted to do. A Classics degree is a pretty useless thing in the real world. It was interesting to do and I enjoyed it, but it hasn't given me any skills I can use for a job. I was intending to wait and look out for something that appealed – an archeological dig somewhere, perhaps, but now I'll have to set my sights on something practical. At the moment, I can't think of doing anything until I've sorted out the mystery of what Dad was up to. I'm determined to find out what has happened to all the hundreds of thousands of pounds he had, shortly before he died. He died of a heart attack, suddenly, he didn't know he was going to die, so presumably he was in the middle of something, some deal or business venture and the money must still be around somewhere. I won't rest and I can't put my mind to anything else until I've found out where it all is. And when I find it, that will sort out Mum's finances, I hope, and then I can think about my own future.'

'Do you have any leads?' Simon asked.

Colin hesitated. He had decided he wouldn't say anything to his mother until he had some results, but working alone meant that he had no one with whom he could discuss any theories or ideas. Simon seemed trustworthy, and had his mother's interests at heart. He decided to confide in him.

'I haven't said anything to Mum,' he began. 'Or to anyone else. But there was this girl at the funeral – Anthea Ransom – Mum didn't know who she was but it turned out she knew my father slightly and *her* mother works at Brightmans. I've been seeing her – only a couple of times, but I'm hoping she or her mother may know something and be willing to tell me. Brightmans have been very cagey about the whole set-up; they wouldn't discuss it with our family solicitor and I'm sure there must be something dodgy about it.'

'It looked that way when your mother told me how the pension had been handed over early,' Simon said. 'I don't want to interfere with your mother's affairs, but any help I can give, I will do gladly.'

'What made me think there was something fishy about this girl was that I found a snapshot of her in an old jacket of my father's, when we were clearing out his things,' Colin said. 'I didn't say anything to Mum, and I don't want her to know about it. The last thing I want is for her to think he might have had a young and pretty mistress on the quiet, as well as all the money problems he has landed us with.'

'I won't say a word to Fiona about anything you've told me here,' Simon said. 'But do you really think she might have been having an affair with Michael?'

'No, frankly I don't. She says she knew him only slightly and I believe her. But her mother worked with Dad and I suppose it's possible they might have had an affair. Dad liked women and they liked him. I suppose he was quite good looking, in the sort of way women like.'

'I hardly remember him myself, only met him a couple of times, but I do remember having a sinking feeling when I learnt he was seeing Fiona. That's my chances scuppered, I thought, and I was right, too. Perhaps I shouldn't have given up so easily, but in those days I hadn't anything to offer your mother, and he had money, charm and good looks. I wasn't in a position to ask her to marry me and he had swept her off her feet before I dared even ask her to wait for me. I'm not blaming your mother; I wasn't much of a catch then and it was a long time before I was financially secure enough to think of marriage. I want to be frank with you, Colin. I hope that, now, I might persuade your mother to marry me, one day when all the dust has settled from Michael's funeral. But I'd like to have your blessing; if you think I'm going too fast for her, tell me frankly. I don't want her to be hurt or feel that I'm offering her support just because I can. I love her truly. I always have.'

'I don't think my father ever did love her, in the sense you're speaking,' Colin said slowly. 'He liked her, yes, she was a convenient, non-interfering wife who didn't meddle with his business interests. And he wanted a son. I wasn't the son he really wanted, but I think he was quite proud of me. His real love, the only thing Michael really cared for, was money and the power and status having it brought.'

Simon nodded. 'You weren't close to him, ever?'

'I didn't see a great deal of him. And now I feel I knew him even less than I thought I did. And I'm never going to forgive him for the mess he's landed Mum in. I can fend for myself, I always expected to have to earn my own living and I never was that interested in amassing great amounts of money, something he could never understand about me, but Mum hasn't worked for twenty-five years. Can you think of anything she could do? She worked in an office when she left school but she'd be totally at sea anywhere like that, these days.'

'She won't have to, if I have anything to do with it,' Simon said. 'But it would be far better if she had the money and comforts she's entitled to, rather than accepting them from me. I never want her to feel dependent on anyone. Look, we'd better drink up and deliver you home before she gets back from Winchester and wonders what we've been up to. I'm invited to Sunday lunch this weekend, to meet you officially, so we'd better pretend we never had this conversation together and that we haven't actually met each other.'

'There's a problem there,' Colin said, draining his glass and standing up. 'The only chance I have of meeting Anthea's mother is on Sunday and I promised I'd be there. Mum is going to be annoyed anyway, she likes to cook on Sundays, but if you've been invited she'll be furious if I don't show up.'

'Don't worry. I'll think of something to cover for you.' Simon gave him a conspiratorial grin. 'You can't miss the chance of talking to someone from Brightmans off the record.'

'This conversation in the pub never happened,' Simon said, as he delivered Colin back to Little Paddocks. 'But I enjoyed it, and I enjoyed getting to know you, Colin.' He clasped Colin's hand in a firm grip. 'Find some way of letting me know how you get on, on Sunday, won't you?'

'I will. And thanks for letting me unburden myself to you. It helped to talk to someone and there wasn't anyone else I felt I could.'

Colin watched the car disappear out of the gate and turn towards the main road. He hoped Simon wouldn't pass Fiona on the way, provoking awkward questions. He decided he liked Simon, trusted him. Fleetingly, he wondered what it would have been like if Fiona had married Simon instead of Michael. He found he liked the idea of Simon as a father. Well, he could very well end up having him for a step-father one day.

CHAPTER 7

'WHAT DO YOU MEAN, you won't be in for lunch? You know I always cook a roast on Sundays.' Fiona glared across the kitchen table at Colin. It was Sunday morning, and he had just broken the news to her that he wouldn't be in at all that day. Fiona was standing by the table, a bowl of flour and margarine in front of her, in the process of making a pie of some kind for dessert.

'I'm sorry, Mum, but something has come up. I have to go up to London today. I know I should have told you before.' Colin had never been a good liar; he simply couldn't come up with a good enough story without telling the truth, and that was something he couldn't tell her yet.

'Can you even get up to London today? Are there any trains running on a Sunday?'

'Yes, but not many, which is why, if I'm to get there by early afternoon, I have to go in the morning.'

'Do you realise I've invited Simon Neville to lunch, especially to meet you? What on earth is he going to think if you aren't here?'

'I'm sorry, Mum,' Colin said again, helplessly. 'But it has to be today and it might lead to something important. I can't miss this interview.' That was the closest he dared come to the truth.

'Who on earth conducts interviews on a Sunday? It's ridiculous,' she snapped. 'What am I going to say to Simon?

How am I going to explain that you've decided not to appear? He'll think it terribly rude.'

'I should think he'd be quite pleased to find that he has you all to himself for the day,' Colin said. 'I don't know that I'd care to play gooseberry for the pair of you, anyway.'

It was the wrong thing to say. Fiona snorted angrily. 'It's not at all like that! Simon is an old friend, nothing more. I don't know what you're implying but there certainly isn't anything like that going on!'

'Like what?' He looked at her blandly, but Fiona began kneading her pastry angrily. She should have asked Mrs Burdett to make something when she was here, Colin thought. The way Fiona was going at it, the crust would be tough as old boots.

'I expect I'll meet Mr Neville another time,' he said, turning away. He wanted to leave the kitchen before she thought up some unanswerable reason why he should not go to London.

'What's wrong with going up tomorrow?' she called after him.

'Tomorrow's no good. It has to be today.' He went to collect his coat and get out of the house as quickly as he could. He'd have to wait ages on the platform but that was better than staying and arguing with his mother. As he closed the front door she called after him, 'What are you going to eat for lunch, then?'

'Don't worry; I'll be having something.' He didn't know what, or where, but there were sure to be places in London where he could eat before seeing Anthea. Three o'clock, she'd said, which sounded as if there might be tea, but not lunch, at the mews house.

Fiona was still fuming when Simon arrived, earlier than she had expected, so that she was still in her apron, with a smudge of flour on her cheek.

'Oh, that son of mine! I particularly wanted you to meet him and now he's just told me he has to go off to London! On a Sunday, I ask you! That's the kind of behaviour one might expect from a teenager, not someone of Colin's age! I am so sorry, Simon. It's so rude of him.'

'I'm not sorry, I'm delighted,' Simon said, kissing her. 'Now I can have you all to myself for the rest of the day, and I won't have to mind my ps and qs in front of the boy. I'll doubtless meet him again another time, so don't give it another thought. He looked a nice lad, that brief glimpse I had of him rushing out of the door when I arrived after the funeral. I shall look forward to meeting him properly some other time.'

'Well, if you really don't mind,' Fiona said, mollified. 'Though what he can have to do that can't be done in the week, I can't imagine.'

'Perhaps it's some exciting job interview,' Simon said innocently. 'You know, these high powered business managers take no account of weekends. They work round the clock, day in and day out. Classics degree, I think you said he had? Then perhaps he's meeting some professor who is only here over the weekend.'

'He could have said.'

'You know youngsters. Don't want to get your hopes up until it is safely in the bag.' Simon made a mental note that he should warn Colin that he was supposed to be at a job interview today.

'I've brought the wine. Thought you might be sick of tawny roses or run out of vases,' Simon said, producing a bottle.

'That's a very good vintage. I hope my cooking lives up to it. Thank you, Simon.'

'I'll open it, shall I? And you can tell me how you got on at the estate agents last week.' Simon steered the conversation into safer channels.

'I've put this house on the market. They think it could be worth about eight hundred thousand, but of course, they'll need to come and survey it before deciding on any definite figure. And even if it is worth that much, practically all of it will go towards paying off both mortgages.'

'Did you enquire if they had anything that would suit you, while you were there?'

'I don't want to live as far away as Winchester. I was hoping for something in the village. I like it here, and I'm not worried about any "how are the mighty fallen" attitude some of the locals could have. It's a beautiful area, and a pretty village. It was the size and fake opulence of Little Paddocks that I never cared for. Michael bought it for show, not for comfortable living, but then, he didn't live here all that much.'

'Is there much choice of smaller property round here, then?'

'Not much. But I suppose there's always somewhere changing hands. They're building along the main road at the moment; nice semi-detached houses but I don't know if I'll be able to afford even one of those. I'll have to see what Nigel Williams can tell me about how much money I'll be able to raise. Michael's pictures and some of the pieces of furniture might sell for a bit.'

'You could always come and live with me,' Simon said, and regretted his hastiness when he saw the expression on her face.

'Sorry. That was tactless of me. But what I meant was, my place is big enough so that if you wanted, you could have a separate flat and be totally independent. I know it's not all that near; the other side of Winchester, in fact, but as an emergency temporary home you might consider it. I was hoping you'd come and see it one day next week. Come and have lunch with me. My Mrs Eggerton would be cooking, you wouldn't have to take pot luck with any efforts of my own, though I do do a mean shepherd's pie.'

Fiona giggled, her good humour restored. 'And I suppose I would need to be vetted by Mrs Eggerton as a suitable companion for you? I know what housekeepers are like, very protective.'

'And have I passed the test with your Mrs Burdett?'

'With flying colours. She thinks you have beautiful manners and are so appreciative of her cooking. If she hadn't approved of you I wouldn't have dared invite you here again.'

'You won't have to worry about Mavis Eggerton. She has a family to look after and she's made it clear she'll be quite happy to bow out if there is ever someone else to look after me. She came to us when cooking and housework became too much for Margaret and not long after that she was confined to a wheelchair. Mavis made a promise to Margaret then, that she'd continue looking after me, but I know it's becoming too much to ask of her, with a demanding family as well.'

'I'd love to see your home,' Fiona said. 'You know, I often wondered what happened to you, when all our group began going their separate ways.'

'You are tempting me to tell you my whole, very boring life story,' Simon said, taking her hand. 'After that splendid lunch I shall want to lie back in one of your comfortable chairs and you will have the choice of me either droning on or dropping off to sleep, neither of which will be very much fun for you, so why don't you take me for a walk round this village you seem to like so much, and we can see if there are any properties on offer that you might like to live in.'

Colin reached London on a stopping train by one o'clock, and found the station buffet open. He bought a baguette and a cup of coffee and spun out the time with the Sunday papers until it was nearly two-thirty. He had given great thought to what he was going to ask Moira Ransom, nothing too confrontational, he mustn't appear too indignant at the way his mother had been treated by Brightmans. After all, the arrangements regarding the pension couldn't have had anything to do with her, he doubted she was Managing Director status, though Anthea had given the impression that her mother knew about the situation and presumably why it had been sanctioned.

He arrived at the mews house at three o'clock, and rang the bell. Anthea ushered him inside and at once he noticed the woman sitting in one of the armchairs. She was dark haired and strikingly handsome, with the same cornflower blue eyes as Anthea. No one could have mistaken them for anything but mother and daughter. Moira must have been in her late forties, but skilful makeup made her look younger. Her clothes were smart, expensively casual. Immediately, Colin was sure she must hold quite an important position at Brightmans and his hopes were raised. She could tell him what he wanted to know, if she chose, but not if he antagonised her in any way.

'Mother, this is Colin Latimer, Michael's son,' Anthea introduced him. 'Colin, this is my mother, Moira Ransom.'

'How do you do, Mrs Ransom?' Colin put out a hand, which was ignored.

Instead, Moira looked at Anthea. 'Why has he come?' she asked. 'Did you tell him that I would be here? Are you setting me up to disclose the Company's arrangement with Michael Latimer?'

'Colin's mother has been left virtually penniless because of the Brightmans' debacle,' Anthea said. 'He wanted to have a few answers and I thought he deserved some.'

'Virtually penniless!' Moira scoffed. 'The man had millions. Hasn't his wife seen any of it?'

115

'No. We were told my father was given nearly two million in advance pension but there wasn't any of it to be found anywhere. I don't know what he did with it, and I find it hard to believe he could have disposed of it in such a short time before he died,' Colin said. 'He must have stashed it away somewhere but we have no idea where. My mother has no money except what will be left from the sale of her home after two mortgages are paid off, and what we can raise from selling some furniture. She has no skills that would be of use in a modern workplace; no means of earning more than a pittance at some unskilled drudgery. I'm not asking for her pension rights to be restored; I assume that would be impossible, though I suspect they should not have been granted to my father in the first place. What I would like is some sort of explanation as to why he was given the money in the first place. And what reason he gave for wanting such a sum. I suppose he did have to give a reason for wanting it?'

There. He'd said it. And kept his cool. He sat facing Moira and waited for her reply.

'Your family solicitor was asking much the same questions, though not quite so politely put,' she said. 'May I ask, first of all, how you come to be here? How you know my daughter, who seems to be supporting you in your request?'

Colin hesitated, not knowing what to say, but Anthea spoke up promptly. 'I went to Michael's funeral,' she said. 'I wanted to. I'd always liked him. I met Colin there, and when he found out what financial arrangements Michael had made, he asked me to help him find the answers to some of the questions he and his mother were asking.'

Moira nodded. 'Yes, I suppose you would have gone to his funeral. I didn't think of that. And now you, Colin, want to know why this extraordinary arrangement was made with Brightmans?'

'And what he wanted the money for, and where it all is, now,' Colin answered. 'If you know that. I am beginning to wonder if anyone other than Michael knew what he wanted so much money for. Certainly we had no idea what he could have been up to.'

Moira took a deep breath. 'Everything I shall tell you here is highly confidential. Understand that. Brightmans do not want a whiff of gossip getting out, to the Press or anyone. You'll have to tell your mother, I accept, but make sure she knows she mustn't say anything to that solicitor of hers, or anyone else. Brightmans' shares would sink without trace if any of this got out. We have our shareholders to consider, and, more than that, it's possible Brightmans would go under completely if the facts ever became publicly known.'

'I understand. You have my word that any information you give me will be treated in the strictest confidence,' Colin said formally. He'd have to tell Simon Neville, but he hoped the man would be sensible and not want to take things further. 'All I want to know is, what happened to the money my father had from his pension rights?'

'There was no money,' Moira said at once. 'Michael never had that money as such. About a year ago he was caught embezzling funds from the company. It was estimated that he had being doing some illegal trading in stocks for at least three years before the matter came to light. Now, there were two things Brightmans could have done. They could have had him arrested and charged, taken to court and the whole thing would have been spread over the front pages of every tabloid in the land, probably every tabloid in Europe and America, too. That wouldn't have done Brightmans' image any good and confidence in the company and therefore shares, would have plummeted. The alternative was to make him pay it all back. Well, he couldn't, of course. The kind of money he had been squirrelling away – and, before you ask, I *don't* know what he wanted it for or what he did with it – ran into a couple of million. And Michael Latimer didn't have that kind of money any more. We made very sure of that before we did anything else. So we did a deal with him. Took his pension entitlement in lieu of the debt. The accountants estimated that he would have about that amount of pension gross if he retired at the normal time and lived to a reasonable age. Of course, he was dismissed, and there was a shortfall, which I understand he managed to cover to some extent by remortgaging his home. Brightmans was determined that he should suffer some discomfort, at least. Now, I'm not at all sure whether Brightmans acted within their legal rights, but it saved a great deal of company scandal and could be hushed up, kept strictly within the company. I am the Personal Assistant to the Chief Executive, which is how I knew all about the arrangement. Now, does that answer your question satisfactorily?'

'Thank you. You've been very frank and I shall respect your confidentiality,' Colin said. 'You will appreciate that there's a lot to take in. We had no idea he had been involved in anything crooked. Embezzling Brightmans' funds for three years! It's unbelievable.'

'True, nevertheless. He admitted as much when he was caught. I don't know what he was doing with the money he acquired I supposed he used it to buy your home and furnish it expensively. I know he had expensive tastes.'

'If he did, he didn't use as much as two million pounds. Our home had a mortgage and I always imagined he could pay that out of his salary. He did earn quite a high salary as a broker, didn't he?'

'Yes. Enough, I always thought, for him not to need to steal more from the company, but some people are compulsively greedy, and the opportunities were there. It was too easy to cheat, so he did.'

'I can assure you that whatever extra money he took from Brightmans, he didn't spend on us or our home,' Colin said. 'My mother lived comfortably, but not ostentatiously. What she had was all well within what Michael's legal salary could have afforded. Now she has nothing, yet he must have money still, hidden away in a secret bank account abroad, perhaps. We've looked, but there are no papers, no financial documents of any sort. In fact, surprisingly few personal papers at all.'

'I'm sorry about your mother's situation,' Moira said. 'What we hadn't bargained for, was for Michael to die so suddenly, so soon afterwards. Had he lived out his normal life span, which everyone expected, since there was no record in his company medical notes of any health problems, then he might well have been able to earn elsewhere sufficient money to enable your mother to have a reasonable annuity. Not as much as a Brightmans' company pension, but sufficient for her to live on. As it was, I assumed that Michael would have used some of the money he had taken from the company to ensure that his wife would be financially secure, whatever happened to him. If he thought he might be caught and end up in prison, one might think he would have made some arrangement for cash that couldn't be touched by the courts, that would come to his wife.'

'If he did, we haven't had as much as a pennyworth of it,' Colin said sourly. He looked straight at Moira. He had, if not all he wanted, all the information he was likely to get from her. 'How well did you know my father?' he asked her bluntly.

She hesitated before answering and Colin did not miss the quick glance she cast towards Anthea. 'We were both working at Brightmans for some years. I knew him as a colleague but we were, of course, in different departments.'

'Did you have an affair with my father?' He knew he shouldn't ask such a direct question, but he felt he had nothing to lose now.

'Michael was a very attractive man,' Moira said. 'And, since you ask, yes, we did have a relationship, but it was a very long time ago, and it had been over for years. I liked him and I was sorry when his dishonesty was discovered. There wasn't anything I could do to save him, he was in far too deep. Once the extent of his embezzlement was known, there was nothing anyone could have done. He was lucky; he might have been sent to prison if Brightmans hadn't been so worried about what the disclosure would have done to their image.'

'Thank you for being so frank.' Colin was sorry he'd asked, but glad that what he had suspected had been confirmed. It was long past four o'clock now, and he was wondering if Anthea would produce any tea. The baguette he'd eaten at the station buffet seemed a long time ago and he was thirsty.

'You've had the information you wanted. There's no more my mother can tell you. In fact, she's told you more than she need have done. I don't have to tell you that she's put her job on the line to tell you all this. It must *never* go further. Impress on your mother that she mustn't say anything to anyone about what has been said here today.' Anthea glared at him. 'I think you ought to go, now. There's no more to say.'

Obediently, Colin stood up. 'Thank you again, Mrs Ransom, for being so frank and explaining what happened. You can rely on my discretion not to let any of what you've told me go any further.'

'Perhaps, but what about your mother? Is she a gossipy woman?' Moira asked sharply.

Colin thought of Eleanor. His mother would want to discuss the story with her, but must certainly be prevented. Fiona might be discreet, but he didn't trust Eleanor not to gossip, especially with a tasty piece of scandal to regale the locals with.

'My mother doesn't gossip. She can be discreet,' he said stiffly. 'And I'll make sure she discourages our family solicitor from making any further enquiries at the company.'

'He won't get very far if he does,' Moira said laconically. 'Goodbye, Colin. It was interesting to meet you. You don't look anything like your father, but you must know that. I gather you don't have any of his financial interests, either.'

'I'm not obsessed by money, if that's what you mean,' Colin replied. 'All I'm interested in is justice for my mother and to ensure that she has enough to live on for the future.'

'Perhaps you should pursue investigations as to why Michael embezzled money from the company, and what he did with it,' Moira suggested. 'It was a sizeable amount, and he died only a few months after he was caught. It might well be that he still has a good deal of it, in some foreign bank account somewhere. Brightmans wouldn't be able to claim it, but then it might be difficult for you to do so, either, even if you located it. Think about it.'

'I will.' And think about what Michael could have been doing, still leaving regularly for work, long after he'd been sacked, Colin thought. That would be a cover, of course, to hide from Fiona the fact that he wasn't at Brightmans any more, but what would he do, each day? Did he have another job, that he didn't want to tell anyone? For a moment, a ludicrous image swam into his mind of Michael working behind the counter in a McDonald's takeaway, or selling tickets on the underground.

This time Moira shook his hand as he left. 'Goodbye, Colin.'

Anthea saw him to the door. 'Well, you got what you wanted,' she said. 'and I hope you'll have the sense to keep it to yourself. I'm trusting you, Colin.'

'You can trust me. I think you ought to know that by now. Well, if you hadn't thought you could trust me, I suppose you wouldn't have let me meet your mother.' He kissed her on the cheek. Anything more intimate felt out of place in the circumstances. 'When can I see you again? Would you care to go to the theatre next week, some time?'

'No, thank you, Colin. This is it. You've done what you wanted to do.' She made as if to close the door, but Colin stopped her. 'I really do want to see you again, quite apart from my father's business. That has nothing to do with it. Let me telephone you tomorrow and arrange something.'

'No, Colin. It's over. Do you understand what I'm saying? I don't want to see you again.' This time she shut the door and left him on the step, staring after her.

Was it because her mother was there, and she had been warned to be careful of him? He didn't understand it. She had seemed to like him, and enjoyed the couple of evenings they had spent together. He'd leave it a few days, then telephone her and invite her out, or invite himself to her house. He thought about getting theatre tickets, but didn't know what her tastes were, or if she would already have seen the show. Finally, he shrugged and began to walk towards the main road and the tube station. He liked Anthea; more than liked her if he was to be honest, and he wasn't going to accept a brush off just like that.

He took another slow train and arrived back in the village by six-thirty. He hadn't stopped for anything else to eat and was feeling very hungry by the time he walked down the drive of Little Paddocks and saw Simon's car still parked beside the front door.

'Colin, is that you?' Fiona called as she heard the front door open. 'We're in the study.'

He found his mother and Simon in the two relaxer armchairs with a tea trolley between them. Simon had his shoes off and Fiona's jacket was tossed across the desk.

'So, you've managed to come home in time to meet Simon after all,' she greeted him. 'Was your interview a success? I certainly hope so, after all that fuss.'

'Fuss?' Colin stared at her blankly.

'Colin, this is Simon Neville, a friend of mine from a long way back,' Fiona indicated Simon, who scrambled to his feet. He took Colin's hand gravely, and with a deadpan face, said 'I'm delighted to meet you at last, Colin. Your mother thought you had to rush off to a job interview. Sounded exciting, but I don't expect you want to discuss that just now. Would you like some tea? I think there's some left in the pot.'

'I don't suppose you had any proper lunch. There's plenty of cold beef left in the kitchen. You could cut yourself some,' Fiona fussed.

Colin sat down on the window seat. 'Thanks. I'll eat later. But a cup of tea would be nice.'

Simon poured him one, saying 'Your mother and I have been walking for miles, working off a large lunch. We've been looking round the village and beyond, to see if there's any suitable property she might like to move into.'

Fiona did not take up the hint to change the subject. She was still mildly annoyed with Colin for missing lunch, and said 'Did you have a successful interview? Have you found yourself a job that you like?'

Colin drank his tea thirstily. Anthea could at least have let him stay long enough for that, he thought crossly. 'I did go to a kind of interview,' he said at last. 'But it wasn't for a job. I've been trying to find out why Dad's pension was arranged as it was and I've found out some interesting things.'

Simon stood up, pushing his feet into his shoes. 'If you are going to discuss family business, I'll leave you to it,' he said. 'It's about time I thought of leaving, anyway. You only invited me for lunch, Fiona, and I've stayed well past tea time.'

'No, please stay, Simon,' Fiona urged. 'That's if you can bear to listen to all our troubles. You already know all about how Michael's will was left.'

Simon glanced across at Colin. 'I'd like you to stay and hear what I have to say, Sir,' Colin said. 'In fact, I'd like you to be fully in on all of it. We can do with another head to plan what we can do next.'

'If you're really sure. I'd like to be whatever help I can.' Simon sat down again. 'Colin, please don't call me Sir,' he murmured.

'I met someone who worked with Dad at Brightmans,' Colin began. 'She told me why the pension arrangements had been made that way. You're not going to like this, Mum, but Dad had been cheating the company for years. Some months ago he was caught embezzling funds.'

Gradually the story came out, and with it the fact that Colin had been seeing Anthea. Fiona rolled her eyes, but said nothing.

'So depriving him of his future pension rights was intended to claw back what Michael had stolen from the company,' Simon said, when Colin had finished. 'Sounds fair, in return for not prosecuting. Michael couldn't know that he'd be dead within a few months, before he had had time to make some alternative arrangement for Fiona's future.'

'There is still the question of why he was embezzling money from the company, and what he did with it all,' Colin said. 'It's clear we've never seen any of it here. Have you any ideas, Mum? Did you notice anything different in Dad in the last year or so?'

Fiona shook her head. 'Only that I never seemed to see very much of him. He said he was working longer hours, seeing clients in the evening, that sort of thing. I accepted that, but now you tell me he wasn't. In fact, he wasn't working at Brightmans at all. He'd been sacked months before. I can't take any of this in. Why would Michael want to steal money from the company? We had enough to live comfortably on what he earned legitimately. I knew what his salary was – well, I knew what his salary was five years ago, when we moved here, and that would have been ample to keep us and pay the mortgage on this house. I simply don't understand any of it.'

'Could he have had debts, do you think?' Simon asked gently.

'Debts? What kind of debts? He didn't spend ostentatiously. If he had, I would surely have noticed. He bought those pictures we have, but that was a long time ago and I was with him when he did. They weren't terribly expensive, but he said they were by up and coming artists and would increase in value. And they have. He bought good clothes, but not a great many over the years. If he'd bought anything big for the house, I'd have known. There was nothing like that.'

'He didn't gamble, did he?' Simon probed.

'I'm sure he didn't. I would have noticed. We had the odd flutter on the National and the Derby, but it wasn't ever more than a tenner. I'm sure, if he had been a secret compulsive gambler, I'd have known, after twenty-five years of marriage. But then, I'm beginning to think there's a great deal I should have known, and didn't, in all the years I thought I knew my husband.'

Fiona looked close to tears, and Colin came across to put an arm round her shoulders. 'It's been a shock to all of us,' he said. 'We've barely had time to recover from the news of his death, then we have all these revelations about things he was doing that we had no idea about. I wanted to protect you from knowing, but you had to know.'

'I don't want to be protected from knowing anything,' Fiona said firmly. 'Please don't keep anything from me, either of you, because you think it'll be too upsetting. I'm beginning to think this Michael who died recently was a stranger to me, and the Michael I married was someone quite different, who died a long time ago. You don't need to protect me from anything that's happened now. He can't hurt me any more.'

'Simon, how can we find out if my father had any offshore bank accounts that he put money into? It doesn't look as if he spent much of the money he embezzled over the years. He must have put it somewhere.'

'The short answer is – we can't,' Simon said. 'If we don't have any idea which bank or even which country he used, we don't know where to begin. There are plenty of places – the Cayman Islands, Jersey, Switzerland, Monaco – and even if we knew, the whole point of using banks like those is that they are discreet and wouldn't tell us anything.'

'There must be papers he left, detailing bank transactions,' Fiona said thoughtfully. 'He wouldn't have destroyed everything. He didn't know he was going to die. Colin, what about his flat in London? He would keep his private things there, wouldn't he?'

'I've been there,' Colin said. 'It was virtually bare. Nothing at all, not even his house keys or his briefcase, which I found distinctly odd.'

'Would the staff who service the flat have taken those for safe keeping?' Simon asked. 'Or even the undertaker or the ambulance people who found him, perhaps?'

'The porter at the flats said not. He took nothing, he said, except some milk and perishable food from the fridge. And as for anyone else who had the authority to handle Michael's personal effects, surely they would have returned them to us, long before now?'

'I think you should have another look in the London flat,' Fiona said. 'And take Simon with you. There must be something you've overlooked.'

Colin wanted to argue that he had looked over every inch of the flat, but saw the sense in returning again with Simon. 'Will you come with me?' he asked, turning to him.

'Gladly. Let's make it as soon as possible next week. I'm virtually retired now, so my time's my own. I'd like nothing better than to be involved in solving this mystery,' Simon said eagerly.

'I'm coming too,' Fiona spoke up. 'You're not going to leave me out of any of this. And do you realise, I've never, ever, been to this flat of Michael's? I'm not even completely sure where it is.'

'We'll all three go tomorrow,' Colin said. 'We need to go soon, before the end of the month, when the tenancy runs out. After that, they'll clear out everything for the next tenant and we'll have lost any opportunity to find anything.'

'Tomorrow it is, then.' Simon stood up. 'I'll be round early to catch the train with you. Now, I must go home. You've given me a great deal to think about, Colin. I'll be on to the financial advisers in my old company and see what they can tell me about offshore accounts and how to trace them, if it's at all possible, with the lack of information we have. And you, Fiona, my dear, must see to it that this young man, who has been doing all the work so far, has a plateful of that excellent beef as soon as possible. He must be starving.'

CHAPTER 8

THEY MET AT THE STATION as soon as the morning commuter rush had subsided. Simon bought tickets and they were soon on their way. Colin took them directly to the block of flats where Michael had stayed when in London.

'He lived here?' Fiona asked, gazing up at the dingy looking Victorian building. 'It looks so drab, so gloomy. Couldn't he have found somewhere more – well, nicer looking?'

'It's really very much better inside. He had quite a nice apartment. Small, but all he needed for overnight stays. He never lived here, remember,' Colin said, leading the way towards the glass-fronted porter's room.

The man on duty was not the same one as Colin had spoken to on his previous visit. Colin wasn't sure whether he was sorry or relieved about that.

He explained who he was, showed his driving licence again, explained this was Michael Latimer's widow, and that they would like the key of Mr Latimer's flat so that they could clear out the rest of his personal things before relinquishing the lease. The porter handed over a key at once, without further question, and Colin led the way up the stairs to Michael's flat.

'I suppose it isn't so bad, once you're inside,' Fiona conceded, looking round. 'But no lift! How on earth do they manage with furniture?'

Colin opened the flat door and stood aside for Fiona and Simon to go inside. 'It's really quite nice,' Fiona said. 'I wish I'd thought of coming here and staying when I came up on shopping trips to London.'

What would the secretive Michael have thought if she had turned up unexpectedly, Colin thought. He was increasingly coming to suspect that Michael had led a double life that he would not have wanted Fiona or himself to learn about. In the flat he felt uneasy, as if he was expecting Michael to be there, sitting in the living room watching them, or worse, lying on the floor where the porter had found him, as if there was going to be some ghastly re-enactment of the last few weeks, and they would all relive the funeral and its subsequent revelations.

'It looks very bare,' Simon said. 'I suppose you brought away most of Michael's personal things when you came here before?'

'I didn't take anything. It's just as it was then,' Colin replied. 'Hardly anything of his was here, except a few spare underclothes and socks in a drawer.'

'There'll be shaving kit and his washbag in the bathroom,' Fiona said, going towards the bedroom. 'Must be. Oh, of course. They'd have taken that with him when they took him away in the ambulance. No, I forgot. He was already dead. The porter found him dead, didn't he? In his bed, I suppose.' She was looking at the bed as she spoke, neatly made up and looking as impersonal as a bed in an unoccupied hotel room.

'In the living room,' Colin said in a low voice to Simon 'I didn't say anything to Mum, but it wasn't quite like that. That was the story that was given out, but the hall porter on duty told me that Dad was still alive when he came in and found him. He was lying on the floor in this room, and when the porter said he'd telephone for an ambulance, Dad said "No, I've already called them, they'll be here in a minute." Something like that. Then he lost consciousness and the porter thought that must have been when he died. Two men arrived with a stretcher shortly afterwards and confirmed that he was dead, and took him away. The porter assumed to the local hospital, but in the confusion and shock of the moment, he didn't ask where.'

'That's very interesting,' Simon said thoughtfully. 'I'm glad you didn't say anything to your mother. Better not now; it might be a bit upsetting for her.'

'There are some of his things in the drawers here,' Fiona called. 'Colin, can you find a bag or something we can put them in? Only a few shirts and pants, but we might as well empty everything.'

Colin went into the kitchen and in one of the drawers found a couple of supermarket carrier bags. Without thinking, he glanced round the room and saw a small frying pan lying on the draining board. He stared at it. He was sure it hadn't been there when he'd been here previously. In fact, on that occasion, he had been surprised by how tidy the kitchen had looked, everything put away and not even any washed-up crockery lying draining beside the sink, as one might have expected if Michael had spent the evening here and then been suddenly taken ill later, but before he had gone to bed.

The uneasy feeling he had experienced on first coming into the flat deepened. It felt eerie to be here. Someone had been here since the last time he had seen it. It might, of course, be merely that one of the porters had let someone stay for the odd night, knowing the place wouldn't be occupied. That was illegal, but understandable in the circumstances. Easy enough to make a few extra pounds if you knew it was unlikely the flat would be used again until the lease ran out. Colin began to look more closely at each room, trying to remember how things had been that last time he had been here.

There wasn't much to the place; a small living room with a sofa and a couple of chairs, a television and a coffee table in front of the sofa; a bedroom with bed, chest of drawers and wardrobe and a bathroom leading off. The kitchen led off the living room, a narrow slip of a room where one wasn't expected to do much in the way of cooking, though there was a small cooker and a microwave. And a refrigerator. Automatically, he opened its door, and saw a carton of milk sitting inside. Hadn't the porter said he'd removed all the perishables weeks ago? This must be smelling foul. He picked it up and sniffed. It smelt fresh.

At the back of the fridge was a carton of half a dozen eggs and a packet of butter. He looked inside the egg carton and saw that two had gone. The sell-by date on the outside was a week ahead. Colin closed the door and leaned against the edge of the sink, breathing deeply. The explanation that the porter had let someone stay here unofficially was the most likely, the most reasonable, yet his mind couldn't accept it.

Gradually, he was coming to an incredible conclusion. His father had been shown to have lived a secret life on the proceeds of embezzled money. Was he, perhaps, still doing that? He thought over the attempts he had made to track down the ambulance crew who had attended here, the hospital they must have taken Michael to, and the blanks he had drawn at every turn. There was one inescapable answer. Michael was not dead. He had faked his own death for reasons of his own and was still alive and visiting this flat from time to time.

'Colin, are you all right? You look very pale.' Fiona stood at the kitchen door. With an effort, Colin pulled himself together and handed her the carrier bags. 'Yes, I'm all right. I just came over a bit faint. I think it must be the stuffiness in here. There can't have been any windows open for weeks.'

'I know how you feel. The place does seem oppressive.' Fiona came into the kitchen and looked round. 'The porter or someone must have tidied up. I can't imagine your father leaving it so clean.'

'Mum – I think I'll go downstairs and have a breath of fresh air. I'll be back shortly.' Colin stumbled over to the door. He had to get out of the flat before he found himself blurting out something which he couldn't say yet, not to anyone.

'We could open a window.' Fiona's voice floated to him but he was already at the main door of the flat.

'I'll be back in a moment,' he called as he passed Simon, who was staring out of one of the windows at a blank wall opposite.

Downstairs, he went to the porter's room and knocked on the door. 'Has anyone else asked for the key to Mr Latimer's flat?' he asked.

'Not that I know of.' The man consulted a ledger on a shelf beside the door. He turned back a page. 'Not since you came ten days ago. That was you, wasn't it, a Mr Colin Latimer?'

'That's me. But suppose someone had a key. Do you record everyone's coming and going?'

'Oh, no. If the tenants have a key they come and go as they please and we don't make a note of it. Good Lord, we'd never have time for anything else. And why should we note it? We're not MI6.'

'No. Silly question. But you weren't here when I came last. There was another chap. Don't know what his name was.'

'That'd be Harry. He's not here now. Gone on holiday, so I've been told. I've been here just since last week so I haven't met him yet.'

'Thanks.' Colin turned away. Michael would still have his key so could come and go and probably this man wouldn't even know who he was. He stood on the steps and took some deep breaths, calming himself while he thought what he should do. He needed to talk to Simon about all this, but not in front of his mother. Time enough to break the news to her when they had some proof, not mere suspicion.

When he returned to the flat Fiona greeted him eagerly. 'I've solved the mystery of Michael's keys!' she said. 'There was an old raincoat in the wardrobe, not one I've ever seen him wearing, but he probably kept it here for years. And there was a bunch of keys in the pocket! So that's why they weren't returned to me when he died!'

Fiona didn't seem to have thought about Michael's briefcase, so Colin kept quiet about that. 'Let's have a look,' he said. 'We ought to be sure they are his.'

'But why ever would they not be his?' She held out a bunch that contained several keys. Colin picked out one and compared it with the housekey in his own pocket. That was definitely not the front door key of Little Paddocks, but what of the others? He flipped through them, one that looked like a car key, another large Chubb-style house key, two Yales and a couple of smaller keys. He went to the main door of the flat and tried both the Yale keys in the lock. Neither fitted.

'I never remember him having a bunch as large as this,' he said, handing them back to her. 'Were they the ones he normally carried on him, do you think?'

'Of course they must be. I expect there are keys from his work here too. Office keys. Maybe he still kept some Brightmans' keys when he left.'

Colin thought that was highly unlikely. The last thing the security men would have done would have been to let Michael leave the premises without handing in all the company keys. He might, of course, have already had duplicates cut, if he expected to need to re-enter Brightmans for any purpose.

'I think we might as well go now. There's really very little for us to clear up in here,' Fiona said. 'What do you think, Simon?'

'Yes, the place looks pretty bare. Must have been rather depressing to stay here by himself often,' Simon said. 'Gloomy view out of most of the windows. They look out onto some kind of interior well. Nothing to see but the wall of another block of flats.'

'We'll be able to take a reasonably early train back home,' Fiona continued. 'We'll be back in time for a late lunch, unless we eat here in London before we go.'

Simon looked embarrassed. 'Look, my dear. Do you mind if I go straight on to Winchester? I have some business to contract with my accountant and I promised I'd see him as soon as I could.'

'Of course you must. Perhaps you could come over for dinner later in the week. I'll telephone you. Or you can call me when you're free.'

Fiona went into the bedroom to pick up the carrier bags containing Michael's clothing, and Colin said to Simon quietly 'Simon, I need to talk to you, alone. Do you think we could meet up at that pub we went to the other day?'

Simon nodded. 'Yes, I think that would be a good idea. Say nothing to your mother yet, but I think you and I may be thinking along similar lines. Shall we say tomorrow, early evening, about seven?'

They took the first available train back to the village and arrived in time for a late lunch. Mrs Burdett, who had her own back door key and came and went independently, had left a cold salad for them. Colin tried to distract Fiona from the subject of the flat, or Michael, as he was afraid he would blurt out his suspicions if they talked about it. Instead, he tried to encourage her to tell him about the houses she and Simon had looked at in the village and surrounding countryside.

'I saw some pretty little cottages,' she said. 'Nicely modernised, too. It wouldn't be like going back to the days when I was a child and lived in one of those awful two up, two down places with a toilet at the bottom of the garden.'

'You'd like a cottage here, roses round the door and everything?' Colin prompted.

'Well, yes I would. But ought I to go ahead and buy one? You see, I have this feeling that Simon – well, he always was sweet on me and I *think* that perhaps he might still be. And that he'll ask me to marry him, now that I'm free. And it would be a pity to go ahead and then find... The only thing is, though, he's such a gentleman, and so sensitive to the situation – too sensitive, really, that I think he'll think it's far too soon to ask me, and he'll dally for ages until he thinks I've got over Michael's death. Except that I don't feel there's anything to get over. I didn't love your father. Not really. Do you think that's an awful thing to say? And now that I know he was a crook – and was so secretive about what he was doing – I feel justified in not being upset at his death. Do you think that's dreadfully callous of me?'

'No, I don't. I was aware for years that you and Dad weren't close. I just thought that's what happened to married couples after a few years. Lots of chaps at school had parents who barely even spoke to each other. At least, neither of you had affairs with other people and an awful lot of chaps' parents did.' Colin thought briefly of Moira, but she had said that was a long time ago. Michael might not even have been married to Fiona then.

'I suppose I should be thankful for that. Though I've wondered – if Simon had turned up a few years ago – I might have been tempted. But would he have let me be tempted? He's such an honourable man. And as for Michael, well, I really don't know what he was doing. He must have been doing something after he left Brightmans, something that brought in money, presumably, yet I haven't the faintest idea what. He might have had a string of girlfriends and mistresses and I wouldn't have known. And yet I thought I knew him so well.' She sighed.

They were interrupted by a thump on the back door and a 'Cooeee!' followed by the handle rattling as it was tried.

'That's Nell. I thought she would be round to see us before long,' Fiona said, brightening. 'I haven't seen her for some days.'

'Now, Mum,' Colin said urgently. 'Not a word about Brightmans and what I was told. It's terribly confidential and I promised I wouldn't let anyone but you know the situation. And Simon,' he added, to himself. 'You know what a gossip Eleanor is.'

'But Eleanor wouldn't – ' Fiona began.

'No, Mum. Don't say a word. Please,' Colin begged. He determined not to leave the room while Eleanor was here, and be prepared to kick his mother's shins if it looked as if she was likely to be indiscreet.

Fiona went to open the back door and bring Eleanor to join them at the kitchen table.

'Still having lunch. My, you do keep strange hours,' Eleanor said, sitting down. 'Hallo, Colin. How is your latest girlfriend?'

Colin, caught unawares, stammered 'W-what?' and blushed furiously.

'Aha! Thought so! I've seen you nipping up to town pretty frequently these last few days. When are we going to meet her? Is she pretty?'

'There isn't a girlfriend. Not in the sense you were hoping to hear about, anyway,' Colin said. 'I had some business in town, that's all. A few job interviews. Nothing's come up so far.'

'Oh, pity. Still, I bet there is a girl in the background somewhere. There always is with you young men.' Eleanor reached out towards a plate on the table. 'Is that one of your Mrs Burdett's quiches? May I pick at it?'

'Help yourself. Have a cup of tea with us,' Fiona invited. 'Colin, put the kettle on, will you?'

Colin went reluctantly into the scullery, giving his mother a warning glance as he passed. He could hear their conversation from there, and decided that he would have to drop the teapot, or spill the hot water to create a diversion, if Fiona said anything about Brightmans to Nell.

'I won't ask you how you are,' Eleanor said, cutting herself a slice of quiche. 'I know you think everyone is treating you like an invalid when they do. Anyway, I can see how you are. You look positively blooming. Would it be tactless to say that widowhood suits you?'

'Frankly, I don't feel any different as a widow than I did when I was a wife,' Fiona shrugged. 'I've been looking at houses in the village and I think I might enjoy choosing a much cosier place.'

'You may not feel any different as a widow, but you must surely be feeling a great deal poorer,' Eleanor said. 'What's the latest about that abominal pension arrangement? Has your solicitor managed to sort out anything?'

In the scullery, Colin moved nearer to the door.

'I've accepted that nothing can be done about that now,' Fiona said. 'I'll have enough to live on, once I've sold all the furniture here that would be too big for a smaller place anyway. I'm not too worried.'

'Well you should be! It's outrageous! If that ga-ga solicitor of yours hasn't managed to put the frighteners on to Brightmans and force them to give you the pension you're entitled to, then you ought to sack him straight away.'

'I can hardly do that. And he's doing his best to maximise as much income for me as he can,' Fiona replied mildly.

'And line his own pockets at the same time, I wouldn't be surprised! The man's incompetent! He should never have let that situation happen in the first place! If he won't sort it for you, you should go and see the MD at Brightmans yourself, demand an explanation and your rights!'

'I can hardly do that,' Fiona shrugged. 'I wouldn't know who to see, and they wouldn't see me, anyway.'

Colin came back into the kitchen. He sat down opposite his mother and glanced at her anxiously.

'Fee, you are being spineless! Go up to their head office and demand to see the boss man. Their most senior executive. Stage a sit-in until they agree to listen to you! Look, I'll come with you! Together we'll make them sit up and take notice!' Eleanor was becoming animated.

'My mother doesn't want to. She is quite happy to leave things as they are,' Colin said. He thought he was speaking mildly, but Eleanor rounded on him furiously.

'Colin, you ought to be ashamed of yourself! You should be championing your mother, not letting a big company get away with cheating a poor widow out of her rights. Why aren't you up there, speaking your mind to them?'

'Colin did go and speak to someone at Brightmans,' Fiona said. Colin gave her a warning look. 'And now I understand that there won't be any money from Michael's pension, so there's no point in pursuing the matter further.'

'There's every reason! It's totally illegal, in any case! Doesn't your solicitor know that? They can't *do* that with a pension. It's against the law. Look, I know of a good man, a really clever lawyer, who'd sort this out for you and you'd get half what Michael's salary was when he died. That's what you're entitled to. Let me give him a ring, explain your situation and ask him to get in touch with you. He's not cheap, but the amount you'd receive would more than compensate – '

'Eleanor, please don't interfere.' Fiona spoke gently, but her voice was steely. Eleanor looked as if she had just received a slap in the face.

'What? But I was only trying to help.'

'It's none of your business. My mother can deal with things her own way, thank you.'

Eleanor stared at Colin with a mixture of indignation and dislike. Then she turned to Fiona. 'Oh, I understand now,' she said coldly. 'It's that Simon Neville that's been influencing you, isn't it? Well, I did warn you to be careful where he's concerned. He clearly has some devious plan of his own to make you so dependent financially that you will be glad to fall into his arms and marry him because there won't be any alternative.'

'How dare you, Eleanor! It has nothing to do with Simon Neville!' Two angry red spots appeared on Fiona's cheeks. 'And Simon Neville is nothing to do with you, either! I wish you'd keep your opinions to yourself!'

Eleanor stood up. 'Very well, then, if that's the way you feel. I'm sorry that years of friendship between us have had to end like this, but if you won't listen to well-meant, good advice from your oldest friend, someone who cares about you and only has your welfare at heart – ' Eleanor's voice cracked. She brushed a hand across her cheeks. 'When you've had time to reflect on what I've said, when you realise that what I'm saying to you is for your own good, and that I'm right, then perhaps you will give me a call and apologise for your words. You've hurt me deeply, Fiona. I may forgive you in time, but you will have to learn to come to your senses first.'

She swept out of the kitchen and a moment later they heard the front door slam shut.

'Oh, dear,' Fiona said sadly. 'I do seem to have upset her deeply. Perhaps I should have told her about the Brightmans' situation. After all, we've been friends for so long, and we've never had secrets from each other before.'

'No, you were right not to tell her,' Colin said. 'If she had said anything to anyone, and in her state of righteous indignation she might easily have shouted it from the rooftops, then Moira Ransom would have been in deep trouble. Lost her job, no doubt, and Brightmans would have been in great financial trouble. You ought to know Eleanor well enough to know that she wouldn't be able to keep something like that to herself.'

'I suppose so. Do you think I ought to telephone her in a day or so, and apologise?'

'No, I don't. You were in the right, and she had no business to interfere when you had said clearly that you didn't want her help. She's angry because she's jealous of Simon. That's the truth.'

'Jealous of Simon? But she was never interested in him like that,' Fiona said in astonishment.

'Not because she wants him for herself, but she's put out that he seems to be your confidant nowadays rather than herself.'

'Colin, you know, you may be right. How perceptive of you! I hadn't thought of that! But what am I to do about it? I can hardly stop seeing Simon because Nell has made it plain she doesn't like him. That wouldn't be fair, and, besides, I don't want to stop seeing Simon. But I don't want to quarrel with Nell, either. Colin, what am I to do?'

'Leave Eleanor to calm down for a couple of days. You know, she needs your friendship more than you do hers. She'll be round again soon enough, and either she'll apologise or she'll pretend the whole thing never happened at all. But when she does come round, do, Mum, please be careful that you don't say anything indiscreet to her. She'd latch on to just a hint that there was something you knew that you weren't telling her.'

'You really think she will come round in a day or so? I hope so. I hate quarrelling with anyone, especially someone I've known as long as I've known Nell. Dear Colin, you are a comfort to me! I'm beginning to think I should have asked you to come with me to look at those houses in the village, if you think you are likely to want to come and live in one of them with me. I am determined not to be one of those possessive mothers that widows so often turn into, and I know you must have a life of your own, but you are such a wise person, so sensible. I don't know what I'll do without you.'

'You won't have to do without me,' Colin said, feeling embarrassed by his mother's words. 'You know I'll be here at least until you are securely settled in a new home, or until you marry Simon.'

'You won't mind if I do marry him? You know, he hasn't any children of his own. He'd like the idea of a step-son, I'm sure, even though he doesn't know you very well yet.'

Simon and I know each other a lot better than you think, Colin thought. Aloud, he said, 'What are you going to do with all those underclothes you brought back from the flat? We've cleared out most of Dad's things already. Surely you didn't want to bring more of his stuff here?'

'Oh, heavens, yes! I wasn't thinking. I just thought we needed to clear the place ready for the next tenant. I suppose Mrs Burdett's everlasting jumble sales will be glad of them.' Fiona bent down to pick up the carrier bags she had left by the kitchen door. 'She's coming tomorrow. I'll leave them here and she can take them then.'

Colin suppressed a smile. If what he thought was true, and Michael was still using the flat and living there, he was going to get a nasty shock to find he had no clean underwear or shirts in the bedroom drawers. Serve him right. And, what might be even worse, he might find he was missing some vital keys.

CHAPTER 9

THE FOLLOWING DAY COLIN made two attempts to telephone Anthea, but her answering machine was on and he couldn't think of a suitable message to leave, so put down the receiver without speaking. He wanted to ask to see her, but if she refused he was unsure what to do next. Finally, he decided he would telephone the following day, check whether she was in, and if so, go up to Chomley Mews without telling her he was coming. She could hardly refuse to see him if he arrived on her doorstep, he reasoned.

He pottered around the house for the rest of the day, pleasing Fiona just by being there to keep her company. He was beginning to realise how lonely life must have been for her when he had been away at university and Michael had worked long hours. Nobody but Eleanor or Mrs Burdett to talk to, he guessed. Fiona had never made many close friends in the village, mostly because the people her own age were at work in the day, commuting from London, and the elderly retired had little in common with her, a cliquey group with their pensioners' clubs and weekly bingo in the village hall, nothing that would have interested Fiona. The other residents on the outskirts of the village were mainly farming people, wrapped up in their own world of crops and livestock and no time for someone like Fiona. Colin wondered why it was that she was so keen to stay here, if she had so few friends. It was a beautiful part of the country, of course, and Fiona liked to walk in the woods and fields that surrounded the village. And where else would she live, he wondered? The alternative was to go back to London, where they had lived before, but current house prices in the capital would make that impossible, unless she were to live somewhere that was all too like the home she had lived in as a child, in an East End terrace. She could afford a modernised version, of course, but would she make friends there, now? She'd have very little in common with people in London, Colin suspected.

At half past six he put his head into the study to tell her that he was going out for a short while. 'I'll be back in time for supper,' he said.

Fiona was reading. She could hardly complain when he had spent the whole day with her. 'All right, dear. If you're sure you won't be late, I'll make you an especially nice supper. I think there are some salmon steaks in the freezer. How about that, with some hollandaise sauce and asparagus? That'll have to be frozen, too, I'm afraid, but there's a good brand which tastes very nice.'

'Sounds delicious.' He debated whether to ask if he could borrow her car, but the Farrier's Arms was only a couple of miles up the road, and a walk there would clear his thoughts.

He saw Simon's car as he crossed the car park. Simon was sitting in a corner, some way from any of the other drinkers. Since it was early the place was practically empty, just a couple of farmers leaning on the bar in hearty conversation with the landlord.

'I got you a pint,' Simon greeted him.

Colin sat down at the table. 'Thanks. You know, someone had been in that flat since I was last there. Things had been moved.'

'I thought that was what you were going to tell me. I saw the expression on your face when you were in the kitchen. Fiona didn't notice; she just thought you were feeling a bit faint from the stuffiness.'

'I was feeling faint. There was *fresh* milk in the fridge. There might, of course, be a reasonable explanation for it. One of the porters might be using it, or letting it out to a friend – '

'But you don't sound convinced about that?'

Colin shook his head. 'No. I think – I think he's coming back there to stay from time to time. I don't think Michael's dead at all. I think he faked his death for some reason. Perhaps because he is now planning to lead a new life. Perhaps he has another wife and family somewhere. He may even have had them for some time. That would explain his need for extra money. Now, he wants to break free from Mum and lead a new life with someone else.'

'Hey, steady on, now! Those are a great many assumptions to make. Why didn't he simply divorce her, if that's what he wanted?' Simon asked.

'I don't know. I don't think Mum would have made any objections if he had asked for a divorce. But the way they were, well, they weren't quarrelling or anything like that.

You would have thought they were quite friendly. Not affectionate, but friendly. It didn't look as if they were the kind of couple who would have wanted to divorce, just two people who had grown apart and lived fairly separate lives. I don't understand it.'

'But then if Michael *is* still alive, there must be some other reason for his wanting to disappear,' Simon said. 'It sounds almost too fanciful to be true. But I've been thinking about it all. There's the porter's story, that he found Michael alive and that when he went to call an ambulance Michael said he had already done so, and then two people with a stretcher turned up very soon afterwards and took him away. I can't think that *bona fide* ambulance men would behave like that. And you said you couldn't trace where they had come from, or find any record of any hospital having taken delivery of anyone from those flats. If anyone dies suddenly, like that, there's always a post-mortem. If they were genuine ambulance men they would have had to take him to the local hospital. And Fiona would have seen a coroner's report on the post-mortem. The whole story is very odd. Didn't Fiona think it was strange?'

'She was in such a state of shock when she heard about him having a heart attack and dying, that I don't think she thought about the details. Not at the time, anyway. Now, I think she has been trying to put it all out of her mind.'

'How, exactly, did she hear?'

'I don't really know. I suppose the porter at the flats must have telephoned her. He didn't know where they'd taken Michael so he couldn't be much help, but very shortly afterwards an undertaker got in touch and said that Michael had taken out a funeral plan some time before and that all costs were already paid. He would provide a coffin and would bring Michael in it to her local church for burial if she would make the funeral arrangements with the vicar. It was the first time she had heard anything about Michael having made a funeral plan, but it is quite a common practice, I believe.'

'But Fiona must have known who this undertaker was,' Simon said.

'I suppose there was an address on the letter, but she says she threw it away, along with other papers that I think now might have been useful if she'd kept them,' Colin shrugged. 'She was in something of a state, you must remember. Not that she was upset, it was the shock of him dying so unexpectedly. He was a very fit person and as far as we knew, no history of any heart problems at all.'

'If someone wanted to fake a death, a heart attack is a good way of doing it. Sudden, unexpected and wouldn't show up as a problem on medical records,' Simon said. 'I think I am beginning to come to your conclusion, though, that Michael *isn't* dead. That had been a thought at the back of my mind but I rejected it, it all seemed far too preposterous. Now, with what you have been saying, and the state of the flat, I am forced to think you may be right. Problem now is, where is he and what is he doing? And why is he doing it?'

'Looks like he's still staying at the flat,' Colin said. 'Though he can't be for much longer. The lease is up in a week or so and he can hardly renew it without giving himself away. I had a word with the porter when I went downstairs to have some fresh air, and he said he wouldn't know if any of the tenants with their own key came or went. And he's new; he wouldn't know Dad anyway. The man I spoke to the first time I went there, the one who found Dad, seems to have mysteriously gone on holiday.'

'One thing I feel, is that we shouldn't say anything to Fiona just yet,' Simon said. 'It's going to come as a shock to her. It's a bit of a shock to me, too. I was planning on asking your mother to marry me. Now, I can't risk making her a bigamist.'

'I can search through all his stuff again at the house. We might find a clue there,' Colin said. 'Mum told me to burn it all, but after I'd found Anthea's photo I wondered if she was a girlfriend, so I kept all his diaries in the garden shed. I'm pretty sure now that she hadn't ever had an affair with him, but her mother admitted that she had, a long time ago.'

'Is he with her, do you think?' Simon asked.

'No, somehow I don't think so. She was very frank about Dad embezzling money and what Brightmans did about it. I think she would have been less so if there had been anything still between them. But what was he embezzling money *for*? I don't know exactly what kind of money he was earning at Brightmans, but I know it seemed to be plenty for keeping us in a better state than we needed to be. I'd have thought he could have kept another woman without needing to embezzle two million from Brightmans. And I don't think Mum would have noticed, either.'

'Colin, you'd better search through everything in the house and see what you can come up with, though frankly I doubt if he'd have kept anything really private there. I'm planning on taking your mother to dinner at my house in the next day or so, so you will have the place to yourself for the evening. There must be something that's been overlooked. From what you've told me, the amount of diaries and letters in his room don't ring true. That's another reason for thinking he might have planned to disappear. Everyone accumulates papers and stuff they never clear out. It sounds like he deliberately removed a great deal of it before he planned his "death". Perhaps not all of it; you may get lucky if you go through everything carefully.'

'I'll do that. I'd better go home now. I promised I'd be in to supper and she's doing me something special as a reward for not sloping off to London today,' Colin grinned, standing up.

'I'd give you a lift back, but she'd see the car and ask awkward questions. At least, I can take you to the end of the road. God, I hate deceiving her, but I daren't say anything until we're absolutely sure.'

'We are sure,' Colin said gloomily. 'It's proving it that's going to be the problem.'

After Colin had left the house, Fiona read until it was too dark to see. The days were drawing in now, only a week of September left and summer was well and truly over. She closed her book, but didn't turn on the light. Sitting here in the gathering dusk, she gave herself up to daydreaming, remembering past times and small incidents that had happened in this house.

On balance, she thought she had been happy here. The flat in London, though in a good, expensive area, had been small and London was becoming stifling and claustrophobic. She had been eager to leave, delighted with her first sight of the village when they had come to look round here, and happy to fall in with any plans Michael wanted. She had thought the house too big and opulent for the three of them, but Michael seemed to have set his heart on owning it, and assured her they could well afford it. After the flat, the space seemed vast, and the grounds almost as big as a park. It had taken her weeks, she remembered, smiling, to explore the whole of their land and she had been excited at first, to be able to step outside and wander at will through lawns and flowerbeds, a small wood bordered by a stream, and pass a pair of tennis courts on her return, knowing that everything she had walked through was owned by them. Later, when the complications of finding a gardener willing to keep even the lawns cut, had become a problem, she began to feel they had taken on more than they had bargained for. It was about this time, Fiona remembered, that Michael had begun spending more time at work, staying up in London overnight because he was entertaining clients, or going away for weekends, sometimes Amsterdam, sometimes Paris, he'd said. Sometimes it was somewhere more prosaic, like Manchester, or Birmingham. She had thought she might like to have gone with him to Paris or Amsterdam, but he hadn't suggested it, implying that the whole weekend would be a bore, entertaining tedious clients and with no time to spare for sightseeing. She wouldn't have cared, she thought.

Now, she told herself, she would have wandered happily round the streets of whichever capital Michael had visited, exploring by herself, happy to spend the whole weekend alone, but equally happy to help entertain his clients at dinner. Did these people never bring their own wives? Now she knew that he probably wasn't entertaining clients, or, at least, not Brightmans' clients.

Did he take a woman with him, when he went to these romantic places, she wondered. Hard to imagine that he did, though that seemed the obvious answer. Somehow, she had always thought that, if Michael strayed, she would instinctively know it, but now she wondered. There was so much she hadn't known about him, never even suspected. It was hard to believe what Colin had told her, that he had been sacked from Brightmans nearly a year ago; that he had been cheating the company for three years before that. And she had never suspected a thing, never had the slightest suspicion that anything had been wrong.

She shivered. What else about Michael did she not know, not even be able to guess at? Quite a lot, if she had to fill in the missing gaps in the past three years. What was he doing, all those months when he had left the house regularly at the same time each day, after he had no longer worked for Brightmans? Why had he gone away for weekends to meet clients when there were no clients? Who had he met, then?

Michael was dead now, and there was so much she still needed to know, so much she wanted to ask him. 'Michael, why did you have to escape from it all so completely?' she said aloud. What would have happened if he hadn't had that fatal heart attack? Surely, he couldn't have gone on with this deception indefinitely. She must have found out about it all in the end; someone would have said something, someone from Brightmans would have told her. Unbidden, the words came into her head, 'The wife is usually the last person to know.'

If he could come back now, if she could only have an hour with him, to ask all the questions she wanted to, would it help? Only if he was willing to answer them truthfully and frankly. But it would help her to ask, if only she could have that chance.

Was it all my fault, she wondered, something in my character that was lacking, that made you crave something else, something more than I could give you? Was it the excitement of making more and more money, the buzz of knowing that he was scoring off Brightmans, cheating them and winning, because they didn't know what he was doing. How had they eventually found out? Companies eventually always did find out these things, she supposed. Annual audits, or the appointment of a more thorough accountant, or just some silly mistake that someone noticed, which led to an investigation. It didn't matter now. They'd found him out and he'd paid the penalty. Only, he hadn't paid it, she had.

It was completely dark now in the study, the only light coming from the glow of the fire which she was lighting every evening now that it was becoming chilly. Fiona peered up at the clock, then, not seeing the time, held her wrist towards the fire. She could just make out that it was nearly half past seven, on the pretty, hard-to-read face of the watch that Michael had given her last birthday. She could probably sell that for two hundred pounds, if things got very tough, she thought bitterly. Knowing that it was probably bought with money dishonestly earned took away her pleasure in it.

There was a sound from the other side of the house, she thought it must be the back door opening, though why Colin would come in that way when he had the front door key, she didn't know.

'Colin, is that you?' she called. 'I haven't started the meal yet.'

There was no reply, no response. Perhaps it wasn't Colin after all. Mrs Burdett had a back door key and came and went freely. Perhaps she had forgotten something and called back for it. Not seeing any lights she must have assumed everyone was out.

'Mrs Burdett?' Fiona called. A few minutes' chat with the woman would be pleasant; she was beginning to feel lonely, here in the dark by herself. She'd been thinking too much, that was the trouble, but a small dose of Mrs Burdett's good countrywoman's plain common sense would be just what she needed to help her put the world – her world – into perspective.

There was no response from the kitchen. She must have slipped in quietly and it would have been the back door shutting after her that she had heard. Or, perhaps, it hadn't been anything like that at all. At night, all houses creaked as the woodwork expanded after the warmth of the day. But it could have been Colin. It *was* the sound of a door opening, she was sure. Fiona went to the door and opened it slightly.

'Colin? Is that you?' she called.

There was a stillness in the hall outside, and in it a feeling she had never experienced before. It was as if the house was holding its breath. No, it wasn't that, exactly. It was as if *someone* was holding their breath. She stood by the door, in total darkness, knowing the sensible thing would be to switch on the light and dispel the rather creepy sensation that was enveloping her, but she couldn't. She simply couldn't bring herself to put her hand up to the switch that was no more than a couple of yards away. Instead, she remained standing in the doorway, listening.

Then she heard it. A definite slithering sound, like feet creeping across the carpet of the hall, going away from her, across the hall, towards the stairs.

She told herself she was imagining it, but she waited, knowing exactly what she was waiting for. The fourth stair from the bottom creaked when anyone stood on it. She held her breath. If there was no sound – it seemed a long time, and then – the unmistakable creak as weight was placed on the fourth stair.

Now was the time when she should have reached for the switch; flooded the hall with light and seen who it was who was creeping up the stairs.

She couldn't. Fiona stood, frozen to the spot, listening as she heard someone ascending the stairs, slowly, quietly, secretively. It couldn't be Colin. He never crept around anywhere. It would hardly be Mrs Burdett, she wasn't the kind of woman to snoop around in her employer's house when there was no one around.

Had the back door been left open? She couldn't remember if she'd locked it after the last time she had been outside. Possibly not. She or Colin did a last, bedtime check on doors and windows each night, but earlier in the day doors and windows were mostly left open. Little Paddocks lay in its own grounds, no one could come near the house itself without first coming up the drive. She would certainly hear the crunch of gravel underfoot if anyone had approached.

Fiona wondered what to do. The intruder had reached the top of the stairs now and she sensed, rather than heard or saw, that he was turning left, towards the bedrooms. Should she take the opportunity now, and call the police? But what if it was Colin, or Mrs Burdett, or completely in her imagination? She'd look a complete fool. She could hear the comments, 'Nervous woman on her own – the strain of her husband's death beginning to get to her. She shouldn't be living by herself, it's clearly sending her bonkers. She's imagining all sorts.'

I'm supposed to be a strong woman, Simon said I was. He'd think I was hopelessly wet if I let this get to me, she thought. She went back into the study, shutting the door and switching on the light. The light was comforting, until she thought that, if there was an intruder upstairs, she was making herself vulnerable by advertising her presence. A burglar could take what he wanted and be gone. If he was disturbed, or discovered that there was a witness to him being in the house – well, she'd read about intruders attacking lone women to silence them. She'd be better off hiding in the dark and keeping quiet until he'd gone. Try to get a glimpse of him, perhaps, if she could do so safely, but wait until he'd gone before calling the police. They were over-stretched and busy these days, everyone knew that. Suppose they didn't come right away, and she had let the man know she was here and by herself?

Fiona switched off the light again. She was frightened now. More than anything, she wanted to speak to a friendly voice. She felt her way across to the desk and picked up the phone. She'd call Simon. He'd reassure her. He'd come over and comfort her, even if it turned out that it was all in her imagination.

She knew his number well enough to punch the numbers out in the dark. The ringing tone sounded so loud in the room that for a moment she wondered if it couldn't be heard outside. It went on ringing, then there was a click, and Simon's voice saying blandly 'This is Simon Neville's house. I'm sorry I can't come to the phone at the moment. If you will kindly leave your name and number I will get back to you as soon as possible.'

'Simon – ' It wasn't any use talking to an answering machine. Fiona put her receiver down. As soon as she had done that, she remembered that when anyone used one of the telephones in the house, the others made a clicking sound. There was a telephone in her bedroom, as well as one in the hall. If there really was an intruder upstairs – there *was* an intruder upstairs, she was convinced of it now – then he would have heard the click and know that there was someone else in the house, using the telephone.

She waited in the dark. There were no sounds now, either from upstairs or down. What was he doing, she wondered. Rifling through the bedrooms looking for small, portable valuables, she supposed. She never kept much cash in the house, and neither, she supposed, did Colin. She had quite a lot of jewellery in her room, almost all of it given to her at various times by Michael. They could have that, with pleasure, she thought crossly. She didn't care for any of it, wouldn't wear any of it again. It could be sold to keep her and Colin for several months, though, that would be its only value now.

She went over to the door and eased it open a crack. A sliver of light from the window to the side of the front door left a path of paler darkness across the hall. Nothing stirred and she had almost convinced herself that the whole thing was in her imagination, when she heard the sounds again. There was definitely someone coming quietly down the stairs.

Now, the last thing she wanted was to put on the light and confront him. She stayed, leaning against the door lintel, watching through the crack, and saw the outline of a man cross the hall, passing through the shaft of light from the window. It definitely was an intruder! She watched him pause by the hall table, touch her coat that was hanging nearby, feeling in the pockets. Colin's coat was next to it, he'd gone out in just a jacket as the evening had still been warm.

The man checked those pockets, too. She watched him standing there. He was tall, well-built, not someone she had any desire to confront on her own. Then she remembered she had left her handbag on the hall table. She had put it there when they'd come home from London yesterday, and forgotten about it. There wasn't much cash in it, but there were credit cards and other things like her driving licence and cheque book which would cause great inconvenience if they were stolen.

Was she going to stand there and simply watch this stranger steal from her bag? She looked round for a weapon but there wasn't even a poker by the hearth. Even in her anger at his blatant rummaging through her bag, she knew she would be foolhardy to show herself now. He was tall, strong, if she challenged him he'd undoubtedly want to silence her. If she screamed there would be no one to hear her. Colin might be on his way home by now, but then he might not. The only sensible thing to do was to stay hidden and try to get a look at the man so that she could give a sensible description to the police later.

The man straightened up. She couldn't see if he had anything in his hands but he seemed to have taken whatever he wanted from her bag. He turned and stepped towards the front door and for a moment was silhouetted in the shaft of lighter darkness from the window and she had a brief but clear outline of his profile.

I am going mad, she thought. I'm seeing ghosts. That man looks exactly like Michael.

He opened the front door, stepped outside and closed it very quietly behind him. She heard a brief crunch of footsteps on gravel and then silence as he must have reached the grass verge and walked along that. She came into the hall and peered out of the window. A dark shadow was just passing out of the gate and disappeared down the road.

She was shaking now. Fiona went across to the hall table and opened her handbag. She supposed she shouldn't touch it, because of fingerprints, but she had to know what he had taken.

Her credit cards and cheque book were all there, along with everything else. Even her purse still had notes in it. She wasn't sure exactly how much she had had, but it didn't look as if anything had been taken. Her knees were trembling and she had to sit down on the hall chair. She must have been imagining it. An intruder finding a handbag containing money and he hadn't taken any of it. It wasn't possible; it wasn't believable. What were the police going to say to a story like that? And an intruder who had a profile like her dead husband? She could hear the snide comments, the knowing looks. Well, she could hardly report a robbery if there wasn't anything taken.

She went back into the study and switched on the light. She was shivering and knelt down on the hearth by the fire. Why wasn't Colin here? It was time he was back, he'd said he wouldn't be late. She looked at the clock. It was twenty to eight. The whole incident had taken no more than ten minutes, although it had felt like hours.

She had to speak to someone. Had to hear a friendly human voice and convince herself she wasn't going mad. She dialled Simon's number again, but the answerphone was still on. After a second's hesitation, she punched in Eleanor's number. There had been angry words the last time she had seen her, and they hadn't been in touch since, but Eleanor was her oldest, her closest friend and surely a silly quarrel couldn't come between them for long.

Fiona felt tremendous relief when she heard Eleanor's voice answer.

'Nell, – it's me, Fiona.'

'Oh, yes?' Eleanor sounded cool.

'Nell – oh, Nell, please help me! I think I must be going mad! I'm sorry we quarrelled last time you were here. Please forgive me. Can you come over, now? Something has happened and I'm frightened. Please, Nell. Forgive me and come here.'

'Isn't Colin with you?'

'No, he's out. I'm by myself and there's been someone in the house. An intruder. He's gone now but I'm so frightened. Please come.'

'Have you called the police?'

'No, not yet. I want you to come here first. Nothing's been taken but I'm so frightened. Nell!'

'I'm on my way. Stay where you are and I'll be with you in five minutes.'

To Fiona's relief, Eleanor sounded like her old, brisk, friendly self. She stayed crouched by the fire, shivering and within five minutes heard the sound of car tyres racing over the gravel outside. Only then did she go out into the hall to open the door to Eleanor.

CHAPTER 10

'WHAT HAPPENED? My God, you look terrible! You're white as a sheet! And you feel icy! Haven't you lit a fire somewhere?' Eleanor's briskness was comforting.

'There's a fire in the study. I was sitting there,' Fiona said, leading the way.

'Go and sit down. Where's the whisky? You need a big slug. And I expect I will do, too.' Eleanor was already crossing the hall towards the dining room where she knew the drinks cabinet was. Fiona didn't argue but went back into the study and sat down in her chair. It was a relief to leave everything to someone else, someone who would comfort her and reassure her she wasn't imaging things.

Eleanor came into the study and with two tumblers of neat whisky and thrust one into Fiona's hands. 'Drink it up,' she commanded.

'I can't drink it like that,' Fiona demurred, but Eleanor glared at her and knocked back half the contents of her own glass in one single gulp. 'Go on. Now tell me. What happened? Were you attacked? How did they break in?'

Fiona sipped her whisky and tried to force some down. 'It wasn't like that,' she said. 'I was sitting here in the dark. I'd been reading, waiting for Colin to come home, and when it got too dark I didn't bother putting the light on, just sat here, thinking and daydreaming, I suppose. Then I heard something that sounded like the back door opening. I called out, thinking it was Colin, but there was no reply. Then I heard footsteps, going up the stairs. It was dark in the hall, but I knew there was someone there because the tread creaked. It always does. I didn't know what to do, so I rang Simon but he wasn't there.'

'Men! They are never there when they are wanted,' Eleanor sniffed.

'I didn't dare put on the light and give myself away. I watched through a crack in the door and eventually he came down again. He rummaged through my handbag which was on the hall table and then he let himself out through the front door.'

'So he was after money, mainly. A vagrant,' Eleanor said.

'No, that was the odd thing. He didn't take anything. As soon as he'd gone, I checked. Nothing had been taken, not my credit cards or cash, nothing. But I caught a glimpse of him in the light from the window, as he turned to leave. He looked exactly like Michael.'

'Now, Fee, are you sure? You must have been thinking of Michael earlier and this chap had a superficial resemblance. Heavens, Michael didn't look anything like a vagrant!'

'I didn't say this intruder was a vagrant,' Fiona said.

'How was he dressed? Balaclava on his head, black tracksuit?'

'No, of course not. Don't be ridiculous.'

'Well, then?'

'Dark clothes. A coat, raincoat or something. I didn't see what else. I just caught a glimpse of his profile as he turned his head and stood in the light from the window. I thought I'd seen a ghost.'

'You say you were sitting here in the dark. You weren't dozing, by any chance?'

'I don't think so. I suppose I may have been.'

'I think you were asleep and something disturbed your dreams. A tree branch tapping on the window, or something. That can play tricks with the unconscious mind. It fitted in with what you were dreaming and you thought you'd seen an intruder going upstairs.'

'I did. I know I did.'

'An intruder who doesn't take anything when there's a handbag full of money on offer in front of him? That's unbelievable. You had been thinking of Michael and you fell asleep. A dream analyst would make a clear connection between dreaming of your dead husband and having him appear in an inconguous situation. Your mind is telling you things. Michael is dead, and you want to move on in your life. *Ergo*, your mind is showing you Michael as an intruder in your life. It seems perfectly clear to me.'

'I wasn't asleep.' Fiona was beginning to lose her patience.

'Then why were you sitting in the dark?'

'I was thinking, remembering the good times here and the not so good. Enjoying reliving them. I won't be here for much longer.'

'You were daydreaming. That's as close to dreaming as anything. Fee, you imagined the whole thing.'

'He went upstairs. The treads don't creak unless you step on them.'

'And I'm willing to bet that you won't find anything disturbed upstairs either. Go on, take a look now. I'll come up with you, and if there's as much as a single brooch been taken I'll eat my words.'

Fiona stood up reluctantly. Perhaps the intruder had been looking for something specific, though the only thing she could think of would be drugs, and Little Paddocks seemed hardly the place to find anything like that.

In her bedroom nothing seemed to have been disturbed, though she thought one of two things looked as if they had been moved. Eleanor went straight to her jewellery case on the dressing table. 'Check it,' she demanded.

'Everything seems to be there.' Fiona gave it a cursory look, but if the man had been a thief, he would surely have scooped up the lot.

'I rest my case.' Eleanor went towards the stairs. 'Now, you're not going to call the police over this, are you? You'll only make a fool of yourself if you do. My advice is to see your doctor. Get him to make an appointment with a specialist. You've been under a lot of strain lately and no one will blame you for feeling like this, having these hallucinations. A good tonic would help, too.'

'Thanks for coming, Eleanor.' It was all she could find to say.

'Well, what are friends for? Though I must say, Fee dear, you do put a strain on friendship sometimes. But I still love you.' She planted a kiss on Fiona's cheek and went towards the front door. 'Colin will be back soon, no doubt. Get him to stay in more, not so much gallivanting up to town to see his latest girlfriend. You need him and he should realise that.' She was out of the door as she spoke, and Fiona heard the car's engine start up.

Hardly had Eleanor's car disappeared out of the gate when Colin came in through the front door. 'Was that Eleanor's car I saw driving away?' he asked. 'Has she been round upsetting you? She hasn't been trying to pester you about Brightmans and Dad's missing pension, has she?'

'No, nothing like that. She was really quite kind but she didn't understand at all. Colin, I've had an awful experience. I thought I must be going mad. I still think there must be something the matter with me. There was an intruder – well, I suppose I *thought* it was an intruder, but now Nell has made me wonder if I was imagining things.'

'An intruder? When?' Colin said sharply. 'Come into the study and tell me what happened.'

'I haven't even begun to prepare you any dinner,' Fiona said regretfully. 'I was so frightened. And then I thought I must have dreamt it, because he looked so like Michael.'

'*What?*' Colin followed Fiona into the study. He saw the half full glass of whisky on the desk and picked it up. Fiona saw him.

'No, I wasn't drinking. Nell poured it for me, said I should have it for shock, but I didn't take more than a sip. I hate neat whisky.'

'Tell me exactly what happened.' Colin ushered his mother into the chair by the fire, then bent to put another log on. 'Was Eleanor here when it happened?'

'No. I rang her. I rang Simon but he wasn't there. I wanted to have someone with me, I was so scared and shaken.' Gradually the story came out. 'I was sitting in the dark, and at first I thought it must be you or even Mrs Burdett, but when I called out there was no answer. Then I heard him, going upstairs. The tread creaked, and you know it doesn't do that unless you step on it. He came down after a few minutes and rummaged through the pockets of our coats in the hall. My bag was there, too, and I watched him go through it, but I was too scared to stop him.'

'Just as well you didn't. He might have knocked you down, or worse.'

'He was standing in the hall and for a moment I caught a glimpse of his profile against the light from the window. I was startled, because he looked so like Michael.'

Colin felt himself go cold. 'He looked like my father?' he repeated.

'I know that's so silly. Eleanor said it proved I was dreaming and there hadn't been anyone at all. And I think she must have been right, because there hasn't been anything taken, not even any money from my bag. And all my jewellery is still upstairs, too. Have you ever heard of anyone breaking in and not taking anything? It doesn't make sense.'

'Have you called the police?' Colin asked.

'Well, I was going to, and then, when I found there was nothing missing, I thought I should look such a fool. I've no evidence that I hadn't dreamt it. Perhaps I did; Eleanor thinks I did. She was going on about my wanting to move on in my life and seeing Michael psychologically as an intruder stopping me. Perhaps she's right. All I know is, I was really frightened. But I'm all right now you are back. Look, I'll start making dinner. It won't take long to cook and I'll bring it in on trays in here. Colin, I'm sorry I was so stupid. Now I think about it, I was sitting here reminiscing about all the things that have happened in this house over the years, and I must have fallen asleep and dreamed it all.'

How he longed to tell her that she hadn't dreamed it, that it was more than likely that it had been Michael, coming back to look for something he had forgotten, but he had made a pact with Simon that they wouldn't say anything to her yet about their suspicions. He wasn't going to break that pact, though the suspicion was now a certainty, as far as he was concerned.

What could Michael have wanted, that he needed to risk coming back here to collect? There was very little in his bedroom now; there never had been much that might have had importance. And the things they'd taken from the flat – of course! That was it! Fiona had found a bunch of keys and brought them home with her. They must be what he was looking for. Now, what had she done with them? Colin didn't want to ask her; it would make her think that he, too, thought the intruder was Michael and she would realise that he thought his father was still alive. He thought back to their time in the flat, visualising his mother holding up the bunch of keys, then taking them himself to try them against his own house key, trying them in the lock at the flat. Then what? He'd handed them back to Fiona and she had dropped them into her handbag. The chances were that she had forgotten them by the time they reached home, and they would still be there when Michael had looked through her bag.

If the intruder had been a genuine, if rather unusual robber, keys would be a very useful thing to take. Fiona kept her own set of house keys in her bag, too. If they were still there, but the flat keys were not...

Colin went into the hall and picked up Fiona's handbag. Feeling like a thief himself, he opened it and searched inside. He recognised her own bunch of keys, with front door and car keys, still there, but there was no sign of the other bunch.

It had to have been Michael. This incident alone convinced him that his father was still alive. So, who was buried in the grave in the churchyard? He glanced at his watch. Would Simon be home by now? He needed to talk to him urgently, but he'd have to wait until he could be sure his mother wouldn't overhear him.

He went back into the study and in a short time she appeared with the tea trolley, laden with plates, a bottle of wine and glasses. 'I thought we ought to have something nice to drink with this,' she said. 'And, frankly, I could do with cheering up. Now, can you manage on your lap or do you want to sit up at the desk?'

Colin was hungry, but he was also impatient to speak to Simon. He forced himself to eat and talk to Fiona, soothing her concerns. 'Of course I don't think you are going mad,' he told her again. 'Eleanor likes to think she knows all about psychoanalysis but she doesn't know anything. You know how she reads weird books and comes up with all sorts of strange ideas. You're the sanest, most balanced person I can imagine. She's the batty one.'

Fiona giggled. 'You'd better not let her hear you say that! But then, if I did really see someone come into the house, why didn't he take anything?'

How he longed to tell her! 'Probably decided that the jewellery you have wouldn't fetch much, or too easy to trace. And these days, credit cards aren't so easy to use without being caught. Perhaps he thought we had much more valuable things than we have. I don't know. Perhaps he was looking round to see what we *do* have, with the idea of coming back if he thought it was worth it.'

Fiona shivered. 'Oh, I do hope not! Well, if he does, we might have moved out by then, and all he'll find is an empty house! At least, I'll be sending off some of the pictures to an auction house in a day or so, and I suppose they are the only really valuable things here.'

He let her talk, seeing that she was recovering from her fright. As soon as they had finished eating Fiona loaded up the trolley and took it into the kitchen. Colin heard her clearing up the cooking utensils she'd used, and took his chance to run upstairs to the telephone extension in her bedroom. There was no telephone in the kitchen.

'I've just this minute arrived back,' Simon said, answering Colin's call. Colin briefly told him what had happened. 'Poor girl! It must have been a frightening experience for her!' Simon commiserated. 'Sounds like it was definitely Michael, if the keys were the only thing taken. That's proof enough for me that he's still with us.'

'But in that case, who is in that grave?'

'That's the question. We ought to see if we can't get an exhumation order. Not sure how we go about doing that.'

'I could ask the vicar. After all, he conducted the funeral,' Colin said.

'No, don't do that. It would alert the whole village that there was something up. I'll ask around at my end, in a general way, so that nobody knows why I'm asking. I'll be in touch with you again as soon as I've found out. We'd better meet at the Farrier's again, can't risk telephoning you.'

'Can't we tell Mum? She thought she was going mad, and Eleanor didn't help much, trying to persuade her that she imagined the whole thing. I tried to reassure her she hadn't, without, I *think*, letting her make the connection that it must be Dad. But she's not stupid; she'll realise there's something strange going on. We have to tell her.'

'She'll have to know if he's exhumed,' Simon said. 'But I think we should tell her together. I'm bringing her here to dinner tomorrow night. I won't say anything until I've spoken to you again but I agree, we will have to tell her soon.'

Colin felt dissatisfied when he put the receiver down. All very well for Simon, but he had to live in the same house as

Fiona, talk to her and all the while he felt he was deceiving her. He *knew* Michael wasn't dead, and Fiona had a right to know, too.

Fortunately, Fiona decided on an early night, after her nerve-shattering experience. 'I'll take a book up with me,' she said. 'Something light and absorbing. One of the old Agatha Christies will be just right. Colin, don't worry about me, dear, I really am all right. Whether he was real or a figment of my imagination, he's gone, and it's over, and you are here now so I feel perfectly safe.'

Colin took special care over checking the door and window locks before he, too, went upstairs. He didn't, though, go to his own room straight away.

He went into Michael's room and shut the door quietly before turning on the light. Most of Michael's clothes were gone from the drawers and wardrobe now, just one or two shirts and a pair of casual trousers that Fiona wondered if Colin would ever care to wear. He wouldn't, even though they fitted reasonably well.

He opened drawers in the tallboy, but they were mostly empty. He remembered that he had taken most of the diaries and other papers down to the end of the garden to put on a bonfire, but in the end he hadn't wanted to destroy anything, so had put them in the shed. As far as he knew, they were still there. He must have a very close look at everything again tomorrow.

Fiona seemed quite recovered by the next morning. She claimed to have slept well, due to the bottle of wine with dinner. 'Simon is taking me to see his home tonight,' she informed Colin. 'He's giving me dinner. Not cooking himself, he assured me. I'm looking forward to seeing his place. I've often wondered what it would be like.'

'He is very fond of you, you know,' Colin said. 'In fact, he's in love with you. Touching, really. Like an old teenager.'

'Cynic!' She punched him playfully on his arm. 'You wait until you find yourself someone and then you'll know what it's like. But haven't you found her already? What about this girl you've been going up to London to see? The one that came to the funeral, wasn't it?'

'She's not a girlfriend. Not really.' Colin shrugged, wanting to change the subject. He wasn't sure how the situation with Anthea stood now, and perhaps he ought to try so see her again and find out. He liked her and wasn't about to lose her without doing his utmost to persuade her to go out with him again. It was Moira, he was convinced, who had influenced Anthea against him. Thinking of Moira, it occurred to him that it seemed quite likely that she, too, might know that Michael was still alive. Perhaps, now he had to give up the London flat, she had offered him somewhere to stay at her home. They had been close once. They might still be close. He decided that as well as a visit to see Anthea he would also try to see Moira. The only trouble was, he didn't know where she lived, and, unless he managed to learn it from Anthea, he would need to see Moira at Brightmans' offices, and that might prove difficult.

Simon came to collect Fiona at six o'clock. She was ready for him, dressed in one of her favourite frocks; a dark green silk which suited her colouring well. Colin noticed Simon's look of approval as he stepped into the hall and gave Fiona a formal kiss of greeting.

'What are you doing about a meal tonight?' Simon asked, turning to him. 'You'd be welcome to come along as well, you know.'

'About as welcome as a rainy Bank Holiday,' Colin grinned at him behind Fiona's back. 'I'm going to be busy tonight. I shall go through the whole house, looking for anything we might have missed.'

Fiona caught part of the remark and misheard. 'Yes, it would be nice if you could begin clearing out all the stuff we've accumulated over the years. We'll have to think about doing it soon. I've already told the estate agent to put the house on the market, and he seems to think we won't have any problem finding a buyer. Simon, I'll collect my shawl and then I'll be ready.' She ran lightly upstairs and Colin watched Simon's eyes follow her.

'We'll have to tell her,' he murmured. 'I can't go on deceiving her and I can see you are going to have a difficult evening if you don't tell her yourself.'

'I want us to tell her together,' Simon said. 'That's why I wondered if you wanted to come back with us tonight.'

'And ruin her evening? No, I don't think so.'

'It will ruin her evening if I tell her tonight, anyway,' Simon said sadly. 'Look, we must talk again. Tomorrow at the Farrier's? We'll plan how we're going to tell her. And I'll have found out about getting an exhumation order by then.'

Fiona was coming down the stairs now and even Colin could see how the years seemed to have dropped away from her. She looked so happy, she must have looked very like this when she first knew Simon, he thought. He wondered uneasily how she would react to what they were going to have to tell her.

'Goodbye, children. Enjoy yourselves. I won't wait up,' he teased, seeing them into Simon's car.

As soon as they were gone he was upstairs, this time to the attic, to see if there were any forgotten papers of Michael's that might give him some clues about his father's secret life.

Fiona sat beside Simon as he drove down country lanes in the gathering dusk. She felt a deep happiness within herself. This evening was going to be special, she knew it.

The journey took about three quarters of an hour, and during it neither of them spoke much. Simon was concentrating on his driving, while Fiona daydreamed happily beside him. At last they turned into a gateway with a short drive up to an attractive, detached house in a road of smart, family homes.

'This is it,' Simon said. 'Some people keep saying it's too big for one person and I should move to a flat, but I like the house. I've lived here a good many years now and I don't want to move.'

'It's beautiful,' Fiona said. The house appealed to her at once; it had a welcoming feel and she knew she could feel at home here. There were lights on in several rooms and she looked at Simon in surprise.

'Mrs Eggerton said she'd stay and look after the meal until it was served. She's a good soul,' Simon explained, seeing her look.

'And of course she will need to check me out. I'm sure she's as protective of you as my Mrs Burdett would be of me,' Fiona laughed.

If she had had any qualms about Mavis Eggerton's approval they were dispersed as soon as Fiona entered the warm, welcoming hall. Simon's housekeeper opened the door and beamed at her. 'I'm delighted to meet you, Ma'am,' she said. 'Shall I take your shawl? There's sherry or gin and tonic in the sitting room, and dinner will be ready in about half an hour.'

'Thank you. It's good of you to stay and look after everything. I know you have a family of your own to get home to,' Fiona replied, thus earning top marks in Mavis's book for thoughtfulness.

'Would you like to see over the house?' Simon asked, after they had warmed themselves by the fire and Fiona had drunk a gin and tonic. 'I feel a bit like an estate agent, but you did express an interest in seeing where I live. It's not as illustrious as Little Paddocks, but – '

'I'm glad of that,' Fiona said quickly. 'That place was always wrong for us. I've never liked it and I won't have any regrets when I leave it. I have my eye on one or two places in the village but I'll have to see what Colin wants to do, before I make any decisions about buying.'

Seeing over Simon's well-cared-for house, Fiona couldn't help wondering to herself what it might be like if she were to come and live here with him. She found she liked the idea, she could happily enjoy this house, and, after all, it was less than an hour's drive from the village if she wanted to visit friends. What friends, she asked herself. There was only Eleanor that she really cared about, living nearby. Winchester was a lovely, busy city and she would easily find plenty to do and new friends in the area.

What was she thinking of? Simon hadn't actually asked her to marry him yet, though she had a distinct feeling that tonight would be the night that he would. And she would say yes, and wish he had asked her that same question thirty years ago.

The meal was excellent, just as she had been sure it would be. Mavis Eggerton served it discreetly, then as soon as they were on the main course said to Simon, 'I'll be off now, Sir. Your dessert is on the sideboard with the cheese when you are ready for it. Just leave everything and I'll clear it away when I come tomorrow morning.'

'Mavis, this is delicious,' Fiona said, earning herself even more brownie points. 'At least, we can take all the used dishes out to the kitchen afterwards.'

'I hope you won't try washing up in that dress!' Mavis exclaimed, shocked. 'It's far too good to be wearing going into the kitchen. Really lovely it is, Ma'am.'

After they had finished eating, Simon took her by the hand and led her back to the sitting room. 'Brandy and coffee?' he asked.

'Not for me, thanks. That was a superb meal. I feel replete.' She sat down on the sofa, drawn up to one side of the fire, and leant back against the cushions. Simon poured himself some coffee and came to sit beside her. He left the cup on a side table and took her hand in his. 'Fiona, you know I love you,' he said. 'You must have known I've always loved you. Whatever happens in the future, I never want to lose you, now I've found you again.'

She frowned. What did he mean? Why should he think it was likely that he would lose her?

'When I move from Little Paddocks, I won't be going far,' she said. She had been wondering about the wisdom of thinking of buying another house, if Simon had plans to ask her to live with him here. With or without marriage, she would say yes, though she knew he was the old-fashioned kind of man who wouldn't ask her without an offer of marriage. And now that she was a widow and free, there was no reason for him not to ask her.

'One day, perhaps, we will be together, but not just yet. There are reasons – I can't explain but I will, very soon.' He looked unhappy, and she longed to put her arms round him and say that she loved him too, and she would be his, whenever he wanted, but his words gave her a cold feeling in the pit of her stomach. Did he have ghosts in his past which he needed to exorcise first? Did the memories of Margaret, his first wife, still haunt him?

'Simon, I – I do understand.' She didn't. She had been so sure that tonight he would ask her to marry him, and now he was telling her he couldn't. Instinctively, she had drawn away from him and then saw the hurt in his eyes as she did so.

'There are things we have to talk about. But not now,' Simon said. 'Look, darling, it's getting late. Would you like to stay the night? There's a spare room ready if you want.'

'And what would Mavis say when she arrived tomorrow morning? Our reputations would be in tatters!' Fiona tried to make a joke of it, but she was hurt. Simon was backing away, she could sense it. She had thought that he would have made his intentions plain tonight, at least, but it seemed that he had changed his mind.

'I'd better go home,' she said. 'But it's a long way if you are going to drive and then come back here. If you'd prefer me to stay – '

'No. Of course I'll drive you home. That's why I didn't have a brandy after dinner. And the beauty of retirement is that I don't have to be up early tomorrow.'

Fiona followed him into the hall and retrieved her shawl. Simon picked up an extra rug which he wrapped round her knees once she was in the passenger seat. She felt cosseted, but there was still the lingering sense of disappointment. Her mouth twisted in a rueful smile. In her handbag was a toothbrush and a spare pair of knickers and now she was feeling like the most awful fool imaginable, even worse that the foolishness she had felt when she had described to Simon how she had been dozing in the dark last night and thought she had seen an intruder who looked like Michael. His expression had convinced her that he didn't want to say what he clearly must have thought, that she was beginning to crack under the strain. Perhaps, she thought sadly, that was the reason he had backed away tonight. He wasn't sure he wanted to ally himself to someone who was on course for a mental breakdown.

Colin made a thorough search of the attic while his mother was dining with Simon. He knew she had moved some things there from Michael's bedroom but although he thought there was probably nothing of interest, he needed to be sure.

He scrutinised every scrap of paper, every page of every old diary, though most of the recent diaries were still in the shed in the garden. He'd deal with them when it was light.

There was nothing that looked in the least likely to give any clue about Michael's past activities, or his present whereabouts. Finally, dusty and disheartened, he came downstairs and decided to give up. It must have been the keys Michael had wanted, and nothing more. He wondered what doors they opened and tried to remember what kind of keys they had been. At least two Yale, a Chubb, clearly main door keys, and a couple of smaller keys which might belong to interior doors, desk, anything. It looked, he thought, as if Michael had somewhere else to live, but it might be anywhere.

He decided, while Fiona was not there, to check through the desk in the study. She used it mostly, but Michael might have left something there and forgotten. He felt embarrassed to be looking through his mother's personal papers, but he told himself he really needed to be thorough if he was to be sure not to miss anything which might help tell them what Michael had been doing, and where he was now.

Fiona was not a tidy person. He found old, empty envelopes from letters already long dealt with and discarded. There were old receipts from years back, even old supermarket checkout lists screwed up and left at the back of the desk. He took them all out, hesitated, then threw them away. Fiona had suggested he begin clearing out everything in readiness for moving house so she could hardly complain if he worked on her desk.

The pile of rubbish grew bigger. He tidied as he went. Now he was on to the drawers that ran down one side of the desk. There wasn't much in them, old diaries that he knew were Fiona's so didn't open, some broken pens and a few letters from family and friends that were dated several months previously. Right at the back of one drawer, screwed into a ball so that he nearly missed it, was one more scrap of paper. He was about to throw it straight into the waste paper basket, then stopped himself and smoothed it out.

He stared at it in delight. He had struck oil. Here was the letter, on headed notepaper, from the undertakers, that Fiona had thought she had thrown away. He read it eagerly. The notepaper looked genuine, the address somewhere in the East End of London, and the letter stated that they had instructions to deliver Michael's coffin to her local parish church; they had been in touch with the vicar there and all the funeral costs had already been met from a pre-paid funeral plan which Michael had taken out earlier.

This was something he must show Simon tomorrow, but before that he would pay these undertakers a visit and learn what more he could from them.

When he had finished with Fiona's desk he went back upstairs to Michael's room for a last look round. All the drawers in the tallboy were empty, and the wardrobe, too. He pulled them out, then pushed them back shut viciously. Michael had left nothing for them to find, but he couldn't destroy the undertaker's letter. That was the one and only clue he and Simon could follow up now. Damn you, Dad. Why did you do this to us? he muttered. Where are you? What did you want all that money *for*?

The top drawer of the tallboy was lighter than the others, probably through more frequent use. Colin pulled it out, then slammed it back, but not straight, and the drawer jammed. He pulled it right out again and was about to reclose it along the runners when he noticed something stuck to the back of the drawer. He put it on the bed and turned it round. The oldest hiding trick and one he'd seen in films on TV and never thought of; there was an envelope taped to the outside of the back of the drawer, completely hidden until the whole drawer was removed.

His hand shook as he peeled away the tape. From its brittleness he thought it must have been there some time, months, possibly, and Michael must have forgotten it. He'd made a very good job of destroying everything else.

The envelope was empty, but there was a name on the outside, Harry Sykes, and two telephone numbers, one Colin thought was a mobile. The other had an area code he did not recognise.

Simon's going to be pleased with me over both these, he thought, putting the envelope carefully in his pocket alongside the undertaker's letter and replacing the drawer. Tomorrow morning he would go to London early and see Anthea. Afterwards, he would go to the undertakers and find out what more he could, and finally, being careful not to leave it too late so that the offices would be closed, he would try to see Moira at Brightmans. Already, as he made his way to his bedroom, he was thinking up a scheme to trick his way in to her office. He was determined that she would tell him all she knew and he felt sure she knew more than she had said so far.

CHAPTER 11

COLIN WAS UP EARLY THE FOLLOWING DAY. He had thought his mother would still be asleep, since she had probably come back late from Simon's house. That was, if she had come back at all. She had gone with him last night looking so happy and eager he would not have been surprised if she had stayed the night. Simon would have asked her to marry him and she would have undoubtedly said yes. They would have to wait for the wedding until Michael had been found, so that Fiona could divorce him, but he would be found soon, Colin had no doubt. Simon would have a few problems explaining that, without telling Fiona that he knew Michael was still alive, but Colin was sure he would have managed it.

He put his head round the door of his mother's room without really expecting to see her. She was sitting at her dressing table, fully dressed, brushing her hair with fierce, angry strokes.

'I didn't expect you to be up, or even here,' Colin said apologetically. 'Do you want a cup of tea? I'm having a quick breakfast and then I'm off to London. I want an early start. Have a good night with Simon?'

'Since you ask, no, I did not,' Fiona snapped at him. 'He thinks I'm going mad. I'm sure of it. He doesn't want to marry me. In fact, I'm not sure he even wants to see me any more.'

'Of course he does! He's devoted to you! What on earth happened to make you think that?'

'It's either that or he's still mourning his late wife. He as good as told me he won't marry me. And I thought – I suppose men do get cold feet when it comes to the final plunge into marriage. What do you think, dear?'

'I think Simon adores you and doesn't think you are going mad, or anything of the sort. He just – well, he's not sure whether you are really over Dad's death properly yet. He doesn't want to rush you into anything before you are ready. After all, it's only been a few weeks since the funeral.'

'Have you been talking to Simon about all this?' Fiona said suspiciously. 'How come you know what he's thinking?'

'I'm a man, aren't I? It's how I would think if I was in his situation,' Colin said.

'I feel as if I have been a widow for years. I realise now I didn't know Michael at all. He wasn't the man I married. I don't think I knew him very well even when we were first married; I was swept off my feet by him. Does that sound awfully shallow to you?'

'No, it doesn't. At least you stayed married for more than twenty-five years. A great many marriages don't last anything like that long. Now, do you want me to bring you up a cup of tea? That's what I came to see, not to sort out your love life with Simon.'

Fiona smiled reluctantly. 'Some love life! But I must say, his home is beautiful, and his housekeeper cooked a superb meal for us. I was hoping for too much, too soon. Colin, you're wiser than I am. I'm coming down now and we'll have breakfast together. I won't delay you if you're rushing off to town. I hope your love life isn't as complicated as mine.'

It was easier to pretend that he was going to London to see Anthea and for no other reason. He hoped to catch her at home before she left to visit her first client of the day, and arrived at Chomley Mews shortly after nine o'clock.

There was no reply to his knock. He peered through the letterbox and sensed a feeling of emptiness in the room beyond. Anthea must have had an early appointment and he'd missed her. If he had arrived earlier, she would probably have been too busy to talk to him anyway. He decided to come back in the evening, when she was more likely to be home, and in the meantime, visit the East End and try to track down the undertaker who had dealt with Michael's funeral.

He took a series of underground trains and eventually arrived in a run-down area of east London. He found the street named on the headed notepaper and was surprised to find there was a genuine undertakers at the address given. He had half expected to find that no such place existed.

The shop door opened into a small room with an enquiry desk. There was no one around but there was a bell on the desk, so he rang it. A man in his forties, dressed in a dark suit, answered his summons. He introduced himself as Martin Simmons, and Colin recognised the name as one of three named on the notepaper heading. He produced the letter and asked if he could give some details about the arrangements that had been made and who had made them. He didn't want to explain who he was at that moment; he was not sure who he was dealing with and for all he knew, these undertakers might be in on the plan to fake Michael's death.

The man invited him into a room at the back of the shop, a comfortable sitting room where clients could be dealt with privately and sympathetically. He read through the letter carefully, frowning.

'I don't remember this at all,' he said at last. 'Though the notepaper is clearly ours. Excuse me while I look up our files and see what records we have.' He left the room and Colin looked round while he waited. The place seemed perfectly genuine. Out of the window he could see a yard, where a hearse and two black Daimlers were parked. Beyond them was a workshop and sounds of sawing and hammering came to him faintly.

The man returned. 'We have no record of sending out this letter, though it's on our notepaper,' he said. 'But it couldn't have been written here. This letter was typed; on a rather old machine, I suspect. All our correspondence is on computer. Has been for several years now.'

Colin decided the only way forward was to explain a bit more. Mr Simmons didn't seem as if he had anything to hide, and this place appeared to be a *bona fide* undertakers. He explained about the strange circumstances of his father's death, without suggesting that he suspected the death was faked. 'He died of a sudden heart attack, alone, in his flat in Paddington. Neither my mother or I ever saw him or was consulted about the arrangements for his body. Naturally, she – and I – feel unhappy about the situation. It's hard to grieve when one has been denied the opportunity to say a proper goodbye.'

Martin Simmons nodded sympathetically. 'This is a very strange situation. It would seem that someone has been using our name without our knowledge or consent. We have no record of conducting a funeral outside London in the third week of August. And we don't have any record of a funeral plan in the name of Michael Latimer. I'd definitely know if we did, I deal with them myself.'

'Could there be a rival undertakers' company in the area?' Colin asked.

'We are the only ones around here. And what would be the point of someone else dealing with a funeral that appears to have already been paid for? Why use our notepaper? No, I don't understand this at all. Bear with me a little longer, if you please. I'd like to speak to one of my colleagues about this.'

Colin wondered uneasily if Simmons would realise there had been something illegal going on and would insist on calling in the police. He didn't want the police involved until he and Simon had had a chance of tracking down Michael themselves. It looked as if it had been a well planned operation involving several people in faking Michael's death and any hint that they might be discovered would mean the whole operation would go underground, disappear along with any chance of ever finding Michael or discovering what he had been doing these last months.

Simmons returned, looking puzzled. 'My partner, Mr Craig, remembers something which he thought little about at the time, but in the light of this, seems rather strange. It was about the second week in August, he said. Two men came into the office and asked to buy a coffin. That's unusual, without asking for funeral arrangements as well. He might have thought there was something fishy about it, but the men explained that they were from a small television company and wanted the coffin as a prop. It sounded reasonable enough. They talked a bit about the film they were making and it sounded like a rather good comedy. He says he remembers saying he'd look out for it when it was screened and watch it. He doesn't remember them saying the name of their company, but they paid in cash straight away and took the coffin away in a van they'd brought with them. He didn't think any more about it. We always have spare coffins in the workshop and it wasn't a problem to sell one. We don't just make them to order.'

'But if someone wanted to stage a funeral without having a professional funeral company how would they go about getting a hearse and funeral cars?' Colin asked. 'We had a hearse and two Daimlers, as well as pall bearers who were dressed in dark suits. They looked as if they worked for a genuine company.'

'Easy enough to hire a hearse and cars,' Simmons said. 'There's a car hire firm near here and we often use their services if we have more than two funerals on the same day. And anyone can dress up in a dark suit and carry a coffin. There's not much to learning that, though to be a proper undertaker's assistant there's a lot more to it.'

'Thank you. You've been very helpful.' Colin stood up to leave.

'Are you thinking there might be something irregular about this funeral?' Simmons asked. He seemed loath to let Colin go. 'If so, it might need investigation at an official level.'

'No, I don't think there was anything seriously amiss.'

'There'd be official documents; death certificates. If there was no professional undertaker involved, it would be difficult to produce proper documentation. Don't you think you ought to make further enquiries, if you suspect something is not quite right?'

'I will make further enquiries. It's just that I don't have anything much to go on yet,' Colin said.

'We ought to be asking questions, too,' Simmons said. 'Someone has been writing letters using our own headed notepaper and it wasn't us. I don't like the sound of this at all, Mr – Latimer.'

'Look, I can't take it any further on the evidence and information I have at present, but I promise I'll get back to you and put you fully in the picture if there has been anything illegal,' Colin said. 'But surely, it isn't illegal to hold a funeral service without using a professional undertaker?'

'No. There are these so-called organic funerals, where people are buried in woodland in cardboard coffins and they have some sort of pagan ritual attached to them.' Simmons sounded dismissive. 'We've done some of them, but we know of people who've wanted to cut costs and do it all themselves. So long as there's a proper death certificate – '

'Oh, there is. I've seen it.' Colin was sure it was a fake but he wasn't about to admit that and have Simmons insist on calling in the police.

'Well, then. I must say, we don't much like the DIY methods, but so long as they stick to certain rules, we can't complain. We've enough genuine business to keep us going. But I don't care for their use of our notepaper.'

'Thank you for seeing me. I'm sorry to have taken up so much of your time. I have to go now, I have another appointment at the other side of London.' Colin was halfway through the door as he spoke. 'If there's anything else, I'll be in touch.' Whether he intended to contact these undertakers again or not, he was not sure, but he had to get out of there before he became embroiled in more complications.

He took the tube to the City and arrived outside the imposing offices of Brightmans and Wellings, Stockbrokers and Financial Consultants. The place looked like a fortress; Colin doubted if he would be allowed inside the door, let alone to get as far as Moira Ransom's office. There was only one thing for it, to do what one of his wilder student friends had avocated: use bluff.

He strode firmly towards the main doors. There was a doorman in uniform standing outside. Colin nodded to him briefly and, he hoped, haughtily. 'Charles Bradshaw to see Mrs Ransom,' he announced, using a name he had invented on his way there.

The man stepped aside at once, opening the door and ushering Colin inside. 'The enquiry desk is just ahead of you, Sir,' he murmured.

Encouraged by his first success, Colin walked on purposefully towards the desk. There was a young, smart and very pretty girl sitting behind it. She looked up and gave him a professional smile. 'May I help you, Sir?'

'Charles Bradshaw, to see Mrs Monica Ransom. I have an appointment,' Colin announced. He managed what he hoped was a rather patronising smile.

'One moment, please.' She consulted a list on the desk, running a well-manicured finger down the page. 'I'm sorry, I don't seem to have your name here.' She looked up, the smile absent now.

'That's very incompetent. My appointment was for twelve-fifteen. If you'll tell me which lift to take, I'll go straight up to Mrs Ransom's office. I cannot abide lateness.' The time, Colin had already noticed on the large clock above the desk, was twelve-thirteen.

'I'm sorry, Sir. I'll have to ring through to Mrs Ransom's office and confirm.'

The girl picked up a receiver on her desk. Colin made a mumble of irritation and glared at her. 'And while you are doing that I'll be on my way,' he snapped. He had seen a row of lifts at the back of the entrance hall and that they were manned, again by uniformed staff. He walked up to them, trying not to look as if he were running. 'Mrs Moira Ransom's office,' he told the attendant brusquely. 'And hurry up, I'm late as it is.'

Colin was learning that an authorative tone worked with the uniformed staff, but others were not so easily manipulated. As the doors closed on the lift he saw the girl at the desk stand up and begin to hurry towards him, calling 'Sir! One moment, Sir! You can't – '

'Like an officious bloodhound, that girl you have on the desk,' he remarked to the lift attendant. 'Determined to make me late, just because I'm running it a bit fine, anyway. Now, if you could point me in the direction of Mrs Ransom's office I'd be grateful. I know she hates unpunctuality as much as I do.'

This, accompanied by a conspiratorial grin, did the trick. Colin resisted the urge to punch the air and shout 'Yes!' as the lift attendant nodded sympathetically.

'That Miss Bossyboots always holds people up when they come in to see executive staff. Likes to throw her weight around, that one. Now, if you turn left as you come out of the lift, Mrs Ransom's office is third door down on the right.'

'Thank you very much.' Colin stepped out of the lift on the third floor, hardly believing his luck and how easy it had been. 'Old Jonners Benson was right. Bluff works every time,' he thought, then wished he hadn't tempted Providence. He still had at least one further hurdle to pass. Moira would certainly have a secretary or assistant in the outer office and by now the girl on the desk would have alerted her by phone.

He pushed open the third door on the right, as instructed, to be confronted, as he had expected, with an outer office containing three desks, all staffed by people sitting at computer terminals.

'I've come to see Mrs Moira Ransom,' he announced to the nearest, a woman in her forties who looked discouragingly formidable.

'Are you Charles Bradshaw?' She had definitely been called by the girl on the desk downstairs.

'Yes. And I really do have to see Mrs Ransom.' He stood squarely in front of her, daring her to refuse him.

'I'll speak to Mrs Ransom. You don't appear to be on her appointments list for today.' The woman walked across to a door at the far end and went inside, closing it behind her. Colin was left standing, being stared at by the other two members of staff, a spotty youth with his wrists sticking out of his suit jacket, and a girl keyboarding at a fast speed while she continued to stare. Neither offered him a seat, though there was a sofa and a pair of leather armchairs in a corner.

The woman came back into the office. Colin expected she would ask his business and had begun concocting a story about seeing an advertisement for a trainee. Not knowing exactly what Moira's position in the company was, he thought he would have to be vague. Anything so long as he got to see her for a few minutes; that was all he wanted, all he could hope for.

To his surprise she said, 'Mrs Ransom will see you now. She can only spare you a few minutes because she has another appointment due. Come this way.'

Colin could barely hide his astonishment. The woman ushered him towards the inner office and he could only think that Moira was curious to know who he was and how he had managed to bluff his way this far. He was steered inside and the door was closed behind him.

Moira sat behind a large, impressive looking desk, with a computer terminal at one side and a couple of telephones on the other.

'Hallo, Colin. I thought it might be you,' she said. 'What do you want?'

For a moment he was tongue-tied, too startled at actually seeing her to say anything. Then his practical side reasserted itself.

'Sorry to con my way in to see you like this,' he began. 'But I thought you wouldn't see me if I gave my real name.'

'I knew it was you from the description the girl on the desk gave me,' Moira said. 'What is it this time? I have already told you all I can. Far more than I ought to have done, as you must realise.'

'Yes, and I was grateful for that. But we – I mean I – I mean, a friend and I have been investigating Michael's death and we have come to the realisation that he faked it. That he isn't dead. I wanted to know if you knew about that, and if you know where he is.'

'It's news to me if he isn't dead, but it doesn't surprise me. Nothing that man does is likely to surprise me.'

'We think he was still staying in his London flat, but the lease is up in a day or so, so he will have to find somewhere else. I thought perhaps he might be staying with you.'

'Not a chance! I wouldn't have him stay with me even if I knew where he was! Listen, Colin. I haven't seen your father since he left Brightmans nearly a year ago. Nor have I heard anything about what he has been doing since. I don't want to know. And, before you ask, I know nothing about what he did with the money he took from this company. He wouldn't say. I don't think he told anyone, certainly not anyone here. I can't help you any more.'

'All right, I accept that. But there's one thing you do know, you can tell me. Anthea has given me the brush-off and I suspect it was because you influenced her. Why do you object to me? I'm not like my father, I'm not a crook and I genuinely like and respect your daughter. I would never hurt her. What's your real objection?'

'You think my opinion carries any weight with Anthea?' Moira sounded amused. 'It's true I thought she could do better. You are a jobless ex-student with no prospects, but if Anthea was interested in you there wouldn't be anything I or anyone else could do to influence her. You're typical of all young men, can't accept that you've been dumped by a girl. Anthea is a smart girl and has an excellent career with a good future before her. Why should she be interested in you?'

'I wondered that more than once myself,' Colin said. 'But at first we seemed to hit it off together rather well, and then, suddenly, right after I had met you, she wouldn't have anything more to do with me. Without giving me any reason. You must admit, I was bound to connect the two together.'

'I suppose so. But if you know Anthea at all, you will realise she makes up her own mind about things. She wouldn't have listened to anything I said.'

Something was coming to the surface in Colin's mind. He believed Moira when she said that she hadn't seen

Michael, and now he had nothing to lose. There was one more thing he wanted to know.

'You told me that you had had an affair with my father, many years ago,' he said slowly. 'and you want me to stop seeing your daughter. Is it, perhaps, because she is Michael's child too? Are Anthea and I half-brother and sister?'

He couldn't decipher the expression on Moira's face. It registered shock, but was there guilt there too, or astonishment?

'Is that what you think?' She stared at him, speechless, for a moment, then began to laugh. 'Oh, I like that one! You really have the most fantastic imagination of anyone I've ever met, Colin! First, you think your father has faked his own death, then you think I'm trying to stop you having an affair with your half-sister! Well, I almost wish Michael was around to hear you! I hope you are not going to broadcast either of these tales to anyone, because I can assure you you will be in big trouble if you do.'

'I'm not likely to say anything about my father's past affairs, if only for my mother's sake,' Colin said stiffly. 'But it seems to me that it's the one good reason for stopping Anthea seeing me. Does she know?'

'All Anthea knows is that she isn't interested in you any more. Heavens, are you such an arrogant creature that you cannot be made to believe that she isn't interested in you, never has been and is never likely to be? Now, I have to ask you to leave, because I am very busy and I have no further time to waste on this rubbish. Please leave the building and do not try to see me or my daughter again. If you ever try to come to Brightmans in the future, I shall inform Security who you are and they will remove you at once. They will recognise you, your image has been caught on the CCTV cameras already.'

'Don't worry. I'll go now. Thank you for seeing me. For what it's worth, I believe you when you say you haven't seen my father since he left here. I don't suppose he would want to see you, either. You were responsible for his dismissal, weren't you?'

'I have nothing further to say to you.' Moira's hand was on a buzzer at her desk. She must have pressed it because the woman who had spoken to him earlier appeared instantly at the door. If the doors had not been so stout, Colin might have thought she had been listening, but that seemed unlikely.

'Mr Bradshaw is leaving now. Please see him to the lift, Catherine,' Moira said. 'And ask the lift attendant to see him safely outside the premises.'

The woman gave Colin a contemptuous look. 'This way,' she said.

He felt as if he were being frogmarched down the passage. She summoned the lift and waited beside him until it arrived, then, unnecessarily he thought, relayed Moira's message that he was to be seen off the premises. He tried to make a joke of it to the lift attendant, but received nothing but a surly silence. He was walked to the door, passing the girl on the desk who glowered at him. There was a murmured conversation with the doorman, which sounded suspiciously like 'and don't let him come back in' and then Colin found himself standing on the pavement, wondering if he had really stumbled on one of his father's best kept secrets.

He realised he had not yet had any lunch. He found a café and bought himself a sandwich and a cup of coffee while he decided what to do next.

He wasn't going to go back home without making one more attempt to see Anthea. He thought she would tell him the truth and the more he thought about it, the more it made sense that Moira would want to discourage any friendship between them if Anthea was Michael's daughter.

A romance, yes, of course that was impossible, but friendship? He had often thought he would have liked a brother or sister. On balance, he would have preferred a sister. He didn't know why there had never been any more children and it wasn't something he had ever felt he could ask Fiona. If Anthea was his half-sister, he felt that would be rather nice. A bond that couldn't be broken. It was a pity that he could never make love to her, as he had often hoped he might one day, but a sister meant that at least he could keep her friendship. Anthea must know the truth, it went some way to explaining why she had come to Michael's funeral. The only problem was, what was Fiona going to think about it?

CHAPTER 12

FIONA SPENT THE DAY WITH MRS BURDETT, taking down the pictures that she planned to sell before the move. An auctioneer was coming the following day and she hoped his valuations would mean that she had enough money to pay for the move and keep herself and Colin until they were settled in a new home and Nigel Williams had sorted out how much money would be left for them after selling Little Paddocks.

'Oh, Ma'am, I am sorry you are leaving,' Mrs Burdett said for the umpteenth time. 'I shall miss coming to this lovely house.'

'Perhaps the people who buy it will be in need of someone to come in and clean for them,' Fiona said. 'I'd give you a glowing reference.'

'I couldn't. Wouldn't be the same,' Mrs Burdett sniffed.

'I'll still need some help in my new place,' Fiona offered. 'It'll be smaller, but you know how hopeless I am at cooking and everything domestic. I'll need you to keep the new place looking nice. And without you, how is Master Colin going to have any decent cakes and pastries?'

Mrs Burdett cheered up a little, but she was still rather long-faced when the telephone afforded Fiona some relief.

'Fee, it's me, Eleanor. May I come over? You're not busy, are you?'

Fiona recognised the tone of voice that told her Eleanor wanted to talk about something. She was only too glad that the quarrel which had threatened their friendship not so long ago seemed to have blown over.

'Of course you can come over. I'm not doing anything in particular. Mrs Burdett and I are taking pictures down and dusting them, ready for the auctioneer tomorrow. We'd be glad of an excuse to stop and have a cup of tea.'

'I'll be right over. Give me five minutes.' Anyone else driving between Eleanor's cottage and Little Paddocks would have taken at least ten by car, but Eleanor drove like a racing driver, disregarding the fact that the lanes between their homes were narrow and winding. Fiona was always expecting to hear that she had crashed, driven into a hedge, or, worse, hit another car, but Eleanor seemed to have a charmed life where driving was concerned.

The squeal of brakes and a crunching sound of gravel being scraped along the drive, heralded her arrival.

'My, that Miss Pagett does drive fast,' Mrs Burdett commented. 'Look, Madam, we've taken all the pictures down now, so I can get on with cleaning them by myself. You take Miss Pagett into the study for a nice chinwag and I'll bring along coffee for both of you.'

'You sure you don't mind finishing off by yourself?'

'Lord no, Madam. All the hard work as needs two is done now. I'll stack 'em up in the hall for when the gentleman comes to see 'em tomorrow. Lovely, some of 'em. Real Old Masters, I'd say.'

'Hardly as valuable as that,' Fiona laughed, 'but I hope we'll be able to raise a reasonable amount of money. My husband said when he bought them that they were intended as an investment, and that the artists were likely to become more sought after as time passed. I hope so; I've lived with some of them that I didn't much care for. It would be galling to think I might as well not have bothered.' She opened the door to Eleanor and ushered her towards the study.

'Packing up already? So you really are moving out soon?' Eleanor looked at the bare walls and stacked pictures.

'Pretty soon. I'm sending these to auction tomorrow. I haven't had anyone come yet to look over the house, but the estate agent said he didn't think it would take long to find a buyer. And I've seen a nice place just outside the village that Colin and I might like.'

'So you're not going to move in with Simon Neville? I thought he'd be sure to whisk you off to his place as soon as he could.' Eleanor settled herself in one of the armchairs in the study and stretched her long legs out towards the fire.

'Simon and I like our independence,' Fiona said stiffly. 'Mrs Burdett will be bringing us some coffee presently, but would you like something stronger in the meantime?'

Eleanor shook her head, unwilling to take the hint and change the subject. 'So he hasn't asked you to marry him? I thought he might not, when it came to the crunch. They're like that, men. Shy away from commitment.'

'Michael didn't. And though it's nice to have Simon as a friend, I have my own life to lead and I am enjoying being single again.'

Eleanor nodded absently. 'You're lucky, Fee,' she said after a moment. 'You don't realise how lucky you are. You've managed to bury your past. Even with Simon coming back into your life, your past hasn't gone on haunting you, dragging you back. You can still live like a well-to-do middle class widow and no one need ever know you were once a two-bit typist from the East End who lived in a rented house with a lavvy at the end of the yard.'

'What, exactly, are you getting at?' Fiona asked. 'I've never lied about my background. My family was poor and I had a miserable job when I first left school. We all lived in pretty hard circumstances then, but that was a long time ago and life has changed for me a great deal since then, the same as it has changed for you, too. I'm not ashamed of my origins. If I had to, I'd go back there and it wouldn't worry me. Fortunately, I won't have to, and I have Colin and Michael to thank for that.'

Eleanor was in a very strange mood, Fiona thought. She wondered what had brought these remarks on, but, knowing her friend, she was sure it would all come out very soon.

Mrs Burdett brought in coffee and biscuits, and Eleanor made desultory talk about village matters until she had left, then reverted to their former conversation.

'It's all very well for you. You haven't anyone or anywhere to go back to, in the East End. All your links are gone now. No one there or here to know about your past.'

'Yes, I know my parents have been dead for years and there aren't any relatives living there now, but what has that got to do with it? I never minded anyone knowing where I was born and brought up, simply that no one ever asked me about it. What *are* you driving at, Nell?'

'My parents are still there. In the same road where we both grew up,' Eleanor said with a touch of bitterness. 'And Paul is there, too. You remember Paul, don't you?'

'Paul? Your little brother? Of course! The little tag-along who always wanted to come with us when we went out to places he was too young to go into,' Fiona said. 'You know, you've not mentioned him for years. How is he? Does he still live with your parents?'

'He still lives in the area. And he's not so much the little brother now. He was eight years younger than us, a little ten-year-old monster when we were going out with the gang. Now, he must be – oh, at least forty, I guess. But he hasn't changed much, over the years, from what I hear.'

'He was always getting into scrapes of some kind, I seem to remember,' Fiona said fondly. 'Full of mischief. But that was mostly boyish high spirits. At forty he must be well settled down. What is he doing now? Married, with a family, I suppose?'

'It might have been boyish high spirits at ten, but it didn't stop there. He's been on the wrong side of the law for most of his life, I gather. When I left home and vowed I wasn't ever going back, I lost touch with my whole family. I didn't want to hear from them, any more than they wanted to hear from me. I did hear some things, from time to time, none of it good. Paul's been in Borstal, then Wormwood Scrubs, more than once.'

'I never realised.' Fiona stretched out her hand to clasp Eleanor's in sympathy. 'I admit, I have often wondered – you broke away so completely from your family and never once mentioned them, I thought they must have died too, like mine. I'd forgotten about Paul completely.'

'I wish I could,' Eleanor said bitterly. 'I heard a couple of days ago, from one of our old neighbours who "thought I ought to know". The interfering busybody. Paul has apparently got himself into real trouble this time. Involved in some gang or other, hard men. He'd be out of his depth with them. He was never more than a car thief and burglar, but this, seemingly, is something different. I'm worried, Fee. If he's in real trouble, he might go down for a long time. And it would be in all the papers. You know what journalists are like, dig out all the dirt and scandal they can, especially if they can't find much in the way of hard facts. My parents' names and faces would be splashed all over the front pages, and so would mine. After all the years I've spent, distancing myself from all that! I couldn't stay here if it all came out. It would be the village scandal of all time. The locals would have a field day! What am I going to do, Fee?'

'Do you really think it's likely to happen? Would anyone really connect you with something happening in the East End of London? Pagett is a relatively common name and you've lived here nearly as long as we have. Surely, no one would think of you having anything to do with crooks?'

'They might dig up anything!' Eleanor said wildly. 'I shall have to go away! Now, before anything happens! Come with me, Fee. We'll flee the country together!'

'Now you're being ridiculous!' Fiona said crossly. 'Here, drink your coffee before it gets cold and calm down. Tell me some more about it all. You know, I've often wondered what you did when you ran away from home. I wasn't there then; Michael and I had just married and we were living the other side of London.'

'The posh side; the expensive side,' Eleanor sneered.

'Hardly posh. It was a poky little flat as I remember it, but it *was* a long way from my old home. I heard you'd gone, and then I didn't hear from you for years. Our little group broke up soon after that; Simon Neville went on to university, he had a wealthy uncle who helped him out financially, and the others disappeared. I never knew what happened to anyone else. I didn't try hard enough to keep in touch. I was so busy being a new housewife, or trying to, and I was happy with Michael and expecting Colin, that I forgot about all my old friends, even you. What did you do? How did you manage? You must have succeeded in whatever you did; you have a very nice house here now and enough money to keep you comfortably.'

'It wasn't always like that,' Eleanor said. 'I had some terrible jobs, far worse than you ever had. I worked at three jobs at once at one time, just to make enough to live. I had a day job in a shop; worked evenings in a pub, and did night shifts as a cleaner in an office.'

'I simply had no idea! Whenever did you sleep?'

'On the job, whichever job I was doing when I fell asleep. That's why they didn't last long. Trouble was, I didn't have any skills, I wasn't trained for anything, like you were. If I'd been sensible, I'd have learned to type and do shorthand like you, then at least I'd have been able to find a decent job.'

'But – you managed in the end. Look at you now, with a nice house in a lovely part of the country. You don't need to work and you wear good clothes and have an expensive car. How did you manage to succeed in the end?'

Eleanor didn't meet Fiona's eyes. She looked down, fiddling with the pleats on her skirt. 'Well, I had help,' she said evasively.

'You mean a legacy? Or you won the lottery and never told me?' Fiona was half joking, but she was nevertheless curious. She was discovering a new side to her friend, one she had never suspected, and she was intrigued.

'No, of course not. Who was there to leave me money? I had a friend, a man friend, and he – helped me get on my feet.'

'I had no idea,' Fiona said. 'You had a man friend but you never told me anything about him. Were you going to marry him?'

'It wasn't like that. Look, I shouldn't have said anything about it. It was all a bit – well, I had to be discreet and I never said anything to anyone. There was never any question of marriage. If it had been that sort of relationship, of course I would have told you. I'd have shouted it from the rooftops. But this wasn't. It's over now, anyway. Been over for some time, but he left me with enough money to live comfortably for the rest of my life, if I'm careful, and I'm grateful to him. Very grateful. I'd never betray him, break his confidence or mention his name to anyone. I really shouldn't have said anything to you about it. Just forget I ever mentioned it. I worked my socks off and had a lucky break. That's all you need to know about me.'

'Of course I won't say anything to anyone,' Fiona said. 'You know I don't discuss things with the people round here. I hardly talk to most of the locals, except to pass the time of day when I meet them in the village.'

'Let's talk about something else,' Eleanor said abruptly. 'I had to come and sound off about Paul. I've been so worried about him, ever since I heard what he'd been up to. I know you must think I'm a selfish cow to be thinking of myself and worrying about people knowing my background isn't as respectable as I've tried to make it look, but it isn't only that. I *am* worried about Paul. He's always been a drifter, and he didn't get lucky like I did. He's mixed up with the wrong sort of people, and there are a lot of them around, where he lives. If he went to prison for years, I don't know how he'd cope. And I don't know what I can do to help him.'

'Are you going back to London to try to see him? Perhaps you could talk to him, try to persuade him to break with them while he still can? He hasn't been arrested or anything yet, has he?'

'Not as far as I know. I don't know many details. I haven't been in touch with Paul, but I know where he is.'

'Could you bring him down here? Away from trouble, until things blow over a bit?'

Eleanor gave a contemptuous laugh. 'Here! That really *would* be asking for trouble! Half the Met might be hard on his heels! And he's not some Cockney kid from the slums who would benefit from a nice holiday in the country, you know! Fee, you simply have no idea how the other half lives!'

'Yes, I did once,' Fiona said gently. 'But perhaps I've forgotten, since I seem to have been far luckier in my life than you have. Nell, I wish I could help you, but I'm clearly out of my depth here. I can't advise you; all I can do is listen and sympathise, and reassure you that I'm sure nobody is going to point any fingers at you, in this village or anywhere. I certainly won't. We've been friends for more than forty years, and I hope we'll always remain friends. I'm sorry about Paul, but it's his problem, not yours. He made his own choices, just as you did. Keep thinking of that.'

'Thanks, Fee. You're a good friend. The best. I really don't deserve you.' To Fiona's surprise, Eleanor flung her arms round her neck and burst into noisy sobs.

Colin arrived outside the cottage in Chomley Mews at half past five, prepared to sit on the doorstep if necessary until Anthea arrived home, but to his surprise, the door opened when he rang the bell. Anthea did not look pleased to see him.

'What are you doing here?' she said.

'I've come to see you.' He wondered if Moira would have telephoned her and told her about his Brightmans' visit. He supposed he would soon find out.

'Colin – it's no use your coming round and pursuing me like this. I've told you – it's over. I don't want to see you again.' She was about to shut the door but he quickly put his foot over the step.

'I understand that. And I've no intention of being a pest. But there's something I want to talk to you about. It's important. Please, may I come in?'

Anthea shrugged. 'I suppose you'd better. I don't want the whole street seeing us arguing out here.' She stepped back and Colin walked into the sitting room. She had clearly not been home long; her coat was thrown over the back of a chair and her briefcase and portfolio of samples lay on the sofa. He moved them aside carefully and sat down.

'Well?' She didn't offer him any refreshment, he noticed.

'First of all, we have reason to believe that my father isn't dead. That he faked his own death, for reasons that are unclear at the moment. I wondered if you knew anything about that?'

'Why on earth should I? I came to his funeral, saw his coffin put into the grave. What on earth makes you think he didn't die?'

'He – or someone – is still using his flat in London. And my mother is certain it was him she saw at our house a few days ago. He was looking for something. Some keys that we'd taken from the flat. They weren't there later.'

'Doesn't sound very convincing. Are you going to suggest I'm hiding him here? Under the bed, perhaps?'

'No, of course not. But I thought, as you knew him, and seem to know more about him and his business than any of us do, that you might know something. If you do, I wish you'd tell us. This uncertainty is not doing my mother any good. It's worrying for both of us.'

'I've told you. I didn't know him all that well. I met him a few times, mainly at Brightmans' functions and things like that. I came to the funeral because I'd liked him. And I suppose, I have to admit, I was curious to see his home and his family. That's all. I didn't come because I wanted to see if anyone noticed he wasn't in his coffin, if that's what you are thinking.'

Colin decided to be blunt. 'I went to see your mother at Brightmans today, to see if she knew anything about him.'

'You went to Brightmans?' Anthea's eyes widened in astonishment. 'And they let you in to see her?'

'I gave a false name. And bluffed my way in. They threw me out afterwards but I did manage to see her.'

Anthea giggled. 'Wow, that was impressive! That place is harder to get into than Fort Knox! And what did she tell you?'

'That Dad being still alive was news to her. And I think I believed her. But she also said something else. I told her I thought it was her influence that made you stop seeing me, and she gave the impression that it was because Michael was your father as well as mine. That you and I are half-sister and brother.'

'She said *that*?'

'Not in so many words, but I asked her if that was the reason and she didn't deny it. I can understand now why she was wary of me, but we could still be friends, couldn't we?'

'I don't believe my mother would have told you anything like that!' Anthea said emphatically. 'It's ridiculous! I know my mother and Michael had an affair a long time ago but it wasn't as long ago as that. My father and mother separated when I was seven. My mother was at Brightmans but Michael hadn't come to work there and I am sure they didn't meet before then. My first memory of meeting Michael was when I was about ten, I think. We went to the seaside on holiday, rented a little beach hut or cottage on the beach or something on the south coast and he was there.' She paused, thinking, then said, 'There was someone else there, too. A woman with him, I think. But it wasn't your mother.'

'A woman with my father?'

'I could have been mistaken. I wasn't of an age to pay much heed to grown-ups in those days. All I wanted to do was make sand-castles and swim in the sea. Except there wasn't much sand to make sandcastles, only shingle. I remember there was a big lighthouse there and he took me to see it, all by myself, one day. Huge, towering thing. My mother couldn't stand it because it was a bit misty for a couple of days and the thing hooted like a banshee every few minutes and kept everyone awake. I didn't see Michael again until my mother took me to the office one day some time later and he was there. I remembered I'd seen him before. I saw him once or twice at Brightmans' functions, office parties and that sort of thing. The affair was long over by then, but he was nice to me and talked to me when I didn't know many people there. But he was not my father! That I am quite sure about.'

Colin let out a long sigh. He didn't know whether he was relieved or sorry. If Anthea *had* been his sister there would always be some link, a connection that couldn't be broken, but since she was not, could there, perhaps, be a chance that they might become something else, just as permanent, but more rewarding?

'If that was all you wanted to know, then you might as well go. I'm going to be busy this evening,' Anthea said. 'Be quite clear, Colin. Whatever my mother might want you to think, I am *not* Michael's daughter. I can't believe she tried to let you think I might be. And it may be true that she wasn't keen on my dating you, but it certainly wasn't for that reason. And, also, it isn't because of what my mother says or thinks that I'm not seeing you again. I don't let her, or anyone, run my life for me. I don't want to see you again because I don't want to see you again. It's as simple as that.'

'I get the message. I won't trouble you again,' Colin said stiffly. 'Thank you for your help. Without you I wouldn't have been able to meet your mother and find out about the situation with Michael at Brightmans.'

'Oh, I daresay you would have managed to bluff your way into their offices and find out whatever you wanted to know, without my help,' Anthea said sarcastically. 'Goodbye, Colin. I am glad I met you and your mother, but I don't think I want to continue the acquaintance.' She walked over to the door and opened it, stepping aside pointedly.

He wanted very much to kiss her goodbye, even just a brief touch of his lips on her cheek, but he didn't dare. 'Goodbye, Anthea. I hope everything goes well for you in the future,' he said, stepping outside.

'And you, Colin. I hope, if your father really is still alive, that you and your mother can come to terms with it and that it won't cause too many problems.' She held out her hand. 'We might as well part friends, not enemies.'

He shook the proffered hand, then quickly turned away and strode up the lane to the main road. He did not look back.

Colin went directly to the station and took the train home. On the journey he had a great deal to think about, a great deal to discuss with Simon when he saw him. The train was a slow one, stopping at every small station on the way, and it was gone five o'clock when he arrived in the village. He debated whether to go straight to the Farrier's Arms and wait for Simon, or whether he should call in at home first, and risk being delayed by Fiona wanting to know how his day had gone.

They would have to tell her about Michael soon. Every time he saw his mother, he was tempted to say something, or something in the conversation cropped up where he had to dissemble or give away what he knew. It couldn't go on like this. He had better not call in to Little Paddocks, particularly if he then would have to think up some excuse for going out again soon after, to meet Simon. The decision was made for him when he put his hand into his inner jacket pocket and found the envelope that had been stuck at the back of Michael's drawer. He needed to show that to Simon, but if he already had it with him, there was no reason to drop off at home first. By the time he had walked through the village and along two miles of country lane to the pub, Simon would be there, waiting. Leaving the station, he turned his back on the road towards Little Paddocks and began to walk directly towards the Farrier's Arms.

CHAPTER 13

S IMON WAS SITTING IN HIS USUAL SEAT IN THE CORNER, as far away from the other customers as possible. He had a pint of beer in front of him and another, full glass on the other side of the small table, clearly a good way of discouraging any of the friendlier locals from joining him. Colin was surprised to see that he appeared to have come directly from working in his garden. Instead of the usual grey flannels and blazer, Simon wore old, faded jeans and a heavy tweed sweater.

Colin sat down heavily in the chair opposite, and took a long pull at his beer. He'd walked a good few miles today and he was tired. 'I have a few interesting things to tell you,' he said at last.

'So have I, to tell you,' Simon replied. 'I haven't been idle. I enquired about exhumation orders and it seems there is a department of the Home Office which deals specifically with these things.'

'So we apply to them?'

'I've telephoned them, told them the situation. Apparently, suspicion isn't good enough. I told them about the flat still being used, and that his wife was sure she'd seen him, and they practically laughed their socks off. Apparently, many people think they've seen a dead person alive after a funeral. They call it something like "wishful thinking" or "fear of being haunted" depending on whether the person wants the corpse to be alive after all, or not. Happens all the time, I'm told.'

'But we are sure,' Colin said.

'We haven't any proof. And even Fiona is beginning to doubt whether it was Michael she saw. Eleanor persuaded her that she was imagining it, and we didn't see him.'

'Of course it was him! Who else would break into our house and take nothing but a bunch of keys, the keys that we had taken from his flat?'

'*We* may be sure, but they are not going to do anything without a great deal more evidence, evidence that I can't see us finding, as things stand. How about you? Have you any better news?'

Colin produced the undertaker's letter. 'Mum hadn't thrown it away. I found it in her desk. I visited them, and they seem perfectly genuine undertakers. Someone bought a coffin from them, shortly before we heard the news of Michael's death. Said it was a prop for a TV production and sounded plausible. And the undertaker told me it was easy enough to hire a hearse and funeral cars from someone round there. That's what they must have done, as well as taking a few sheets of their headed notepaper. They didn't write this letter, and, looking at it again, I can see they didn't. It's typed on an old machine, whereas these people have a computer. And I bet they faked the death certificate and any other documents they might have needed for the burial.'

'We could go into that; it shouldn't be all that difficult to prove a fake death certificate. The Home Office might take more notice if we produced that.'

'That can wait a while,' Colin said. 'What happens if we prove he's still alive, and they act on it? He'll go to ground, unless the authorities find a good reason why they should arrest him. No, we need to get to him first, before he realises anyone is on to him, otherwise he'll disappear and we'll never find him.'

'You are right. We still have to keep quiet about this. After my phone call, I began to realise that we can't go public about him still being alive. We have to do it all ourselves.'

'We'll have to tell Mum,' Colin said. 'I really can't go on deceiving her any longer. I'm having to lie, and I'm not good at that. Not to her, anyway. She's always known when there's something up.'

'We'll tell her tomorrow. Together,' Simon said. 'And in the meantime – '

'Wait! There's something else I have to show you. Something I found amongst Michael's things when I did another search yesterday evening.'

'I thought you had gone through everything with a fine toothcomb.'

'Back of the drawer. I'd never have found it if I hadn't pulled the drawer right out.' Colin produced the envelope and laid it on the table between them.

'This it?' Simon picked it up and looked inside. 'There's nothing here.'

'No, but there's a name and two telephone numbers written on the back. And on the front it's addressed to Dad at Brightmans. The postmark is smudged but it looks like several years ago. I think I can make out that it's not a 2000 date.'

'Hmm. Rung these numbers?' Simon was staring at them.

'No, not yet. I wanted to show you first. And to discuss what we say if we ring and someone answers. Do we ask for Michael, or pretend it's a wrong number?' Colin was thinking of his trick on Anthea with the Telecom engineer. He thought he had better not try that twice, or leave himself open to having the call traced.

'One's a mobile, but that's a land line. The code is Kent, I think.'

'Kent? So he might have contacts there?'

'Could be. Worth investigating. Ask Fiona if she knows of anyone Michael knew who lived in Kent. It's a long shot, but don't lose that envelope. It must have been important to him or he wouldn't have hidden it away.'

'So what do we do now?' Colin asked, leaning back in his seat.

'What the Home Office won't do. We do a bit of digging ourselves, and exhume Michael for them.'

'*What?*' Colin nearly fell backwards off his chair.

'Tonight. That's what I planned, when I couldn't get anywhere with them myself. There's a reasonable moon tonight so we'll have sufficient light. The churchyard has a high wall round it and Michael's grave is tucked away. No one's going to see us.'

'But digging up a grave is illegal! We can't do that!' Colin was aghast.

'If we discover what I hope and think we'll discover, then the illegality won't be an issue. Who is in that grave? We might be uncovering a murder, for all they know, and they'll thank us for it.'

'So that's why you're dressed for work,' Colin said, realising at last that Simon was deadly serious.

'Yes. I have a spade in the back of the car, but I haven't a second one. You'll have to slip back and fetch one from Little Paddocks, and change into something more suitable for digging, if you don't want to get those city clothes spoilt.'

'My God! I never would have thought you'd be like this!' Colin whispered. 'I had you down for a conventional, law-abiding citizen who'd have been shocked to the core if I'd suggested digging my father up.'

'Perhaps I would have been, a few months ago,' Simon said. 'But I'd do anything for Fiona. And this is the only way I can see of setting all our minds at rest.'

'Very well. I suppose we'd better get on with it.' Colin stood up. 'If you can drop me at the end of the drive I can sneak into the house and change without Mum knowing. I'll pick up a spade from the shed on my way out.'

Simon grinned. 'Good lad! But it's too early to start now. We'll have to wait until it's completely dark and the moon's up. Go back now and have something to eat. I'm going to eat here at the pub. We'll meet at the church lychgate at around eleven. Can you bring a powerful torch or lantern of some sort, so we can have a good look inside the coffin when we reach it?'

In spite of himself, Colin shivered. 'There'll be something in the shed,' he said. 'There's a load of stuff there, or the garage. But how much digging will we have to do? Don't they bury coffins deeply?'

'Traditionally, six feet down, but I believe it isn't as much as that, these days. What are you worried about, Colin? I thought you wanted to be an archaeologist. Plenty of digging involved in that. This'll be good practice for you.'

Colin gave him a sharp look. There was a macabre sense of humour about Simon that he had never suspected. He felt as if they were co-conspirators in some plot and the thought made him feel closer to the older man.

As he trudged along the lane towards Little Paddocks he wondered what he was going to say to Fiona. She would certainly ask him about his day in London and there was little he could tell her at present. He would insist, whatever tonight's outcome, that Simon and he told her all their suspicions and put her fully in the picture regarding Michael. It was impossible to continue lying to her. That was something he had never done, even as a small boy, and it was becoming increasingly difficult to do so.

They ate in the kitchen, and Colin spun some vague tale about an interview in a big office in the City, trying to give the impression that he had gone there enquiring about a job. At least, the interview in the big offices was true, though he was careful not to go into too much detail or mention any names.

'That's interesting, dear,' Fiona said absently. 'I didn't know you wanted to work in London. You never showed any interest in anything like that when your father suggested it.' She paused, then added 'but if it's anything like the kind of work he did, I don't suppose you would ever be offered anything. The name Latimer must have spread round the whole City by now.'

'It doesn't matter. I'd hardly been there long before I realised I'd never want to work in a place like that,' Colin said truthfully. 'I still think I might like to work at an archaeological dig somewhere, though of course I know there isn't the money to study the subject. I wouldn't mind being a dogsbody and just mucking in and helping out somewhere. I like the idea of finding things that have been buried for ages.' He was suddenly struck by the incongruity of what he had said, and nearly choked on his dinner.

'I had an interesting day today,' Fiona began, and with relief he realised she was less interested in hearing his own exploits than in telling him her own piece of news. 'Eleanor came round in quite a state. It seems her brother Paul has got himself into trouble again, serious trouble this time, and she's worried sick about him.'

'Paul? She has a brother Paul? I never knew that. She's never talked about her family and I've always thought she didn't have anyone.'

Colin showed interest. Anything to steer the conversation away from his own business.

'Eleanor has a family still living in the East End, but she never speaks about them and she wouldn't thank me for mentioning the fact to anyone,' Fiona said. 'She ran away from home when she was quite young, and never went back. Her parents lived a few doors away from mine, but while I kept in touch with mine after I'd married, she simply disowned hers. Actually, I think it was more she wanted to disown Paul at the time. He was always in trouble with the law; thieving, stealing cars, breaking into places – all the forms of petty crime that you could name.'

'Really? Did you know him in those days?' Colin was becoming interested.

'We all knew Paul. There was a group of us that used to go round together, out to dances and trips to places, that sort of thing.'

'Was Dad one of the group?'

'No, not at the beginning. There was Eleanor and me, and Simon, who worked with a couple of the boys, I think, and two other girls. About six of us altogether. Paul was a lot younger, about eight or ten years younger than Nell, but he liked to hang round us all the time and sometimes he was a real pain, wanting to come with us to places where he was too young to be let in. I lost track of all the others a couple of years after we'd left school and the group began to break up and pair off with boys, but I was closest to Nell and stayed in touch until she left home. That was shortly after the time Michael appeared. Paul seemed to hero-worship Michael; he was always hanging round him and Michael didn't seem to mind. I suppose I hoped that he would prove a good influence and Paul would grow out of his delinquent ways, but he seemed to get worse after Michael and I married and moved away. Nell says he has been in prison more than once, and now he's involved in something really serious. As if burglary and theft weren't serious enough. She didn't say what, but she's worried that if he's arrested, the Press will discover that she's related to him and come down here to interview her, or something. She's afraid that the locals will find out she has a less respectable background than she's always pretended. Well, I don't know what she's worried about. If they ever got wind of what Michael was up to, the Press could have a field day with us.'

'Does that worry you?' Colin asked anxiously.

'Not really. He paid for what he did, and he's dead now. The local people here aren't the sort to point the finger at us for London cheating. If Michael had been rustling cattle or stealing sheep, they would be angry, but most of them aren't interested in what goes on in London. Most of them believe that stockbrokers and financial advisors are on the fiddle anyway and all out to line their own pockets.'

Colin laughed, and nodded in agreement. Fiona was naive in many ways and he was not about to point out that many of the people who lived in the village had worked in London, or still commuted there, and would have a very great interest in what went on in city companies. The farming community might not be interested in what went on elsewhere, but there were plenty who were. Once it became public knowledge that Michael was not dead, his mother might find it difficult to continue living here. He only hoped that Simon would whisk her away with him as soon as possible.

'There's a good play on the television tonight,' Fiona said, picking up the dinner plates. 'We can watch it together in the study. Be nice and cosy by the fire with a bottle of wine.'

Colin's heart sank. He wondered how he was going to explain the necessity of going out again tonight. 'How long does it go on for?' he asked.

'Until half past ten, I think. Why?'

'It was just that I was thinking of an early night. It's exhausting traipsing round London.'

'Half past ten is early enough for you, I should think. And if you found one day in London exhausting you certainly couldn't cope with a daily commute there. Give me a hand with the dishes, dear, and then we'll be cleared away before it starts.'

Colin helped wash up, then found a bottle of wine and glasses and settled in the study with Fiona. He made sure she had at least three quarters of the bottle, leaving himself with a clear head for the work later. As soon as the film was over he stretched, yawned expansively and stood up, 'Well, I'm for bed. I can hardly keep my eyes open.'

'I think I must have dozed off, too,' Fiona said. 'I'll go up now as well. No point in staying up by myself.'

He saw her to her room, wished her goodnight, then hurried to his own bedroom. In a moment he had changed into old jeans and a sweater, crept downstairs and collected the shed keys and a torch from the kitchen. Within ten minutes he was striding down the road towards the churchyard, the spade over his shoulder and a car lantern swinging in his free hand.

He saw Simon's car, parked on the verge across from the church wall. Simon himself was standing in the shadow of the lychgate, a spade in his hand. He straightened up as he saw Colin approach. 'Lucky most people go to bed early in a place like this,' he said. 'There's been no one around ever since the Farrier's shut at eleven. Now, I had a reccy earlier today while it was still light, but if you remember, I never actually got to the funeral, so you'd better make sure which is the right grave'.

Colin led the way through the churchyard, towards the enclosing wall at the back. 'This is it,' he said. 'Still with turves piled on top. Lucky it's too soon to have erected a stone, we'd have had a problem moving that.'

Simon surveyed the plot, casting his torch over the oblong mound. 'Better remove the turves first and pile them up by the side. Don't want to make too much mess.'

It occurred to Colin to wonder what they would do after they had dug up the coffin. Look inside, then put it back again? But then, there would still be their word alone that it was not Michael buried there. But what if it was? What if they had both been misled by events and had got the whole thing completely wrong? He was relieved now that they hadn't yet told Fiona of their suspicions. She'd be horrified and shocked to learn that her son and her lover had dug up her dead husband from his grave. He looked across at Simon.

'What are you going to do when we've dug him up?' he asked. He had assumed, all along, that Simon had his plans all worked out but now he was not so sure.

'Find out who or what is buried in the coffin,' Simon grunted, lifting a large slab of turf and heaving it to one side. 'Come on, get moving. You're younger than I am and so far I'm doing all the work.'

Colin picked up another turf, surprised at how heavy it was. After a moment he straightened and leant on his spade. 'How do we open the coffin?' he asked. 'Aren't those things screwed down?'

Simon looked startled. Then he said abruptly. 'Toolkit in the car. There'll be screwdrivers and levers in it. But we've got to reach the damn thing first, so get digging.'

They worked in silence for some time by the light from the two lanterns, placed either end of the mound, taking spadefuls of soil and piling them up beside the grave. From time to time, Simon produced a bottle of water and they took turns to drink from it. Colin was hot and took off his sweater, draping it over a tombstone beside Michael's grave.

'Let's have a look and see how far we've gone.' Simon straightened up and lifted one of the lanterns, holding it high above the grave. Colin took advantage of the break and stretched before glancing down at his feet.

'Doesn't look very deep,' he said. 'Not more than three feet at most, and it's a bit lop-sided. We must have been at it for over an hour, too.'

Simon peered at his watch by the lantern's light. 'It's nearly one o'clock,' he said. 'We've plenty of time before it gets too light. I suppose people are early risers round here, but no one's likely to come this way. This isn't a short cut to anywhere, is it?'

Colin shook his head. 'No, and there aren't any houses nearby. Only the vicarage. I didn't see any lights on when we passed it so I suppose the vicar is an early-to-bed man. He's in his sixties, I should think, and a bit conventional, so he probably goes up to bed with a mug of cocoa by ten o'clock.'

'Let's hope he's a sound sleeper. Not that he'd hear anything from the vicarage,' Simon said. He began to laugh. 'Lord, I feel like we're Burke and Hare, the Irish body-snatchers.'

'Didn't they get hanged for stealing bodies?' Colin asked uneasily. His back ached and he had developed a blister on one hand. He also had an uneasy memory of Michael's coffin being lowered a long way down into his grave. It seemed a great deal deeper than six feet, more like ten. Perhaps they had dug a double grave, room for another coffin on top, and still have it six feet below the surface. They weren't going to manage that far without a ladder. He doubted if they could dig much further anyway, without some mechanical help. He began to have great respect for professional gravediggers, remembering the straight sides of the neat oblong. So far, the pit they had dug was anything but neat.

'Simon, this isn't going to work,' he said. 'There must be another way.'

'There isn't another way. We can hardly borrow one of the farm diggers,' Simon snapped.

'No, I mean another way of proving that Michael isn't dead. Search for him.'

'Where do you suggest we look? He could be anywhere. He must have left the flat by now, the lease is up. That was our only chance of locating him. On reflection, our best bet was if one of us stayed there permanently until he turned up. He must have come back soon after we were there, to find we'd taken his keys so he had to come to Little Paddocks and retrieve them.'

'I wish I'd been there,' Colin said. 'I'd have tackled him, rugby fashion if needs be. And then made him tell us what he'd been up to and why.'

'He probably watched the house and saw you leave. Fiona said she was sitting in the dark so he must have thought the place was empty, otherwise he wouldn't have risked her seeing him.'

'He must have another place he's living in. Two of those keys were house keys,' Colin said. 'He probably has had somewhere else for years. And he never bothered with a car when he was at home. He went off by train, or, if it was a short, local trip, he'd use Fiona's.'

'Do you think he was the sort of chap to have another woman?' Simon asked. 'If he's got a wife and perhaps a family, tucked away somewhere, what do you think Fiona's going to feel about that?'

'I don't think anything we find out about him will surprise her now. When we have proof that he's still alive I think she'll have mixed feelings. She was sorry he died when he was young and fit, but I think it was almost a relief, too, though she would never admit it. Now, she's used to the idea that he's gone, and if he's back he's bringing a load of new problems with him.'

'Not least the fact that I can't marry her,' Simon muttered. 'We must find him. And not just to know what he's up to. I want him around so that Fiona can divorce him properly. If he simply disappears and we never find him, she'll be in limbo for the rest of her life.'

'You could still marry her, now,' Colin said. 'We have a death certificate. If we don't rock the boat who else is to find out that he's not dead?'

'I couldn't do that to her, marry her, being virtually certain he's still alive. It would inevitably come out eventually. She doesn't need to be saddled with two husbands breaking the law.'

'I suppose we'd better press on with the digging,' Colin said reluctantly.

'Heavens, yes! We've been talking too much and not getting on with it.'

Simon picked up his spade. 'Pass the water bottle will you, please?'

He turned towards Colin but was dazzled by a sudden bright light shining directly into his face. 'What the – !'

'And what in God's name do you think you are doing?' said a stern, very angry voice.

Dazzled by the light, Simon could see nothing beyond it, but Colin, standing to one side, saw the outline of a man in what appeared to be a long robe. He knew at once it was the vicar.

'Oh, Lord!' he muttered. 'Now we're really in a mess! Simon, it's the vicar!'

Simon had a reputation as a quick thinker. 'Ah, Vicar! I don't think we've had the pleasure of meeting yet!' He stuck out a hand, then, looking at it, withdrew it quickly. 'Sorry, I'm a bit muddy to shake hands.'

'What on earth do you think you are doing? You two are desecrating a grave. What is this all about? Are you performing some sort of black magic ritual, or is it plain theft? You won't find anything of value here.'

'Vicar, we can explain,' Colin said desperately. 'I'm Colin Latimer, and this is my father's grave. You buried him about a month ago. But we have reason to believe that it isn't my father buried here. We are sure he is still alive.'

'And so you take it upon yourself to interfere with the grave and try to disinter the coffin? If you had serious reasons for this ridiculous idea then you should have gone through the proper, official channels.'

'We tried,' Simon said. 'They wouldn't listen. We have approached the Home Office's exhumation department but we haven't sufficient evidence at the moment to prove Michael Latimer is still alive, though we have every reason to believe he is.'

'And who are you?'

'I'm Simon Neville, a long-time family friend,' Simon said. 'Look, I'm sorry to be doing all this in such a secretive way, but we couldn't think of any other way. We've tried not to make too much mess, and we'll clear it all up as soon as we've finished.'

'Are you saying you really intended to dig six feet down to the coffin? With spades? In the dark?' The torch played over the piles of earth and the gaping hole. Colin saw that it still looked no more than three feet deep and was shallower at his end. Suddenly, he wanted to laugh. The whole situation seemed like something out of a slapstick film comedy. How could he and Simon have believed they could dig down to Michael's coffin without at least a ladder and some buckets or something in which to put the soil? And if they did reach the coffin and succeeded in opening it, what then? Leave whoever was inside uncovered, as evidence?

'You realise you have committed a criminal act?' the vicar said.

'Yes, I suppose we have. But it was necessary. We can explain exactly why we've had to do it,' Colin said.

'If it wasn't you, Colin, and your own father's grave, I would have no hesitation in calling the police immediately,' the vicar said. 'I think I may have to inform them anyway. But I will listen to what you have to say first. Not here. I have no intention of standing out here longer than necessary. You had both better come to the vicarage and explain yourselves.' He turned away, gesturing with a wave of his torch that they were to follow him. Simon glanced at Colin, shrugging. 'Sorry, old chap. I seem to have landed you in a right mess. Can we persuade him not to involve the police, do you think?'

'I don't know,' Colin replied. 'I don't know him terribly well, but probably when we explain why we're here...' He tailed off, not at all sure now that any reason they could give would satisfy the man. It had struck him that digging up a grave in the middle of the night was a crime, and a serious one, whatever the reason. He just hoped Simon had good powers of persuasion and looked respectable enough to convince the man that they had no criminal intentions. He glanced across at Simon as they followed the vicar towards the vicarage gate, set in the churchyard wall behind the church. He had to admit, with their muddy jeans and old sweaters, they looked far from respectable.

The vicar unlocked his front door and ushered them inside. Both stopped to remove their muddy boots before stepping over the threshold and Colin hoped that would dispose him kindly towards them.

'Come into the study.' He led the way through a door to the left, into a book-lined room with a desk and some comfortable armchairs. Colin guessed this was where he took his parishioners who wanted to talk through their problems with him.

'Sit down, please.' He indicated the chairs in front of his desk. He took a seat behind the desk and looked at them keenly. 'I don't know you, do I?' he said to Simon. 'You certainly aren't one of my parishioners and I don't remember seeing you in the village.'

'No. I live the other side of Winchester,' Simon said. 'I'm a long-time friend of Fiona Latimer. But I don't know your name, either, and I can hardly keep calling you vicar.'

'My name's Eric Marsden. I've been vicar here for ten years or more. I know Mrs Latimer quite well, and Colin, too, though I am aware that they are not regular worshippers at the church.'

'No, well, I've been away at university a good deal,' Colin mumbled, embarrassed.

'No need for excuses. I am aware that the congregation at divine service here is always small,' the Reverend Marsden said. 'I am happy to be of service to the whole village, not merely those who come to church. Now, will you please explain to me exactly what you thought you were doing in the graveyard, and why?'

Between them they told him of their suspicions that Michael was not dead, that he had faked his heart attack and was still alive, living somewhere, where, they didn't know. Why, they didn't know, either. Even to Colin's ears it all sounded rather implausible.

'But the funeral was perfectly straightforward,' Eric Marsden said, frowning. 'It was all completely above board, and I've officiated at a good number of funerals in my time.'

'The undertakers were a genuine company,' Colin said. 'But they had no record of writing to my mother regarding the funeral. Someone used their headed notepaper. It was typed, and they assured me they've used their computer for all correspondence.'

'You must have had a letter from them. Do you still have it?' Simon asked.

'No. Actually, they telephoned me to make arrangements and asked me to confirm with Mrs Latimer – your mother, Colin,' said Eric. 'But everything about the funeral itself was authentic. Except there was one thing,' he added thoughtfully.

'Yes?' they both said together.

'The undertaker paid me immediately after the service. That's unusual, but very welcome, all the same. And it was in cash. Money for the service, the organist and the grave-diggers. Even a tip for the churchwarden and a donation towards the church on top. It was very generous.'

'So you have no record of who these people were?' said Simon.

'They did give me their name, but I've forgotten. As I said, the whole thing appeared perfectly normal. Some people prefer paying by cash and so long as they do pay, I've no objection.'

'So what happens now?' Simon said.

Eric looked thoughtful. 'By rights, I ought to inform the police that I've discovered you desecrating a grave,' he said. 'But since it is your father's grave and you appear to have thought you had good reason, I'm prepared to turn a blind eye. But you must give me your word, both of you, that you won't attempt anything like this again. It's highly unlikely that your father is still alive. I'm totally convinced that he is buried in that grave and there he must remain, undisturbed. The evidence you have produced is very flimsy. You admitted yourself, Mr Neville, that the Home Office didn't take you seriously. Why should Michael Latimer have faked his own death? Has anyone actually seen him since the funeral, apart from your mother, who only thought she did, in the dark? A very unnerving experience she must have had, to find an intruder in her house. No wonder she seemed unclear about the incident.'

Colin opened his mouth to say that his mother had not been unclear, and, although he hadn't seen the intruder himself, he was quite convinced that it must have been his father, come to take back his keys. Simon pressed hard on his foot to shut him up, and he realised that he was being unwise to argue. The vicar was letting them off, and probably risking trouble for himself in doing so.

'Tomorrow I'll tell the gravediggers that there seems to have been some damage in the night. They'll put it right and no one will be any the wiser as to who did it or why. But I must have your word that you won't go round spreading stories about Michael Latimer. Does Mrs Latimer know about this?'

'She doesn't know what we were planning to do,' Simon said. 'And we haven't said anything to her about our suspicions. We wanted proof first.'

'And how do you think she would have felt, to hear that you had interfered with her husband's grave? That poor woman has had enough shocks without anything of this nature on top.' Eric stood up. 'Go home, the pair of you. And I don't want to see you anywhere near the graveyard again. Do not enter these premises unless you intend to come to a church service.'

'Thank you, Mr Marsden,' Simon said meekly. 'We're very grateful that you aren't going to take this any further. Colin?'

'Yes, thank you, vicar. I realise now that wasn't the way to deal with things.'

'Accept, Colin. Accept.' Mr Marsden spoke in a gentler tone. 'Your father died very suddenly. You must miss him a great deal, and you may feel the loss more because you had no chance to say goodbye. That is understandable. It's very common for those left to find it hard to accept that they will not see their loved ones again. Not in this world, anyway. Perhaps if you were to come to a service one Sunday, you might find solace and the peace you so clearly lack.'

Colin gulped. 'Yes. Perhaps I will.'

'Bring your mother. I understand she may be moving from Little Paddocks soon, but will still be living in the village. Wise of her, not to dwell on sad memories, but still stay close, where all her friends are near her.'

He showed them to the door, watched them cross the graveyard and pause only to pick up their spades and lanterns. 'I feel like a schoolboy just come from the headmaster's study,' Simon whispered, as they trudged through the lychgate.

'He hasn't a clue,' Colin said. 'But we were lucky. He could have made it very awkward for us.'

'Don't suppose the local Bobbie would have appreciated being called out at three o'clock in the morning to arrest us,' Simon said. 'But, you know, I don't think we'd have been able to dig that far down in any case. We'll have to think of some other way of finding proof. The best way would be to find Michael himself.'

CHAPTER 14

THEY REACHED SIMON'S CAR, parked on the verge opposite the church.

'You're not planning on driving all the way back to your home at this hour, are you?' Colin asked. 'You must be exhausted.'

'Well, I am a bit tired.' Simon looked drawn. He hardly seemed to have the energy to walk through the churchyard to his car.

'Come back and sleep at Little Paddocks,' Colin said. 'We can explain in the morning and it will help if you are there anyway. We can tell her everything as soon as she's awake.'

'It's tempting. Yes, I'd like that, if it's no trouble,' Simon said.

'You can have Michael's room, the bed is made up ready in there. Or, if you'd prefer not, there's the spare room and I'll easily find some sheets and a spare duvet.'

'I don't mind where I sleep. At the moment, I feel I could sleep on a clothes line.' Simon held out the passenger door for Colin. 'If I park just inside your gate, do you think it'll be all right? Fiona won't hear me?'

'She'll be sound asleep. She said she was tired and went up to bed before I came out. We can easily sneak into the house without disturbing her,' Colin replied.

Simon parked the car as quietly as he could. They walked up the drive on the grass verge and Colin opened the front door. 'Don't tread on the fourth stair,' he whispered. 'It creaks. Not that Mum'll hear anything. She's bound to be sound asleep.'

They were at the bottom of the staircase when the lights went on, both upstairs and down in the hall. Fiona stood, in her dressing gown, at the top of the stairs, Colin's cricket bat in her hand.

'Who's there?' she demanded. 'I warn you, I'm armed.'

'Whoops,' Simon muttered softly.

'Colin? Is that you? And – *Simon*?' Fiona came down the stairs. 'What on earth has happened? You're both covered in mud. Has there been an accident? Simon – what are you doing here?'

'I brought Simon back to stay the night. It's too late for him to drive home now,' Colin said. 'He's tired. We both are.'

'I thought *you'd* gone to bed ages ago,' Fiona said. 'And why are you here, Simon? Not that I'm not pleased to see you, but I hardly expected to, at this hour.'

'I think we should tell her – now,' Simon said. 'If we wait until tomorrow, none of us will sleep.'

'Tell me what?' Fiona looked from one to the other, bewildered. 'I think you'd better come into the study and explain. I suppose you thought I didn't know something was up between the pair of you, but you've been acting oddly lately and I think it's about time you told me exactly what's going on. Is it about Michael? What more revelations can there possibly be?'

Simon took her arm and steered her to the armchair in the study. He looked ruefully at his muddy jeans, then picked up that day's paper from the desk and spread it over the second chair before sitting down.

'Would you like a hot drink?' Colin asked.

'Later. I want to know what all this is about, first,' Fiona said.

'We think Michael may still be alive,' Colin said bluntly.

She stared at him, white faced. 'And you were in the churchyard, digging?' she whispered.

'No, no. Not buried alive! Good lord, no!' Simon said hastily. He took both her hands in his, finding them cold. 'When we went to his London flat, Colin thought someone had been living there since his last visit. And there was the time you thought the intruder looked like Michael. You weren't imagining it; we're convinced now it was Michael, come to take back the keys we took from the flat. They were the only things missing.'

'You actually mean to say you've both thought for some time now that he wasn't dead but you never said anything!' Fiona sounded indignant.

'We wanted to be sure first. But we haven't any real proof. Not proof that would be believed by anyone else, but we are both sure,' Simon said gently.

'You mean – the whole funeral was a pretence? I can't believe that! The whole thing is utterly preposterous!'

'That's what I thought at first, too,' Simon said. 'We were trying to dig up his coffin to check what was in it, but it wasn't possible, and the vicar came along and caught us before we'd come anywhere near to discovering anything.'

'You were digging up his grave! But that's a criminal offence!' Fiona was shocked.

'Yes, but we had no alternative. And we didn't want to alert anyone official because if Michael knows we know he isn't dead he'll go to ground and we'll never find him. We have to get to him first, before anyone else does.'

'But why would he want to pretend he was dead? What possible reason could he have?' Fiona looked genuinely puzzled. 'And why must you find him before the authorities do?'

'I have to find him. We need to force him to agree to a divorce so that we can be married,' Simon said. 'If he disappears we may have to wait years before we can presume death and be free to marry.'

Fiona stared at him. 'So you do want to marry me?' she asked. 'You don't think I'm going mad because I thought I saw him – *you* knew I was right and it was Michael I saw!'

'Of course I do want to marry you. I've wanted to marry you for thirty years, but I was too slow off the mark then,' Simon said gruffly. 'I'm not going to miss my chances a second time.'

'But I'm technically a widow,' Fiona said.

'We're convinced the death certificate, like the funeral itself, was a fake. I'm not going to make you a bigamist. We have to find Michael before he realises he's wanted by the fraud squad as well as us. Otherwise, he'll disappear off the face of the earth and we'll never track him down.'

'If he's really still alive, then I want to see him, too,' Fiona said. 'There are a great many questions I want to ask him.

There were a great many questions I wanted to ask before, when I thought I would never have the chance. I don't know what I think about what you've both just told me. When someone dies, so suddenly and unexpectedly, one's mind cannot take it in properly. I found it hard to believe he could really be dead, harder still because I wasn't given the chance to see him, to say goodbye. I remember when my father died. He was much older, of course, and ill, and his death was not unexpected. I saw him in the hospital and I knew that was the last time I'd see him. I said my goodbyes to him, silently, because we were still all pretending he might get better. With Michael, it wasn't like that. He was young and fit and there had never been any kind of heart trouble. His death was simply unbelievable. I think that's one reason I wasn't upset at the funeral. I simply didn't believe it, even then.'

'And now? Are you shocked to know that he's almost certainly still alive?' Colin asked gently.

'I – don't know what I feel,' Fiona said slowly. 'Part of me feels I ought to be relieved, pleased. After all, he was my husband. But after all he's done, I can find nothing but anger for him in my heart. I think I'm only glad that he's alive because it means I can ask him why he did all the things he did, what he did with the money, and why he needed to.'

'We have to find him first,' Simon said grimly. 'Have you any idea where he might have gone? Did he have anywhere where he might go, to friends, to hide out?'

Fiona gave a harsh laugh. 'Why ask me? I knew him less than anyone. It seems I didn't know him at all.'

'Does the Kent coast mean anything to you?' Colin asked.

'Kent coast? No, nothing at all. I don't think I've ever been anywhere like that. I don't know anyone who lived in Kent. When we went on holiday it was usually abroad, Majorca or the Canaries, or Scotland. You remember, Colin. You always came with us.'

'I wasn't thinking of family holidays,' Colin said. 'But Dad went away quite a lot, didn't he? Paris, Amsterdam, places like that.'

'He always said they were conferences, or meeting clients. Now, according to what that woman at Brightmans told you, he wasn't meeting clients. He was always cagey about my going with him, said I'd be bored, or it was just business, nothing else. It annoyed me sometimes, but I accepted it.'

'So he might be anywhere in Europe by now?' Simon said. 'Whatever his business was, he must have had contacts there. With the new European regulations he'll be even more difficult to find if he's left the country.'

'Let's hope he doesn't realise he needs to hide yet,' Colin said. 'He's clearly faked his death for a purpose. My guess is that he's done that so that he can carry on doing whatever he was doing, under another identity. The fact that he carried on using the flat for as long as he still held the lease, showed that he didn't think it necessary to leave London after the funeral. He must have thought he was safe. I think he's still somewhere in this country, still doing whatever he was doing when it became necessary to disappear by dying.'

'You may be right. I certainly hope you are.' Simon stifled a yawn.

'Look, it's nearly dawn and neither of you has had any sleep.' Fiona stood up. 'I'm going to make us all some cocoa and then we're off to bed. But before I do,' she looked at both of them in turn. 'I want you to promise me you will not keep anything else from me, concerning Michael, ever again. I suppose you thought you were protecting me, but, heavens, I'm not a stupid woman who is likely to collapse with shock, especially after all the things I've learnt about Michael's behaviour these last weeks. I want to be in on everything you are planning, and to come with you if you are going to search for him. Is that understood?'

'Understood,' they said together. Simon added 'I'm sorry I discouraged Colin from telling you everything earlier. I think we both realised independently but at much the same time, that he had to be still alive. And, for me, it was hard to believe; even harder to accept.'

'Oh, come to bed, both of you,' Fiona said. 'I don't want you sleeping in the spare room, Simon. The bed's not made up, anyway. What's wrong with my own, comfortable double, upstairs?'

'How could I refuse an offer like that?' Simon took her hand. 'But I warn you, I'm practically dead on my feet, after all that digging. I'll be asleep as soon as my head touches the pillow. No use to anyone.'

Fiona giggled. 'It doesn't matter. There will be plenty of other times. Now I'm going to be a full partner in the search for Michael, I expect you will be spending quite a bit of your time here anyway.'

Mrs Burdett behaved like the perfect discreet servant when she arrived the next morning, to find Simon, Colin and Fiona at breakfast at the kitchen table. With no more than a brief nod and a murmured 'Good morning, Master Colin; Sir. Shall I start on the study, madam, or would you rather I did the dining room first?' she raised not a single eyebrow, though it must have been clear that Simon had stayed the night. Fiona wondered if explanations were necessary, decided that they were quite impossible, and answered her question as if nothing else was amiss.

'I think the dining room could do with a dust, though it hasn't been used much lately. We might be in the study after breakfast. We have a few things to discuss. About – er – my late husband's affairs.'

'Very good, Madam. I'll leave you to it. All right if I go upstairs to do the rooms later?'

After she had left, Simon said 'What tact! The woman's a wonder! Can we keep her when we're married, even if we're living in Winchester?'

'I'm sure she'd come. But you haven't asked me to marry you yet,' Fiona said with spirit.

'And you know why not. Until this Michael business is sorted out, I can't. And, frankly, I haven't had a chance to tell you my intentions.'

'I think Mum knows them. Or she should do, by now,' Colin muttered. 'And perhaps we ought to make your staying here look official. If we're going all out to work out where my father is, and track him down, we'll need you here with us to make plans. Can you come and stay here for the next few days?'

'Of course, if that's all right with Fiona. I'd like nothing better, and it would make things easier.' Dropping his voice, Simon muttered to Colin 'much better than the saloon at the Farrier's Arms. I never really took to their beer.'

'You'd better have Michael's room – officially, that is,' Fiona said. 'And what was that about the Farrier's Arms?'

They told her, rather sheepishly, about their meetings. Fiona looked serious. 'That just goes to show – I never notice what's going on under my nose. Michael could have been up to anything – *was* up to all sorts, and I never knew. And now you two tell me you were plotting and scheming in the local pub and never said anything.'

'Sorry, darling. We'll never do anything like that again without letting you know what we're up to,' Simon said.

'You'd better not. You promised last night that I'd be in on everything from now on and you wouldn't hide anything from me. I want him found as much as anyone, probably more urgently than either of you. I've got questions to ask, answers to demand, and I'm determined that he shall answer them fully before the police lock him away. When I've finished with him, he may even be relieved to escape to a cell for some peace.'

Simon began to laugh. 'What am I letting myself into marrying? I can see I shall have to be the perfect husband to avoid the wrath of your vocal rolling pin. We three together will find Michael, I'm sure. And then you can ask what you like, and Colin and I will hold him down if necessary until he's given you answers. And now, if I'm to move in here, I'd better drive home, tell Mavis I'll be away for a while and pack a bag, collect some decent clothes so I don't have to stay around in muddy jeans and upset Mrs Burdett. I could see she was dying to put them in the washing machine for me.'

Simon went out to his car and Fiona turned to Colin. 'You don't mind him staying here, do you?' she asked.

'Good Lord, no! Why ever should I? I'm glad and relieved that he's going to be here and helping us find Dad. He has some good ideas and knows people who could be helpful. We need him here.'

Fiona looked relieved. 'I just thought – '

'He's a splendid chap. I'll be delighted when the pair of you get married. Just don't expect me to call him Dad, will you? He's Simon, a mate, and the word Dad has bad connotations for me, anyway.'

Fiona went upstairs to make up the bed in the spare room, though they both knew Simon wouldn't be likely to use it much. She hummed softly to herself as she worked. It had been a delicious feeling, waking up that morning with someone warm and responsive beside her. Simon had fallen asleep as soon as he'd tumbled into bed last night, but this morning they had wakened together and it had felt so *right*, so good to see him there beside her.

Colin took the opportunity to visit the shed and look again at the papers and diaries they had taken from Michael's room. He was sure now that his father had removed anything that would have given a clue to his secret life, but there was always the chance that he *might* have missed something.

Now that they knew he had been planning his own death, it was plain that he would first have made sure there was nothing left at home or at his flat that might be traced to his present whereabouts. Colin didn't hold out much hope that he would find anything; he had already looked through everything once before, but he did it again, particularly looking for any references to Kent, or the telephone numbers which had been on the envelope at the back of the drawer. When he went back to the house, over an hour later, he saw the van from the auction house parked in the drive.

'They are taking all the pictures,' Fiona said. 'And I must say, I'm not sorry to see them go. They remind me too much of Michael. They were all his choice. All I hope is, that he was right and they will fetch a decent price that will tide us over until we've sorted all this muddle out.'

'Even if we do find Dad, there's no guarantee that he'll still have any of the money, or would give it up if he did,' Colin warned her. 'I bet that Brightmans will still be interested in getting their hands on some, if there's anything left.'

'I know. But at least we'll have whatever I can raise from selling these and some of the furniture that will be too big for a smaller place,' Fiona said. 'And if I do move into Simon's home I can get rid of the lot, just leave enough for you to set up a place of your own somewhere. I suppose you'd like to live in London, though?'

'Why should you think that? I don't want to work there.'

'But isn't there still this girl – the one who came to the funeral – aren't you keen on her?'

'No. Not any more. She was very useful in introducing me to her mother, who told me about Dad embezzling from the company, but she's not my type. I don't suppose I'll be seeing her again.'

'There'll be someone else soon. You'll see,' Fiona said lightly. She looked happy this morning, prettier and younger than Colin had seen her for some time.

Simon arrived back shortly before lunch time. He came into the hall, clutching a suitcase in one hand and a newspaper in the other.

'Mrs Burdett has left lunch for us, laid in the kitchen,' Fiona greeted him. 'Cold, I'm afraid, just salad, but I can warm up some soup – '

'Lunch can wait!' Simon said excitedly. 'Have you seen this morning's papers yet?'

'No, and I really don't bother much. The TV news is enough. What is it?'

'Where's Colin? Let's go into the study and I'll show you.' Simon led the way, then spread the newspaper out on the desk in front of him. It wasn't the front page headline, but there was a prominent article just inside. A London gangland mob had been infiltrated by the police and a series of raids had resulted in several arrests. Among those now in custody was Paul Pagett.

'Oh, poor Eleanor! This was what she was dreading would happen!' Fiona said. 'Does it give any more details, any background?'

'Not a lot. But it's definitely Eleanor's brother all right. The police seem to think the people they have arrested are small fry, they are still looking for the Mister Big who has been masterminding the operations.'

'Do you think Michael could be involved in all this?'

'I think it may be possible. But there is more than one gang of criminals in the East End and these may not have anything to do with him.'

'What were they involved with, these people?'

'All kinds of crime, it would seem. The article is a bit vague but I imagine the police aren't giving much away if they are still looking for the main criminals.'

'I must telephone Nell!' Fiona said. 'She'll be worried sick, if she's seen this article.' She picked up the telephone and keyed in Eleanor's number.

'No answer,' she said after a few moments, replacing the receiver. 'She must have gone to London to be with her parents.'

'They still live in that part of London?' Simon asked.

'In the same house as they did when my parents lived just a few doors away. Nell was telling me that she left home soon after Michael and I married, and never went back, never had much contact with them, but of course when something like this happens, family ties are still strong. You know what East-enders are like, blood ties are everything, and she was always close to Paul.' She was looking in the desk as she spoke. 'Now I must still have their telephone number somewhere. I'll ring them and speak to her there.'

'The number will have changed, Mum. All the London telephone numbers are different now,' said Colin.

'Then Directory Enquiries will tell me their current number.' She was keying in numbers as she spoke. 'I remember the address perfectly well.'

Several moments later she was at last connected with Eleanor's parents.

'Mr Pagett? This is Fiona Latimer. You might remember me as Fiona Ellis, my family used to live at number forty-six, a few doors down from you. Oh, years ago now, I know, but I'm a friend of Eleanor's. We were at school together. Is she there? Could I speak to her, please?'

The man at the other end of the telephone sounded annoyed. They heard him clearly, saying crossly 'She's not here. Hasn't been here for years. I don't know where she's living now.'

'But I thought she might have come to see you. You must be so worried about Paul – ' Fiona got no further.

'Bloody nosey reporters!' Mr Pagett growled down the receiver. 'Mind your own business! I've nothing to say to you!' The telephone went dead.

'Perhaps she's still at home. After all, the news broke only this morning. Shall I go round and see her?' Fiona wondered.

'I'll drive you if you like,' Simon offered.

They didn't suggest Colin came with them, and he felt all three of them might be too much, especially if Eleanor had already expressed concern that her neighbours would discover Paul's connection with her.

There was no reply to Fiona's knock on Eleanor's cottage door. She peered through the windows but could see little. Finally, Eleanor's helpful next door neighbour put her head out of an upstair window to call down, 'If you're looking for Miss Pagett, she's not there. Went away a day or so ago. Piled her car up with suitcases and all sorts. Looked like a long holiday somewhere, if you ask me. She didn't say anything, didn't even put a note out for the milkman, but I told him it was no use his leaving anything because she looked as if she wouldn't be back for weeks. Very nice for some, I dare say she's off sunning herself somewhere hot while we're stuck here as the cold nights are drawing in. And chilly days, too.' She banged the window shut as if to shut out the encroaching winter chill.

'I wonder, did she know about Paul before it reached the papers?' Fiona said. 'Nell told me she was scared stiff about the neighbours knowing about her background, about her crooked brother.'

'Probably she did,' Simon said. 'Well, we can't do anything more for her. She's gone, and my guess is she's back in London, even if not with her parents. If she and Paul were close, she'll want to see him.'

'Will the police let her, if he's been arrested?'

'I should think they might. It's more than likely she will ring you when she's seen him, and fill you in with what has happened. We'd better go back and wait for a call. And have some of Mrs Burdett's lunch, if Colin hasn't eaten it all himself.'

CHAPTER 15

T HEY HEARD NOTHING FROM ELEANOR THAT DAY. Fiona wondered if she should telephone Mr and Mrs Pagett again but it seemed unlikely that Eleanor would be staying with them, in the light of Mr Pagett's remarks.

'She must have other friends or more sympathetic relatives living near there who she can stay with,' Fiona said. 'I'm sure she's there in London to be near Paul. Well, there's nothing I can do for her now.'

'Does anyone know what Paul has been charged with?' Colin asked. 'The papers gave little detail apart from the report of his arrest, with two other men, and the fact that he was part of some criminal fraternity.'

'I can try to find out,' Simon said. 'I've some contacts in the newspaper world. Give me half an hour with your telephone and a London directory and I'll see what I can do.'

They left him alone in the study. Fiona wandered aimlessly round the house with Colin. 'The place looks so bare without the paintings,' she said. 'Even though I didn't much care for them, I'm missing them. I wish the estate agent would send someone to look over the house. He said it ought to sell quickly but so far no one's shown any interest.'

'It hasn't been on the market long. Autumn is a bad time for moving house anyway,' Colin said, aware that he wasn't being terribly helpful.

Simon came out of the study, calling to them. 'Not a great deal more news, I'm afraid,' he said. 'But I have a few details which didn't get into the papers. It seems Paul's home was raided after an anonymous tip-off and a quantity of guns and ammunition was found there. More than one would expect for an individual going in for armed robbery.'

'It really is serious, then,' Fiona said.

'The police think the gang was planning something big, and Paul might have been in charge of the weapons. They don't want to release too much information yet as the main criminals, those masterminding the operation, are still at large. They want to put pressure on Paul to give them names, tell them what the intended target was. The police have been thinking along the lines of a really big break-in somewhere and they think it still could go ahead in spite of Paul's arrest, unless they can persuade him to talk. Trouble is, he probably doesn't know very much. Someone asked him to store the weapons in his flat and so far he is saying that's all he knows about anything. They'll get more out of him before long, but whether the police will pass any more details on to the Press is doubtful. They are playing it down very much, which makes my reporter friend think there's something pretty big involved. Sorry, that's all I could find out. That's all he knows at the moment but he says if he learns anything else that he's allowed to pass on, he will ring me here.'

'Do you think Michael could be involved in all this?' Colin asked. 'Mum, you said he knew Paul well when you and Eleanor were in London.'

'Michael has surprised me a lot lately, but an armed robber!' Fiona said. 'That doesn't sound like his style at all. I suppose I ought not to rule out anything where he's concerned, but I can't see him as a Great Train Robber or breaking into the Bank of England. Sitting at his desk altering figures in a ledger or on a computer screen to embezzle hundreds of thousands of pounds at a touch of a button is much more like his style.'

'He might have bankrolled the operation,' Simon said thoughtfully. 'I remember Paul when Michael came on the scene. He hung round him all the time. He had some sort of hero-worship crush on him, I used to think. Ironic, really. I was quite glad that he did, at the time, because I thought he would distract Michael away from you and Eleanor.'

'I remember,' Fiona smiled reminiscently. 'Paul used to hang around whenever Michael was there. He could be a bit of a pest, sometimes. Eleanor used to give him money to go to the cinema and leave us in peace.'

'I'm sure your stroll down memory lane is very enjoyable for both of you,' Colin broke in, 'but it doesn't help much now. Dad *must* still have money stashed away somewhere, enough to pay people to help him fake his own death; enough possibly to fund masterminding a big armed robbery. I can't see him being actively involved in anything like that, but he could see it as an investment. He might supply the money for guns and vehicles, things like that, in return for a cut of the proceeds when the robbery was carried out.'

'He must also have sufficient money to enable him to disappear successfully if things become too hot for him,'

Simon said. 'Which it would appear they have, with Paul's arrest. The police have ways of persuading suspects to talk and Paul already has a criminal record. They've only to threaten him with the prospect of a long stretch in a tough prison, and he'll tell all he knows. Michael must have left London as soon as he heard about Paul, and that would have been long before the news reached the papers. He might be anywhere now.'

'And very soon the police will be looking for him,' Fiona said. 'We've lost our chance of finding him. He could be anywhere by now, Australia, South America, anywhere at all.'

'If he's involved in all this, the police will find him. And then you will be able to see him in the cells and ask him all the questions you want.'

Fiona shook her head. 'In a situation like that, he wouldn't tell me anything. No, I want to find him before anyone else does; talk to him without him thinking the police are listening in on what we say. I want him to be honest with me and give me answers that he'd only give me if he felt safe. I know this may sound silly; he probably lied to me most of our married life, but I feel that if I had one last chance to speak to him, he might tell me the truth if he thought it didn't matter any more.'

Simon nodded. 'I think I understand what you're saying. I hoped that Colin and I might be able to give you that chance, but now it looks as if it's too late. As you say, he could be anywhere by now and he seems to have had plenty of contacts on the Continent – Amsterdam, Paris, and other places he frequently visited in the last few years.'

There seemed no more that could be done. The following day the estate agent send two possible purchasers to view Little Paddocks, which cheered Fiona, especially as one, a couple with a family of three teenagers, showed great interest and put in an offer on the spot. It was below the asking price, but not vastly less, and the estate agent thought that, if anyone else showed interest, he might be able to persuade them to raise the amount. In between showing people round the house, Fiona and Simon took Colin to see properties for sale in and around the village.

'This is a nice village,' Simon said, after they had toured round several times to look at places suitable for Fiona. 'But I've been wondering. Are you really sure you will want to go on living here, if there's going to be a court case and scandal involving Michael?'

'You mean, you think I'd do better to move away and avoid any gossip? To come to Winchester, perhaps?'

'You liked my house, but it is only a house. No, I was wondering if we shouldn't be looking at somewhere bigger, for both of us, and Colin, too, if he wants to stay. I'd like one of those detached houses on the edge of the village, with a nice garden but small enough to manage. What do you think?'

'It was something like that I really wanted when we moved here, but Michael was adamant that he preferred

Little Paddocks, even though it was far too big for just the three of us,' Fiona said.

'If I sold my house, we could easily afford that place that we passed this afternoon. You said you liked the look of it and it is for sale,' Simon said. 'And we could keep the best of all our furniture. What do you think?'

'But you love your house in Winchester! And you've been there a long time, it must be full of memories for you,' Fiona protested.

'We take our memories with us,' Simon said. 'Perhaps it's time to move on, make a clean break . But if local gossips are going to have a field day over Michael and you, perhaps it's not such a good idea to stay on in the village. Eleanor seemed to think she would be branded a criminal along with Paul if anyone discovered a connection between them.'

'Nell was more concerned that her past background would become known. Over the years she's been here she's built up an image of herself as coming from a well-to-do family, able to live comfortably on an inherited income, hiding the fact that she's from a run-down, slummy area of London and never had much money. She was very cagey about how she managed to buy her cottage and run her car but I gather she had a man friend – I suppose we would have called him a sugar daddy – who bought them for her, as well as giving her enough money to live comfortably without working. He was a married man, much older than her I assume, and there was no question of her marrying him. This was a few years ago now, soon after we came to live here. I think he must have seen the error of his ways and gone back to his wife, or died, because she has never mentioned him and I think she might have told me if she was still seeing him, even if only to warn me when not to visit her.'

'Whereas you've never made any secret of your background?' Simon said.

'No, but then it never arose. My parents died years ago, so they never had the chance to visit here. Pity, really, they'd have loved Little Paddocks and been pleased to see their daughter had apparently done well for herself. What they'd think now, I cannot imagine! I don't have any other connections with the place where I grew up, except for Paul and Eleanor's parents, who don't seem to want to know either of us now.'

It was two days later, as they were sitting in the study watching a television programme and considering a nightcap and snack before bed, that the doorbell rang, followed by a peremptory hammering on the knocker.

'Somebody impatient,' Colin remarked. 'Who would be calling this late? Shall I go?'

Simon followed him out to the hall. Three policemen stood on the step outside. 'Is Mrs Fiona Latimer here?' one of them asked.

'What do you want with her? It's late,' Colin said aggressively. His heart had sunk on sight of their uniforms. He felt at once they had come to tell his mother something unpleasant about Michael.

'I'm Fiona Latimer. What can I do for you?' Fiona had come up behind him and Simon. Instinctively, they moved aside for her and Simon put an arm protectively round her shoulders.

'Mrs Latimer, we understand that the funeral of your late husband took place in the local churchyard in August. Is that correct?'

Fiona nodded. 'Yes, he's buried there. Why are you asking? The vicar could have told you that.'

'From information we have received, we now have reason to believe that the body buried in that grave is not that of your husband. We have a Home Office authorisation to exhume the coffin and examine its contents. We are informing you as a courtesy as we do not require your permission for this, but we may have to ask you to come to the churchyard to identify the body later.'

'I see.' Fiona looked pale, but her voice was steady. 'When will that be? Do you want us to wait up? We were about to go to bed.'

'Shouldn't take us more than an hour to dig down to the coffin. We've a mechanical digger on site and it doesn't take long to rig up screens and lights. We'll come and call for you when we are ready. Should be well before midnight, we expect,' the policeman said.

'Why do you always do these things at night?' Colin asked, puzzled.

'Avoids having an audience of curious neighbours, Sir,' the policeman replied. 'Exhumations are almost always done at night. You'd be surprised at the numbers of onlookers who can gather when we have to work in daytime. Right ghouls some people are, and they get in the way.'

'At last the Home Office is taking us seriously!' Simon said exultantly as they closed the door on the policemen. 'It must have been Paul who told them, which means Michael must be very much involved with whatever Paul has done.'

'And this means the police are already looking for Michael,' Fiona said. 'What hope have we of finding him first?'

Colin made some sandwiches and Fiona brewed a large pot of coffee and they sat round the table in the kitchen, waiting for the police to come back.

'You don't have to look into the coffin, you know, Mum,' Colin said. 'I can do that. And we know it won't be him.'

'I want to be sure it isn't,' Fiona said. 'And I don't mind. If it *is* Michael buried there, I want to know, to be sure. And if it isn't, who is it? Oh, dear, I'm not making much sense, am I?'

The knock on the door came shortly after eleven o'clock. This time it was a gentler, more discreet sound. 'We'll all go,' Simon said, standing up. 'I'm not leaving you to face any of this by yourself, darling.' He glanced apologetically at Colin. 'Not that you wouldn't be a tower of strength to your mother, Colin, I know.'

'We both want you here with us,' Colin muttered. He didn't much fancy the thought of peering into a coffin to look at the decaying remains of a body, even if that body was not his father's, but then his mother must be feeling much the same. And Simon wouldn't be able to identify him, it would have to be someone who was next of kin and had seen Michael recently.

Two policemen escorted them with torches down the road to the church and through the lychgate. In the far corner of the churchyard floodlights picked out a screen of canvases and several figures silhouetted against them. Behind the screens they could see the outline of a mechanical digger, its scoop raised in the air like some strange, prehistoric creature. Fiona began to shiver and Simon put his arm round her, holding her close. Colin, walking behind them, felt nothing except a detached interest in the police procedures. He noticed that, though there were the three policemen who had come to the house, the people actually working on the grave wore overalls and there were four of them, working under strong arc lights. So much for our own efforts, he thought ruefully. How could he and Simon have possibly hoped to dig deeply enough with a couple of spades and only a single torch to see by?

They were led from the site of the grave to a tent, erected by the church wall. Inside was the coffin lying on trestles, and surrounded by bright, hissing gas lights.

'We haven't opened the coffin,' one of the policemen said. 'It needs to be done in your presence.' Two workmen stepped forward at his signal and began unscrewing the coffin lid. Fiona gave a little gasp and Simon stood close by her.

'I can identify the body, if it's that of Michael Latimer,' Colin said loudly. 'I'm his son.'

'No, Colin, it's all right.' Fiona reached out a hand to him.

The men removed the lid and propped it against the trestles. One reached inside, then stopped, looking up questioningly at the policeman standing nearby. 'Never seen anything like this,' he said.

The policeman stepped forward to peer into the coffin. 'What is it?' Fiona asked.

'Looks more like sacking than a normal shroud,' the workman said. He pulled it aside, then stepped back. The policeman looked into the coffin, then drew back and turned to them. 'You'd all better take a look at this,' he said.

There was no body in the coffin. It had been filled with rocks and stones, wedged with earth and old sacks, and covered with further sacks.

'But what happened – ?' Fiona whispered.

'Did any of you know about this? Were you aware of what was in this coffin when the funeral took place?' the policeman looked from one to the other of them. Colin thought policemen were probably trained to look at people in a certain way that ensured they became incapable of lying. He felt like a rabbit facing a fox.

'Of course we didn't!' Fiona said angrily. She was more angry because she had psyched herself up to face – something, a body if not Michael's body – and the sight of the rocks and stones had shaken her badly.

'The coffin came straight from the undertakers – we didn't see it until the hearse brought it here to the church,' Colin said. 'We never saw him dead.'

'We have reason to believe your husband faked his death,' the policeman said. Simon resisted the urge to say,

'Yes, we'd worked that out for ourselves'. Better not to let them know that it was no surprise that Michael wasn't there. Safer, in fact, to say nothing. He hoped Colin would have the sense to keep quiet about what they suspected.

'We have checked the undertakers. There was no genuine funeral firm used, though a coffin was bought from one,' the policeman said. 'The hearse and two Daimlers were hired from a car hire company, who were told they were to be used by a film company making a television comedy. I believe the same story was used when the coffin was bought.'

'You learnt all this from interviewing Paul Pagett, I suppose,' Simon asked. The policeman gave him a sharp look. 'What makes you say that, Sir?'

'I know Paul Pagett has been arrested, and that he was an associate of Michael Latimer. I assume he was in on this.'

'And you are acquainted with Paul Pagett?'

Simon could see he'd said too much, fallen into just the trap that he'd been fearing Colin might. 'I read the papers,' he said stiffly. 'I know that Paul Pagett has been arrested, suspected of being involved with some gangland crime. You also appear to be looking for Michael Latimer, who we now know to have been involved with some criminal activities. It would be natural to think the two people had some links. That's all.'

'That's as may be. We are still investigating the information Paul Pagett has given us. We cannot say any more at present, but if you have any further information, I hope you will tell us.' The policeman treated all of them to his sweeping glare again, daring them to keep silent if they knew anything.

'I assure you, Officer, that neither my son nor I knew anything about the contents of this coffin,' Fiona said. 'Speak to the vicar. He knows I didn't see the coffin until it was brought here. And Mr Neville here didn't come to the funeral. He arrived after it was all over and hadn't seen me or Michael for more than thirty years. He has nothing to do with whatever has been happening here. He's a dear friend who came to support me – and see I wasn't unduly upset or bullied by anyone.' She glared back at the policeman, who had the grace to drop his eyes. Simon could have cheered her.

'I think that will be all for the moment,' the policeman said. 'We shall be taking the coffin and its contents back with us to the Forensic department. That was always our intention but our investigation will doubtless take a different turn now.'

'I suppose they will be able to analyse the rocks and find where they came from,' Colin asked, leaning into the coffin to take a closer look. The policeman gave him a sharp look, as if suspecting he was being facetious.

'That's right, Sir. It's surprising what can be discovered by professional examination of objects like this. We shall discover exactly where these rocks came from, and probably extract fingerprints from inside the coffin. Now, perhaps you'd let one of my men escort you back to your house. I take it you aren't planning on leaving the area in the next few days?'

'Was that a veiled threat, do you think?' Colin asked, when they were back in Little Paddocks and sharing a stiff drink in the study while they discussed the events.

'They always say that. They must have spoken to the vicar and he would surely have convinced them neither you nor Fiona knew anything was wrong at the funeral,' Simon said. 'You wouldn't have been able to put on an act to convince everyone if you had known what was in that coffin.'

'I didn't cry,' Fiona said. 'I didn't appear upset at all. And that was because I wasn't. I was shocked; stunned by the suddenness of it all. I was very, very stupid. I should have realised there was something wrong from the outset. Aren't there always post-mortems when someone dies in circumstances like Michael's? And I dare say the death certificate has a forged signature on it that wouldn't stand up to any real examination.'

'You were in shock, just as anyone in that situation would have been,' Colin said. 'You were in no state to start asking questions. I should have done more.'

'Now, now. No recriminations,' Simon soothed them. 'You had no reasons to doubt anything at the time, and only too glad that someone was taking on the burden of dealing with everything for you. That's what Michael was banking on.'

'He knew I wasn't good at managing things, dealing with official matters,' Fiona said. 'He didn't know I'd have you here to help me.'

'The point is, what are we going to do now?' Colin said. 'Are we just going to sit around and wait until they find Michael, or are we going to try to find him ourselves?'

'How can we do that? We don't have the slightest idea where he is. He could be anywhere, literally anywhere in the world,' Fiona said. 'He probably left Britain before they even arrested Paul, before there would have been any reason to alert airports or docks to look out for him. He has money, and friends abroad who would help him. It's impossible. I doubt the police, even with their contacts, will be able to find him, so how could we hope to?'

'We do have a few advantages that the police do not,' Colin said slowly. 'I've been thinking about it. I know it's a long shot and probably I'm being silly and it won't lead to anything, but it seems to me we can't sit here and do nothing. We have to try anything, however unlikely it seems.'

'What are you getting at?' Simon asked curiously.

'I know it's late and we should be in bed as the good policeman intended, but I didn't like his attitude and I'd like to score one over him,' Colin continued. 'So, gather round, both of you, and I'll tell you what I think we should do.'

CHAPTER 16

'THOSE KEYS MOTHER FOUND IN HIS LONDON FLAT,' Colin
began, as soon as he had all their attention. 'They
weren't keys of that place, nor of this. And a day
later, he came here to retrieve them. That must mean that he
needed them, or currently used them. If they were keys from
somewhere he'd used in the past, he wouldn't have
bothered. That means they were probably keys of the place
he was going on to when the London lease ran out.'

'But that could be anywhere,' Fiona objected. 'He
probably has a flat in Amsterdam or Paris which he uses
when he goes there. Could be the home of a girlfriend abroad
who has given him a set of keys.'

Colin shook his head. 'No, I think not. Those were
English keys, a Chubb and a couple of Yales. Any foreign
keys would have been of different manufacture. What do you
think, Simon?'

'I'm no expert about things like that, but I'm sure you are
right. European keys would be different. And he must have
needed somewhere else as soon as the lease was up. He
couldn't have risked staying on at his flat.'

'But where? How much further does that get us?' Fiona
said impatiently.

'Those keys weren't new. And remember the envelope I
found with the telephone numbers on it? You thought the
area code was Kent, remember, Simon? If they weren't
important he wouldn't have hidden them away. He has a

contact somewhere in that area. That narrows it down quite a bit.'

Simon nodded. 'I see what you're driving at. And we can ring those numbers and see who answers. It's a long shot, but it's the best we have. And it's considerably more of a lead than the police have, unless Paul has told them a great deal more than they are admitting.'

'I don't think Paul will know too much about Michael's personal plans,' Fiona said. 'He was never one for taking anyone into his confidence, always preferred to keep things to himself. That's why he managed to con Brightmans for so long; he never told anyone what he was up to, so there was no one to betray him. He might use Paul, but I don't think he'd trust him with anything that might risk his own safety.'

'So what are you suggesting we do?' Simon asked Colin.

'We can't do much tonight, it's too late. But tomorrow we'll ring the number on that envelope and see where it leads us. We may need to take a trip to Kent and have a look round.'

'It's a big county,' Simon said doubtfully. 'Where would we begin?'

'Anthea told me something. She said she'd been on holiday with her mother in a seaside cottage and Michael was staying nearby.' He avoided mentioning the fact that Anthea had said there was a woman staying with Michael. 'She said there was a lighthouse nearby which made foghorn noises and annoyed her mother. Michael took her to see it, so it must have been on the shore, or nearby. It was a long time ago because she said she was only interested in making sand castles, but it was mostly stony, no proper sandy beach.'

'Sounds like Dungeness,' Simon said thoughtfully. 'Lighthouse on the mainland, shingle, not beach, though there is a beach there. And summer cottages dotted around. It might be worth taking a look round there.'

'But the police implied we shouldn't leave here without telling them. If we go, they'll suspect we know where Michael's hiding out,' Fiona objected.

'If they complain, we'll tell them the strain of the whole business has made you ill and you need a few days' rest and sea air to recuperate,' Simon said. 'I know it's a slander and you are far tougher than that, but it's a plausible excuse and we needn't say exactly where we're going. Let them think we're going to some east coast seaside resort, Frinton or somewhere like that. Whoever heard of anyone hiding from the police in Frinton!'

'I could try telephoning Anthea again to see if she remembers any more details of where, exactly, she and her mother stayed,' Colin said. 'But the whole thing is rather a long shot. She said she was about ten at the time and that would make it anything up to fifteen years ago. Michael may have been long gone. He may only have been renting a place there for that year.'

'We can go on speculating about this all night,' Fiona said wearily. 'And we can't do anything more now. Let's go to bed; it's long past midnight. We'll be fresher in the morning to plan what to do.'

Colin didn't know – or much care – whether Simon and his mother slept well or not, that night. He was aware only that his mind was racing, lying wide awake and sleep refusing to come. He thought up schemes to try to see Moira again, but doubted if she would tell him anything, even if she knew anything useful. The same might be said of Anthea and he had to admit to himself that part of the reason for contacting her would be to see her again. He hadn't given up on the hope that he might persuade her to come out with him, if he could discover something she would really like to do. For one crazy moment he wondered if she could be persuaded to come with them on a trip to Dungeness, but dismissed the idea almost at once. Fiona wouldn't have been happy about that, and even he wasn't entirely sure just where Anthea's loyalties lay. He had convinced himself now that she wasn't Michael's daughter; that had been a rather clumsy ploy on Moira's part to discourage him from trying to date Anthea. Moira had thought he wasn't good enough for her daughter; a jobless layabout with an uncertain future. She was undoubtedly right and he'd have to do something about that situation as soon as this business with Michael was satisfactorily finished. His mind turned to possible careers, jobs that he could do, with no experience and a middling degree in Classics. It didn't sound terribly promising and he could understand Anthea's reluctance to have anything to do with him.

Eventually he slept, and awoke when Mrs Burdett tapped at his door to tell him his mother and Mr Neville were having breakfast and would be expecting him to join them as soon as possible.

They couldn't discuss much over breakfast, eaten in the kitchen with Mrs Burdett hovering nearby, but as soon as they'd finished, Colin went into the study and rang the number on the envelope he'd found stuck to the back of Michael's drawer. He hadn't thought out what he would say, just hoped that inspiration would come to him. As it happened, he didn't need to say anything. The voice that answered had the bright cheeriness of a young man, calling 'Boat Yard!' to be followed by a message, clearly repeated for all calls, though it didn't sound like a recorded one. 'The boatyard is now closed for the winter. We will be open for trade again after Easter. Only essential and emergency repairs carried out over this period.' The line went dead.

Boatyard. So Harry Sykes ran a boatyard somewhere on the Kent coast and if Michael was there, he could be planning to hire someone to take him across the channel, in a small boat that would take him to France without anyone knowing. If the boatyard was closed for winter, either he would have some arrangement with the owner, or he'd steal a boat. It was beginning to look as if his hunch was right and Michael was somewhere on the Kent coast, and planning to cross the Channel in the near future. They didn't have any time to waste.

'Pack a small bag, in case we need to stay overnight,' Simon said. 'I'm going to inform the local police that we're going to the seaside for a couple of days. I'll say Frinton or Clacton, they sound innocuous enough but if we go and don't tell them, they may try to follow us, which would be a nuisance, to say the least.'

'Tell them I'm a nervous wreck and need a change of scenery,' Fiona said. 'You can lay it on thick, I don't mind. Make out I'm a neurotic woman who will take up all your time to look after and pacify. That should allay any suspicions they might have that we're interested in finding Michael.'

'Just so long as we convince you that we know you aren't like that,' Colin said with a grin. 'I know you, Mum. Any suggestion that we're protecting you and you're outraged.'

'Just so long as I don't have to throw a fit of the vapours in front of that policeman,' Fiona said. 'I'm no actress.' She giggled. 'I don't even know what a fit of the vapours looks like.'

'I doubt he does either,' Simon muttered. 'Come on, let's go at once. Will you tell Mrs Burdett we'll be away possibly overnight? She won't be concerned, will she?'

Simon and Colin looked out road maps and held a brief discussion. 'Due east, across country. Shouldn't take us more than two to three hours at most,' Simon said. 'But what do we do when we get there? There's a great deal of coastline in Kent. Short of driving along the length of it shouting "Michael!" I can't see how we're going to track him down.'

'We'll aim for the boatyard first,' Colin said. 'I'm sure he'd be planning to leave from somewhere nearby, like that. We'll scout around the area near the lighthouse. Most of the cottages on the shingle must be summer places, shut up now for the winter. We'll look for somewhere that still has signs of life around, a car outside, or lights on inside. After that, we'll have to see how the land lies. I just don't know what we'll do, I only know we have to do something, however daft it seems.'

They stopped for lunch in Tunbridge Wells then arrived in Rye an hour later. 'Shall we book in somewhere here for the night?' Simon said. 'I can see us searching for days.'

'We haven't got days,' Colin snapped. 'If Michael's here I feel sure it's only until he makes his final arrangements to cross the Channel. Then we'll have lost him completely. He must know by now that the police know what was in his coffin and they'll be looking for him. He won't wait around to be caught, that's for sure. We may even be too late already.'

'If he was going abroad at once, he wouldn't have needed to come to Little Paddocks to take his keys back,' Fiona said. 'He was taking a risk, doing that, especially as soon as he realised I was still in the house. He must have needed those keys very urgently, which means that he was coming here before going abroad. Perhaps he needed to wait for something, confirmation of his money or the right tide, or something. I have a feeling we'll find him here somewhere.'

'Let's drive to the coast and find this boatyard first,' Simon said.

In the event, they found both the boatyard and the lighthouse without any trouble. The lighthouse towered over the surrounding shingle, little shacks and cottages clustering nearby. A little way along the coast road they came across a dilapidated boatyard with the name Harry Sykes painted in fading blue lettering on one side.

'There it is. Looks closed, like they said,' said Colin.

'Everywhere looks closed. This is the most bleak and gloomy place I've ever been to,' Fiona declared. 'Who on earth would come here on a holiday?'

'I suppose it looks better in summer,' Colin said. 'Is it worth having a look round the boatyard anyway? Could it tell us anything useful?'

'There is someone there,' Fiona said, leaning out of the car window. 'I can hear a noise like a drill coming from inside. Suppose I take a look by myself? I can make up some story about wanting a trip round the bay, something like that. Better by myself than all three of us. You two could be undercover policemen but no one would take me for anyone other than a rather dotty old lady.'

'All right, but be careful what you say,' Simon said, to be rewarded with a scornful look. 'We'll take the car out of sight round the corner and wait for you there. And if you're not back in fifteen minutes – '

'Oh, don't be so melodramatic! I don't suppose I'll learn anything useful, but you never know.' Fiona opened the car door as she spoke, gave them a cheery wave, and walked towards the boatyard.

It looked very closed. Fiona walked round it and saw the main doors facing the slipway padlocked shut. She turned back, then saw a small door in the far side was slightly open. The sounds of a mechanical tool were coming from inside. She pushed the door wider and stepped inside. 'Hallo? Anyone there?' she called.

There was no response but she doubted anyone could hear her over the high, whining whirr of the drill. She came further inside, seeing several boats of various sizes pulled up on to metal frames so that they were suspended above the ground. Some were in the process of having barnacles scraped from their hulls, some looked as if they were waiting to undergo more major repairs. Someone was working on a boat at the far end of the shed, and she made her way towards it. On the way she passed the slipway leading down to the big doors opening on the water. On it was a boat, clean and newly painted, looking as if it was ready to go to sea at any moment, unlike any of the others.

There was a young man of about twenty or so, working on a small open boat that had been upturned onto a set of trestles. Fiona was quite close to him before he noticed her, looked startled and switched off his drill.

'How did you get in here?' he asked. 'We're closed. Closed for business until next April.'

'Oh! The door was open and I heard you working so I thought there must be someone around who could help me,' Fiona said, sounding vague. 'My husband and I are staying near here and he wondered if there was a chance of taking a boat out for fishing in the next day or so. He's done a bit of sea fishing before, he isn't a complete amateur,' she added.

'Nah, don't do anything like that. As you can see, all the boats are laid up waiting to be scraped and checked over. Couldn't put them to sea even if we wanted to.' He turned back to his boat dismissively.

'That one looks as if she's ready to sail,' Fiona pointed to the boat on the slipway. 'He so much wants a day's fishing and the weather looks good, the sea's calm. He'd pay over the odds.'

'Not that boat. That one's not for use.'

'She looks quite ready to go, just as she is.' Fiona turned large, hopeful eyes on the young man, hoping she didn't look so much older that mildly flirting with him would be off-putting.

'Yes, well. That one's booked. Can't use that. It has to stay there to be ready for when a customer needs it in a hurry,' he shrugged.

'So you do hire out boats occasionally? Couldn't I book one for tomorrow, or in a few days' time?' Fiona wheedled.

'Nah. Like I said, we're closed. Boss doesn't let any boats out now. Come back in April and you can hire whatever you want.' He switched on his drill again and turned his back. 'Shut the door on your way out,' he called over his shoulder.

Fiona left. She tried to take a look at the boat on the slipway as she passed, but it was too high to see over the side. She had no doubt that it was ready to be launched as soon as the customer wanted, and that the customer was almost certainly Michael.

She almost ran back to the car. If what she suspected were true, then Michael was indeed here, and had not yet escaped across the channel, though clearly he was intending to. Their guesswork had been right. All that was needed now was to find him, living somewhere in one of the little cottages scattered around.

'One boat, on the slipway, ready to be launched at a moment's notice,' Simon said when she had told them what she'd seen. 'Yes, I'm sure you are right. Well, it's all we have to go on. Now we have to find him before he leaves.'

Colin, in the back of the car, put his hand into his pocket and found his mobile phone. 'Why don't I give Anthea a ring?' he suggested. 'Ask her where she stayed when she was here, if she can remember.'

He looked at his watch. She might be home by now. He knew she had a mobile phone but she hadn't given him her number. Didn't trust him not to call her at work, he suspected, and didn't blame her.

She answered on the third ring. 'Anthea Ransom here.'

'Anthea, it's Colin. Please don't hang up. I need to speak to you.' He sounded as desperate as he felt.

'What do *you* want?' she said ungraciously.

'Look, when you went on holiday with your mother and met Michael, do you remember where you stayed? What the place was called?'

'*What?* It was years ago. I was only ten. I hardly remember any of it.' She sounded impatient.

'Anthea, it's important. You said it was by a big lighthouse. Was it at Dungeness, do you think?'

'Dungeness? I – don't know. Could have been. I don't remember. Yes, I think it was. I know it was a funny name.'

'And you stayed in a cottage here, near the lighthouse?'

Anthea laughed. 'Yes, *right* by the lighthouse. It was a bit foggy on a couple of nights and the wretched thing boomed out all night. Mother was furious. She hadn't wanted to come here in the first place, but Michael said it was lovely, just a wonderfully peaceful place for relaxing. One of his favourite places. I suppose I liked it too, but I would have liked a sandy beach rather than all those pebbles.'

'And you stayed in a cottage near the lighthouse? Did Michael have a cottage nearby?'

'What is all this about?' She sounded wary, and Colin decided he would have to take her into his confidence.

'We're looking for Michael. We have to find him before the police do. He's in trouble.'

'I did wonder. I read something in the papers which made me think he might be involved in something big. Well, if you find him, give him all the best from me. He might be a crook, but he paid attention to me when I was there, and that meant a great deal to a ten-year-old.'

'Can you remember anything else? The name of your place? Or Michael's?' Colin asked.

'Are you really there, in Dungeness?' Anthea sounded surprised. 'I told you, it's a long time ago and I didn't pay much attention to things like that. Let me think.' There was a pause, so long that Colin had begun to think she had put down the receiver, when she said 'Driftwood. That was it. I think that was the name of the place.'

'The place where you stayed?'

'No, I mean, that was the name of Michael's cottage.' Anthea sounded impatient. 'Look, I can't talk any more. I have to go.'

'Anthea, you're an angel and I love you!' Colin didn't care that Fiona and Simon heard him. He turned to them triumphantly. 'Driftwood!' he shouted. 'Michael stayed in a cottage called Driftwood. And she says he loved this place, so the chances are he had a permanent home here. It figures, doesn't it? Near the coast with a boatyard where he can hire a boat to put across the channel whenever he wants to slip abroad without going through formalities. Somewhere where not many people come in winter so there's no one to notice him. We've found him!'

'Once we've found the cottage called Driftwood,' Fiona said. 'There are dozens of little cottages all over this area.'

'By the lighthouse. And at this time of year, most of them will be shut up until spring. All we need to do is look for those with lights on, and there can't be many.' Colin was ecstatic; Michael might be no more than a few hundred yards away.

'Better wait until it's dark, then,' Simon said. 'Then we'll take a walk round. But what do we do when we finally confront him?'

'I'll know what to do,' Fiona said grimly. 'I've been waiting for this. Now, at last, I'm going to have my chance to find out all the answers to the questions I've been asking myself all these weeks.'

'And if he refuses to tell you anything?' Simon asked gently.

'I'll *make* him tell me! And why shouldn't he? He's got nothing to lose, if he thinks he's going to be across the channel and safely in France before the police catch up with him.'

Simon looked at Colin. He didn't share either of the other two's confidence that Michael would make any kind of full confession, even when they found him, but they knew him better than Simon did. He only hoped that whatever happened in the next few hours, Fiona would be satisfied and able to lay the past to rest.

They spent the next couple of hours trudging along shingle paths between cottages, looking for one called Driftwood. Though summer was well and truly over, there were still people enjoying the last of the mild weather by the sea.

Simon did not want to knock on any doors to ask for directions, in case they alerted Michael before they found him and caused him to disappear again. It was dark by the time they reached a small cottage set a little apart from the others. At first glance, it looked unoccupied, heavy dark curtains drawn across the windows, but there was a chink of light where they came together.

'There's a name on the gate, a wooden board,' Fiona said. 'Have you a torch?'

Colin struck a match. Holding it up, he was just able to make out the word Driftwood before having to drop it to avoid burning his fingers.

'Bingo!' Simon said softly. 'What do we do now? How do we approach this? What's the plan?'

Colin was very much aware they didn't have a plan. He had hardly dared think about what they would do when they found Michael. It felt very much as if it was *if* they found him. He realised he hadn't really expected that he would ever see his father again, and the thought that in a few moments he would be face to face with him, gave him a peculiar feeling inside.

'We go up to the door and knock,' Fiona said firmly. 'You needn't both come. In fact, suppose I go alone and speak to him first?'

'If you think I'm going to let you go inside alone,' Simon began.

Fiona began to laugh. 'He isn't a monster, you know. He's the man I've been married to for thirty years. Why shouldn't I be as safe as I've always been?'

'We'll all go,' Colin said. 'I want to see him too. And Simon does. It would be silly to leave either of us standing at the gate.'

Fiona led the way up the short path and knocked at the door. There was a longish pause, and then the sound of bolts being withdrawn. The door opened a crack and a face peered out at them.

'Hallo, Michael. May we come in?' Fiona said casually. She might have been tapping on the bathroom door any morning.

'Who's there?'

Colin recognised his father's voice and a shiver ran down his spine.

'Only myself and Colin. And an old friend, Simon Neville. You remember him, don't you?' Fiona said. 'There's no one else here. No one at all around. It's just us.'

A light in the porch over the door came on and they were surveyed under it. Then the door opened wider and the three of them stepped inside, straight into the main living room.

'How did you find me? How did you know I was here?'
Michael said.

'We realised you must have faked your funeral and then
we worked out where you probably were,' Colin said.

'Mmm. You have more intelligence than I gave you
credit for,' Michael said. 'But if you've found me, then others
undoubtedly will. Are the police here?'

'Not yet,' Fiona said. 'Though they are looking for you.
They have been ever since Paul was arrested. You do know
that Paul Pagett, Eleanor's brother, was arrested a few days
ago? We thought that you and he must have some
connection.'

'Yes, I know all about Paul's arrest. He was caught with a
quantity of weapons in his flat. The police jumped to the
conclusion it was to mount a raid on somewhere big – break
into a bank or something. They were way off course but Paul
let them think that. It distracted them from what we were
really doing. Paul has been a great help to me, he helped to
arrange my funeral. He would have liked to have been a pall
bearer, but you would have recognised him and asked
awkward questions. He won't be able to help the police much
even if they persuade him to tell them what we were really
doing; he doesn't know anything about my own personal
plans.'

'And what are your plans?' Fiona asked softly. She was
staring at him and Colin had a sudden sinking feeling in his
stomach. She still cares for him, he thought. Poor Simon, who
is worth ten thousand more than Michael.

'I'm away, out of here. In the next couple of hours,' Michael said. 'You were lucky to find me still here, weren't you? Come to say goodbye? I'm sorry I wasn't able to say it before, when I had to die rather suddenly. But I thought you'd feel better not having to go through all that death scene ritual.'

'I've come to find out the truth, Michael,' Fiona said steadily. 'I want to know why you stole money from Brightmans, why you forfeited your pension rights that should have been mine, too. Why you remortgaged our home and left me and Colin with nothing. I want to know what you needed all that money for. You had a good salary at Brightmans, plenty for our needs. I know you weren't going to rob a bank, that isn't your style at all. Where is all the money you embezzled, Michael? You must still have thousands left.'

'I have very little left,' Michael said with a shrug. 'I should have had far more, but I was swindled out of thousands.'

'Tell me what you were doing, please. I think I have a right to know.' Fiona was still looking steadily at him, and Colin could see Michael was disconcerted by her. So far, he had completely ignored Simon and barely acknowledged Colin's own existence.

'All right. I suppose it doesn't really matter now. Why don't you sit down, Fiona?' Michael gestured towards the sofa, underneath the window. Simon and Colin accepted the invitation and sat there, but Fiona didn't move.

'I want to know everything,' she said. 'After that funeral, when I found out about the money, and that you'd been sacked from Brightmans for embezzling, there were so many questions I wanted to ask and it was so frustrating because I thought I would never know what really happened.'

'I was involved in a way of making heaps of money,' Michael said. 'But, like most schemes, it needed capital to get started. If you really want to know, I was buying arms and ammunition cheap and selling them on somewhere else.'

'Gun running?' Fiona paled.

'Rather a romantic way of describing it, but that's the general picture. Kalashnikovs bought from Soviet countries, sold on elsewhere.'

'Not – not to – '

'No. I wouldn't be that daft. I didn't sell to the Middle East, if that's what's worrying you so much. Africa, mostly. They've an insatiable thirst for weapons there. Trouble was, a consignment went missing. Someone muscling in on the action and helping themselves. I was left with no supplies and a massive bill to pay. That's when it all went pear shaped and I needed to get out, quick. Either that or have one of my own bullets in me. So I rigged up the heart attack with a couple of lads acting as paramedics to cart me off. The hall porter at the flats never suspected a thing, except that he was too keen to call a real ambulance and I had to come to and tell him I'd done it already. Paul and some of my other associates arranged the funeral. I thought you might not ask too many questions if it was all paid for and you had nothing to do but turn up and act the part of the grieving widow. I hear you didn't do much of an act there, you were on to Simon Neville before the day was out.'

'It wasn't like that!' Fiona said angrily. 'Simon saw the death notice in the *Times* and came to give me support. I hadn't seen him since before our wedding, until that day.'

'And I need to talk to you,' Simon broke in. 'Your death certificate is a fake, as any kind of investigation will uncover. I want to marry Fiona and I can't while you are still alive. If you are going to disappear, we may have to wait years before we can be free to marry. Can't you organise divorce papers or something to free her before you go?'

'You don't know much about the law, do you?' Michael sneered. 'I can't start divorce proceedings when I'm officially dead, or at least, missing. Use my death certificate; even if it's shown to be a fake they're hardly going to charge Fiona with bigamy. What's a wedding, anyway? You can call yourselves married and the world won't know any better. I certainly sha'n't come back to bother you. As far as you are concerned, I really will be dead.'

'That's not the point,' Fiona said. 'I don't want to be still married to you and it will take years to arrange a legal divorce if we don't know where you are.'

'And you won't know. No one will find me where I'm going.' Michael grinned. 'So, say goodbye nicely, Fiona dear, like you wanted to, and I'll be off.'

'What's that?' Simon sat up suddenly, his head cocked. 'There's someone else here. I heard a noise in the other room.'

'You didn't imagine I was living here without someone to look after my creature comforts, did you?' Michael said sneeringly.

Colin looked towards the door leading to the second room. It couldn't be Anthea, but was it Moira after all who was with him, or some stranger? He felt sick.

'You might as well come out,' Michael called.

The door opened. Eleanor stood in the doorway, a pistol in her hand. She pointed it directly at Colin. 'If you've brought the police –' she began.

'No, they haven't. This is merely a social call. Put that gun down, Nell. It isn't loaded anyway.' Michael took it from her and laid it down on a table at one side of the room.

'Nell? What are you doing here?' Fiona said faintly.

'What do you think I'm doing here?' Eleanor looked at Fiona with contempt. 'I'm here with Michael. I've always been with Michael. We've been lovers for years. Why else did you think I bought a cottage near Little Paddocks when you moved there? Well, actually, Michael bought it for me, like he's looked after me for years.'

'You – and Michael?' Fiona whispered. She looked as if she was living out a particularly horrible nightmare. 'You were – and it was Michael who...? Nell, I thought you were my most trusted friend.'

'Well, I was. I was a good friend to you, but friendship doesn't count when there's a man involved. You never appreciated Michael, you never really loved him. You've often said so. All you wanted was the trappings and the social kudos that went with money, money that Michael had, to lavish on you, you and your stupid, layabout son. You never knew what it was to know real, desperate hardship like I did. And when Michael came to me, I showed him how I appreciated his help, his kindness. I love him in a way you'll never understand.'

'I never realised – I never thought for one single moment – ' Fiona floundered. 'Colin, I must sit down.'

Colin leaped up and steered her into his place on the sofa. He glared at Eleanor. 'There just aren't words to describe a woman like you,' he snarled at her. 'You're a two-faced – '

'Oh, Colin, don't go all high and mighty on me,' Eleanor said. 'When you're a bit older, you may understand what grown-ups feel, what they do. But don't get upset. You won't have to put up with seeing me around any longer. Michael and I will be gone in a matter of hours and you'll never see or hear of us again. Your mother can marry her precious, saintly Simon, or live in sin with him if she wants. It won't bother either of us.' She turned to Michael. 'Shall I send word to Harry Sykes to launch the boat? This lot will have the police after us if they get a chance. Better tie them up here somewhere to delay them until we're safely away.'

'You can do that. I'll be off now.'

Eleanor frowned. 'But there's my case. I can't carry that. And how am I to catch up with you and Harry if I have to keep an eye on these three?'

'You won't be catching me up, any more than the law will. Sorry, darling, but this is where we say goodbye. I'm travelling alone.'

'Don't play the fool, Michael. Of course I'm coming with you. That was always in the plan.' Eleanor's voice was sharp.

'*Your* plan, not mine. How easy do you think it would be to disappear with you in tow? You'd hold me up, and you know it. Look, I've given you money. You'll manage – '

'I can't manage! The police would pick me up if I stayed! I have to come with you!' Eleanor sounded frightened as she began to realise that Michael was serious. She grabbed his arm but he shook her off.

'Don't be stupid. Let me go. I've already alerted Sykes and he's waiting.'

'In the boatyard?'

'No. Somewhere else. Along the coast. Some place you don't know. And neither does anyone else.' Michael bent down to pick up a rucksack that was lying on the floor by the door. At last it dawned on Eleanor that he had never intended to take her, that he had planned it that she would never be able to find where he was picking up the boat that would take him across the channel. Or perhaps there was to be a rendezvous with another boat, out at sea? She realised she didn't know, would never know, and that Michael was ditching her just as he'd ditched his wife. She looked round wildly, saw the gun that Michael had made her leave on the table, and snatched it up. She pointed it straight at him.

'You'll take me with you, Michael, or you won't go either,' she said.

'Don't be an idiot. Put that thing down. It isn't loaded, anyway.'

Eleanor squeezed the trigger and there was an explosive bang. Michael keeled over backwards with blood pouring from his chest. Eleanor stood, staring at him, the gun hanging from her hand. 'You said it wasn't – ' she said.

Colin crossed the room and prised the gun from her fingers. She didn't seem aware of what he was doing, or of anything else. She still stood, staring at Michael, lying on the floor, the blood welling out of his chest. Fiona dropped to her knees beside him. She seized a tablecloth and screwed it up to press against the wound, though even she could tell it looked hopeless.

Colin reached into his pocket and found his mobile phone. He tossed it to Simon. 'Call an ambulance. Tell them it's a shooting. They'll bring the police as well.'

Fiona pressed the cloth against Michael's chest. He was conscious, just. His eyes opened and he looked up at her. 'You've got your deathbed scene after all,' he muttered.

'Ambulance will be here very soon. Lie still and I'll try to stop the blood as much as I can,' she said.

His breath was coming in great, wheezing gulps. He turned his eyes on her. 'Thanks, Fee,' he whispered. 'I don't deserve this. I'm sorry.'

'Don't talk.' They both knew it was a losing battle. Fiona's clothes were covered in blood and the cloth was soaked.

'Won't – need – divorce. Marry Simon soon. You'll be happy.' The words were an effort and she knew they were the last ones Michael would ever say to her or anyone.

Seconds later his eyes glazed over and his head lolled to one side. Fiona put her hand over his lids and closed them. 'He's gone,' she said. At that moment they heard the sirens of the ambulance coming along the main road.

It was several hours later before they left the cottage, after lengthy interviews and questioning by the police. Michael's body had been put in the ambulance and taken to the local mortuary and Eleanor had been taken away by police car. She seemed in a state of shock, unable to speak or move.

Colin and Simon explained what had happened and, after a phone call to London, the local force seemed to grasp who Michael was and acted as if it was a feather in their caps to have tracked down one of the masterminds of their much-wanted gun criminals. They were also relieved to discover that the guns found in Paul's flat were not intended for use in a major break-in, but part of a consignment destined for abroad.

'Let us know where you will be,' the officer in charge told Simon. 'We'll need to contact you later, but Mrs Latimer looks as if she could do with some rest – and a change of clothes.' He looked at Fiona's blood-spattered coat and trousers.

'I'll look after her. We both will,' Simon said. 'We'll stay tonight at the hotel in Rye where we booked in earlier, and drive back tomorrow. How we'll explain all this blood on her I don't know.'

'One of my men will take you all in a squad car, and another will follow with your own vehicle,' the Superintendent said. 'I wouldn't like to think of you driving any distance after the experience you've just had.'

'I'm all right, really,' Fiona said. 'I look a mess, but apart from that, I'm all right. I've seen Michael again, which was what I wanted. And I was already used to the knowledge that he was dead. But Eleanor – that will take a bit longer to come to terms with. I've been such a fool. I feel I should have known, sensed something not being right, yet I never thought for a moment – '

'Don't, Mum.' Colin put his arms round her. 'You will have to forget Eleanor. She'll go to prison for murder. That's justice; she murdered the friendship and trust you two had together.' He led her out towards the waiting police car and Simon followed close behind.

CHAPTER 17

THIS IS WHERE IT ALL BEGAN, FIONA THOUGHT. She was standing in the churchyard listening to the vicar intone the words as Michael's coffin was lowered into the grave. Today the wind was bitterly cold and flurries of rain blew across the bleak landscape. In a week's time it would be New Year, a time of new beginnings. It had taken this long for the authorities to release Michael's body and everyone had tried to dissuade her from attending the funeral but she had wanted to be here, a kind of closure on all that had gone before. Simon stood beside her, his arm, as ever, round her waist. Technically, she supposed she was chief mourner, the deceased's widow, except that she wasn't a widow now. She wasn't Fiona Latimer but Fiona Neville. She and Simon had married in a quiet ceremony in Winchester as soon as Michael's death had been officially confirmed. Next week they were going to have their delayed honeymoon, a trip to somewhere warm for a couple of weeks, before moving into a new house outside Winchester.

She looked across the grave at the people gathered here. Not so many as had been at Michael's first funeral. That time she had sent Colin to comfort Eleanor who had been crying, looking more distressed than anyone. Now she knew why, or perhaps she didn't. Had Eleanor known even then that Michael was still alive; had she been putting on a rather exaggerated act, for Fiona's benefit? Somehow, she didn't think so, but Eleanor must have learnt fairly soon that Michael was still alive, of that she was sure.

Nell wasn't here today, of course. She was in prison awaiting trial for Michael's murder and would probably receive a life sentence. I must be a very cold and hard person, Fiona thought. I can't feel anything for her now. And we were so close when we were teenagers in London. My only regret is for the passing of those days. The people I feel most sorry for are Mr and Mrs Pagett, with both Paul and Eleanor in prison awaiting sentence for serious crimes.

There was only the police representative and someone from the Home Office standing on the far side of the grave. And Colin, standing a little way apart. He hadn't wanted to come, but he didn't want to let her down. He had a job now, helping out at a prehistoric archaeological dig in Wiltshire. It wasn't much of a job, but he seemed to be enjoying it and it could lead to other things.

There had been someone else at the first funeral, Fiona remembered. A mystery girl who had turned out to be quite a help in the end. And Colin had been rather keen on her, she thought. He probably wouldn't see her again now, there was no reason to do so, though it seemed rather a pity.

There was the sound of footsteps on the gravel path behind them and she looked up sharply. For a second she almost expected to see Michael and realised her nerves were still tense and her mind was playing tricks on her.

It took a moment to recognise the girl who had joined them. She came to stand beside Colin and smiled at him.

'Hallo, Colin,' she said quietly. 'I wanted to come. I hope your mother doesn't mind.'

Colin shook his head. 'No. I think we all needed to finish things properly.'

Anthea slipped her hand into Colin's as the vicar tossed the first scoop of earth on to the coffin. 'Or perhaps we could make it a new beginning,' she said softly.

Fiona didn't hear her but she saw the expression of pure joy on Colin's face and was glad that he, too, was about to embark on a much happier New Year.

The Waiting Time

Sara Banerji

'... she cannot remember the name of the village in which her family lived ... she knows it is not far from the sea ... that a shallow river runs at the bottom of the garden, that in the garden there is, there was then at least, a pear tree ...'

Julia has given up on love in her middle age but is searching for a vanished brother and a lost identity. In doing so, she collides with Kitty, a woman of a different age, life-style and aspirations. The proof of Julia's identity lies somewhere under Kitty's home. The literal digging up of the past changes life for both of them, though what they eventually find is very different to their expectations. Ahead are surprises, conflict, terror, disappointment, love – and unexpected happiness.

Sometimes it is necessary for people to find the strength and courage to dig deep into themselves and their past. Those who do so will not always find what they expected and may even encounter disappointment and sadness. For the brave and the clear sighted, though, such fearless scrutiny can bring fulfilment, love and even happiness.

'Sarah Benerji's view of the world is completely original and vivid ... she is always worth reading.' *Philip Pullman*

ISBN 1 905175 02 7

Turning Point

Bowering Sivers

"I'm going on a cruise in the spring. I've chosen my cabin, the ultimate in luxury, with a king size bed and a Jacuzzi. It's utterly immoral ... but I don't care. Daddy taught me to be very careful with money but he didn't teach me how to live. I'm going to make up for lost time. There's nothing like a coronary to frighten the life into you."

A lively woman with witty, frequently caustic views on the world, Ruth is a talented but overly-modest artist whose secret passion is the stage. After the death of her father Ruth is forced into a humdrum existence with her elderly mother but a heart attack in her forties makes her take stock.

Into her world come two men – one a scenic designer who opens up the possibility of a career in the theatre, the other a young artistic director who falls in love with her. But has she the courage to say yes to either or both of them? Ruth has reached a turning point ...

This novel of conflicting desires by award-winning author Bowering Sivers will find echoes with many women.

'The book is a joy. It bubbles with humour on every page.'
Marina Oliver

ISBN 1 905175 03 5

Scuba Dancing

Nicola Slade

'It was late spring when the angel first manifested himself to Ursula Buchanan in the village shop, just along the aisle from the bacon slicing machine ...
"Go on," he urged, pointing a glowing golden finger at the notice.
"Join the group, Ursula, it'll change your life."'

And so it does.

Ursula's is not the only life to be altered forever.

Walking out on her job in Brussels, her flat and yet another in a long line of disastrous relationships, Finn Fitzgerald decides at 45, it's about time she took herself in hand and found out what she wants from life. Moving in with her sister, and meeting gorgeous Charlie Stuart is great, but how on earth has she ended up working as a clairvoyant?

Julia and her friends are busy raising funds but are very cagey about exactly which good cause they are supporting. Then there's wealthy, gin soaked Delia, ex-Brown Owl, Bobbie, Sue who despairs of her unfaithful husband and Rosemary who despairs of her demented, sex-mad mother.

Soon Finn and Charlie Stuart find themselves drawn into the money-making activities of the older generation and love is in the air. Until that is, they find out more about the alleged good cause, and Finn finds out about Charlie's wife.

'Packed with delightful, unforgettable, eccentric characters and written with humour and deep sensitivity.' *Anita Burgh*

ISBN 1 905175 01 9

Uphill All the Way

Sue Moorcroft

'It was ... unsettling. His eyes told her he desired her, but her clear and sensible head found it difficult to believe. If her ex-husband, Tom, a decade older than her, had succumbed to the tighter, younger flesh of Liza, why should she expect better from Giorgio, a decade younger?'

When 51 year old Judith lost Giorgio, she lost her life in Malta – joy, love, her income, her own space, and her circle of friends. She even lost the view from her sun-warmed balcony of the sparkling blue waters of Sliema Creek. And, she discovered, she'd lost most of her money, too.

What she gained, back in England, was a bed in her sister's spare room in chilly Northamptonshire where she'd been brought up, and a whole host of difficulties and family problems.

But a road that's uphill all the way can bring exhilarating views. It can be fulfilling, too, and a lot easier when you find someone who wants to travel it with you ...

'A strongly written story that many women will relate to.' *Katie Fforde*

ISBN 1 905175 00 0

Pond Lane and Paris

Susie Vereker

'Jack smiled. "Maybe you'd better change out of your wellies before you go to Paris."'

After faithfully nursing her invalid husband for eight years, the widow Laura Brooke is hesitantly emerging into the world. She finds a job with Oliver Farringdon, Ambassador to an international organisation in Paris – he's divorced and needs someone to supervise his teenage daughter. But can Laura cope with her demanding employer and with Paris after her solitary celibate life in the depths of the country?

Leaving Hampshire mud to live amongst chic Parisians is a culture shock. Laura's position in the ambassadorial household is tricky and the servants resent her. Besides, keeping tabs on Charlotte isn't easy. Oliver has strict views about daughters, as well as everything else.

Jane Eyre meets Nancy Mitford in this story of life and love in two countries. During her time in Paris impulsive, over-conscientious Laura comes to realise that adversity has made her a stronger person.

'Entertaining and true to life.' *Katie Fforde*

ISBN 1 905175 06 X

Emotional Geology

Linda Gillard

"I talk to the island. I don't speak, but my thoughts are directed towards it. Sometimes it replies. Never in words, of course. I miss trees. You don't notice at first that there are hardly any trees here, just that the landscape is very flat, as if God had taken away all the hills and mountains and dumped them on neighbouring Skye. But eventually you realise it's trees that you miss. Trees talk back."

Rose Leonard is on the run from her life.

Taking refuge in a remote island community, she cocoons herself in work, silence and solitude in a house by the sea. But she is haunted by her past, by memories and desires she'd hoped were long dead.

Rose must decide whether she has in fact chosen a new life or just a different kind of death. Life and love are offered by new friends, her lonely daughter, and most of all Calum, a fragile younger man who has his own demons to exorcise.

But does Rose, with her tenuous hold on life and sanity, have the courage to say yes to life and put her past behind her?

'Lyrical, intriguing and haunting.' *Isla Dewar*

ISBN 1 905175 07 8

Stage by Stage

Jan Jones

' "That's it. Enough is enough. I'm leaving."
Beth's mouth fell open in surprise. The row hadn't nearly got to that stage yet.'

Teaching full-time and acquiring all the oddball kids in the new intake are only the first of Beth's challenges when Alan leaves her after twenty-five years of marriage. She also has to turn her untidy Cambridge house into a B&B to make ends meet and then counteract the effect of regular theatrical guests on her impressionable teenage children. Alan doesn't even have the decency to stay out of her life. Instead he keeps making disapproving incursions back in with his saccharine-laden new partner.

But Beth's real worry is lodger Owen Pendragon – a touring character actor with wicked hazel eyes, a quirky sense of humour and a tendency to walk around her home sexily damp in his bathrobe.

With attitudes and lifestyles clashing, will Owen and Beth ever find common ground? All they can do is take things 'stage by stage'.

'Warm, witty and down to earth, and a lovely curl-up-and-enjoy read. A sparkling debut from a talented new author.' *Liz Young*

ISBN 1 905175 08 6

Elissa's Castle

Juliet Greenwood

"I thought I knew everything that day I was fifty-two; that I had nothing else to learn, and nothing would ever again arise to shock me. That day I bought Bryn Glas Castle, I was looking forward to a life of single, middle-aged, purple-wearing, self-indulgent bliss, with natters with my friends, and flying visits from my children and grandchildren as the headiest excitement of my future existence."

When Elissa Deryn buys a dilapidated castle in Snowdonia, with the intention of turning it into a B&B to support her in her old age, she has no idea just what she is letting herself in for.

Far from fading away into obscure old age, Elissa suddenly finds herself eminently desirable. Suitors appear at an alarming rate. But is it Elissa's charm, or her castle and its unique Elizabethan garden, that is desirable? Can she find one amongst them all who will love her for herself alone, and not for her assets?

Or is she really having far too much fun as she is?

'Gripping from the very first page, so turn off the phone and open the chocolates before you settle down to this delightful novel.' *Anita Anderson*

ISBN 1 905175 04 3

Forgotten Dreams

Doris Leadbetter

'When they had cleared him completely, they looked at the dead man in silence. Helen traced with her finger the eyebrows, the closed lids, the nose, the full-lipped, gentle mouth. The dead man lay there, black as the peat around him, at one with it. Part of it.'

Sixty year old Helen Lytton, a recently retired research scientist, travels to Australia determined to prove her theory right – that there had once been water in the far, arid north of Western Australia. Along with her husband and an Aboriginal school-teacher who knew the area well, the expedition unearthed far more than they expected.

Helen could not have known that her adventure would coincide with one begun many years ago and many miles away. Perhaps, as a scientist and a mature woman, she should have foreseen the risks that lay ahead as well as the excitement that was about to happen; the threats arising from the ambition and pride, the secrecy and the greed of man.

'A born novelist ... her excellent book keeps the reader interested to the last chapter.' *Iris Gower*

ISBN 1 905175 05 1

Transita books are available through all good bookshops, or you can order direct from us through Grantham Book Services.

Tel: +44 (0)1476 541080
Fax: +44 (0)1476 541061
Email: orders@gbs.tbs-ltd.co.uk

Or via our website

www.transita.co.uk

To order via any of these methods please quote the title(s) of the book(s) and your credit card number together with its expiry date.

For further information about our books and catalogue, please contact:

Transita
3 Newtec Place
Magdalen Road
Oxford OX4 1RE

Visit our web site at

www.transita.co.uk

Or you can contact us by email at info@transita.co.uk